BEAM OF

Alex Hamilton was born in 1930
America, then England and Oxford University. After experimenting with a variety of jobs, he turned to writing full time in the early 1960s, beginning by alternating novels with short story collections such as *Wild Track* (1963), which, although not macabre, caught the attention of Herbert Van Thal, editor of the popular *Pan Books of Horror Stories* series. Hamilton went on to contribute stories to this and other series, including his most celebrated tale, 'The Attic Express', and in 1966 he published his own collection, *Beam of Malice*, which won widespread acclaim in both England and the United States. During the 1960s and '70s, he also edited several collections of macabre and horror fiction containing early works by many important writers, including William Trevor, Anthony Burgess, Robert Nye, and Michael Moorcock, among others.

His last novel, *The Dead Needle* (1969), was a macabre blend of fantasy and reality, but after publishing his third story collection, *Flies on the Wall* (1972), Hamilton, with a growing family to feed, worked increasingly in journalism, most notably for the *Guardian*, where he wrote about books and publishing as well as travel (in which he won several awards) for twenty-five years, and for the BBC World Service. Recently, a collection of Hamilton's interviews with a remarkable array of authors over a fifty-year span, from Dennis Wheatley and John Wyndham to Gunter Grass and Chinua Achebe, was issued by Troubador.

Widely praised when first published, Hamilton's short stories fell into a prolonged period of neglect but are now being rediscovered, with a hardcover collection from the esteemed Ash-Tree Press in 2007 and recent acclaim from Britain's foremost living horror author, Ramsey Campbell.

By Alex Hamilton

FICTION

As If She Were Mine (1962)

Wild Track (1963)

Town Parole (1964)

Beam of Malice (1966) (*stories*)

The Dead Needle (1969)

Flies on the Wall (1972) (*stories*)

The Christmas Pudding That Shook the World (1988) (*stories*)

The Attic Express and other Macabre Stories (2007)

ANTHOLOGIES EDITED

My Blood Ran Cold (1966)

The Cold Embrace (1966)

Splinters (1968)

Best Horror Stories 3 (1972)

Triangles (1973)

Factions (1974)

NON-FICTION

Writing Talk: Conversations with Top Writers of the Last Fifty Years (2012)

ALEX HAMILTON

BEAM OF MALICE

Fifteen short, dark stories

With a new introduction by the author

VALANCOURT BOOKS

Beam of Malice by Alex Hamilton
First published London: Hutchinson, 1966
First Valancourt Books edition 2014

Published by Valancourt Books, Richmond, Virginia
Publisher & Editor: James D. Jenkins
20th Century Series Editor: Simon Stern, University of Toronto
http://www.valancourtbooks.com

ISBN 978-1-941147-26-9 (*trade paperback*)
Also available as an electronic book.

All Valancourt Books publications are printed on acid free paper that meets all ANSI standards for archival quality paper.

Cover by M. S. Corley
Set in Dante MT 11/13.2

INTRODUCTION

In the 1960s, when this, my fourth book, first appeared, I was determined to produce a novel every other year with a collection of stories in between. My second book had been *Wild Track*, in which ten characters working on a film pass the inevitable time hanging around by telling stories of their adventures in other jobs – travelling salesman, secretary, dancer, company director, a terrible teenager. . . . It didn't make my fortune (generally an author will sell twice as many of a novel as of a book of stories), but it brought me to the attention of Bertie van Thal, who collected 'Horror Stories' every year for Pan Books. It was their rule to publish only new stories. From the five of mine that they chose, and used in later years, I took two to figure in *Beam of Malice*.

Many readers prefer to grasp the main theme of a novel and go on to the end, feeling a kind of friendship with it, rather than needing to be wide-awake to learn about entirely new characters, starting afresh every ten or twenty pages. Others, like me re-reading today this book of fifteen stories, tend to skip around, expect some difference between them, give themselves a rest from the last one to be fit for the next. 'The Attic Express' proved to be one favourite, with a life of its own in various anthologies, while the last story in the book has another, quite different, style – a conversation between two men on a beach, which was prompted in my mind by my early life in Rio de Janeiro, and was later broadcast by BBC radio in London.

When I gave the book to my parents in 1966, I added 'Read with caution.' This may be why my father offered me lunch, but not at his house. He had worked much of his life in Brazil, and had the conventional expat's view of his home country, but perhaps by then he had finally forgiven me for writing books rather than get work in the City of London. Now, more than fifty years later, I still take up the chances that come my way. Recently I had the good luck to write a new macabre story that appealed to Johnny Mains, editor of a British Fantasy Society anthology. Introducing the eight contributors, the pundit Ramsey Campbell writes of my story, 'Where is Uncle Philip?', that I had 'always been an original, and while this one belongs to a tradition of eccentric graveyard humour that stretches from Shakespeare to Jerome K. Jerome, it doesn't read like anybody else. Here's to his continuing vigour!' Thank you – I hope so! Ironically I'd written something rather more grim in my introduction to a *Best Horror Stories* anthology thirty years earlier: 'A horror writer might be drawn in a graveyard chipping out his beastly fantasy on a headstone.'

I admit that I had to expand from depending on writing novels and horror stories in order to maintain a family. As a freelance good luck came my way when in my middle years I could interview other writers (and my recently published *Writing Talk* figures a choice of 85 of the best, including many from across the Atlantic such as Kurt Vonnegut, Stephen King, Joyce Carol Oates, John Updike, Margaret Atwood, Gore Vidal, Norman Mailer . . . of the 26 who met me in London.)

Then I was given a wholly different sort of job, which took me away from great writers, and the publishers who drowned me in works they hoped I would review, and going home to my family at the end of the day. It put me in charge of the travel section of the British *Guardian* newspaper, so that for fifteen years I visited all the countries of Europe, and fifty islands of the Caribbean; I felt an earthquake in Mexico, journeyed by rail from Atlantic to Pacific, floated along the great rivers of China.

Yet, for all these foreign experiences my imagination is rarely fired by exotic settings. Today I live in the English county of Norfolk, whose seafaring past bred the adventurers and rebels who colonised Virginia and New England, and Captain George Vancouver, who mapped the furthest northwestern coasts of America, and Captain John Smith, who brought his Pocahontas home to a little port just a few miles from my study. Did the terrors of the unknown haunt their dreams? Did the tales they brought back thrill their listeners in dark village taverns? Maybe not. Maybe there were enough *local* tales of witches, of the spirits of the marshes, of bells still ringing from drowned churches off-shore . . .

And for me, too, the sinister springs from the familiar. Marriages, lovers, neighbours, college mates, children. Mine are tales of unease, not of gothic horrors. But, with a bit of luck, the unease will linger . . . and linger.

Alex Hamilton
King's Lynn, Norfolk

May 10, 2014

BEAM OF MALICE

TO JONATHAN

CONTENTS

THE BABY-SITTERS

All the while she dressed, Muriel worried.

'If they don't come soon, we shan't be able to go.'

'They'll come,' said Selwyn easily; 'they're not like friends, they're professionals. They won't let us down.'

'Makes it a jolly expensive evening out, *hiring* people to look after your kids.'

'Better than paying in kind,' said Selwyn. He lay on his back on the bed, choosing the best route from a map wide enough to have been tucked in with the bedclothes on either side of him.

She turned to look at him, although she could see him perfectly well in the mirror.

'Aren't you going to finish dressing?' she asked. 'I don't want them to arrive and find us both half naked.'

'Stop fussing, Moo. Tie and shoes and jacket and I'm ready for all comers.'

'You haven't even shaved yet!'

'That's not obscene, is it? Baby-sitters have to take you as they find you.'

'Oh, you are selfish! It creates a terrible impression. You don't seem to *think* that we're leaving the children in their charge, and if they think we're sloppy they'll probably be sloppy too. I truly think you're selfish.'

'Sel*wyn*, darling, not selfish.'

'I suppose it'll be left to me to show them everything.'

'The advertisement said they'd done it hundreds of times. I'm sure by now they have a nose for everything.'

'That's just the part of them that I don't want, their nose. I'll show them all they need to put their nose into.'

Selwyn slid off the bed and walked over to her. He kissed her shoulder and swivelled her to kiss her throat and the upper slopes of her breast. He rested the tip of his nose on the bridge of her bra. She stroked the back of his head.

'Darling, I *must* get ready.'

He laid his head alongside hers and looked at the two faces in the mirror.

'I have powder on the tip of my nose,' he said. 'Do you think they'll guess where it came from?'

The bell rang. She jumped up. 'There they are. Oh, Selwyn, I knew this would happen! Will you see them while I get my dress on? Then come back and zip me up. Please hurry, and put your shoes on before you answer the door. *Selwyn!* Your jacket!'

'They won't go away,' said Selwyn, 'they wanted to come. They don't give a damn about us and who we are. It's the kids they're coming to look after, not us.'

'All the same . . .' she sighed.

She listened to Selwyn cheerily greeting the baby-sitters. He was saying *frightful* things, but he was one of those people who got away with remarks that from somebody else would be in terrible taste. He had evidently taken them into the lounge and left the door open, because she could hear his voice booming back as if he were addressing people at the back of a hall.

'. . . little snifter to start the evening, eh? I'm going to draw a line on the bottle after that, but it'll be in pencil, so you can always rub it out and draw another one, eh? Gin or Scotch? That's it, touch of the old gold watch is best on a cold night. Was the house difficult to find? Can't always find it myself when I've had one too many. If you feel hungry, would you work your way through the canned stuff first? The leg of lamb in the fridge is our Sunday dinner. If you want to make love in front of the fire I should make sure the door's properly shut, because even when it is there's a draught like a gale comes in through those windows, where there's a sashcord broken. . . . Here you are. Jolly good health!'

She could not hear the replies, and struggled impatiently with a dress which seemed to have got too small for her since the last party they'd been to. Ever since Mark it had been a problem to stay the same size, while David had been a greedy little chap and she'd almost wasted away. Well, they were both first-class kids, and, professionals or not, nobody could help loving them.

Selwyn came back. He gave her the thumbs-up sign.

'Very presentable,' he said, 'even chronically good-looking.'

'Yes, dear,' she said, 'you'll have to zip me in, this seems to have shrunk.'

She turned round and he obligingly took hold of the zip. It would not budge. He put his hand on her hip to steady her and then pulled again. It remained where it was.

'What are you doing?' she asked, trying to peer down over her shoulder.

'I think I've found the snows of yesteryear,' he replied; 'stop laughing, or are you trying to cause an avalanche?'

'Do be serious and get me into this damn dress. I want to go in and talk to the baby-sitters. We can't just leave them in there waiting.'

'Yes, we can,' he whispered, 'they're the most self-possessed baby-sitters I've ever met.'

'All right, all right,' she said, 'I get the point. I'm sure they're very efficient and reliable and I'm silly to worry. All the same, I worry.'

'You've got cause,' he said. 'I'm going to take you out tonight and seduce you.'

'If you have as much trouble getting me out of my dress as you're having getting me into it I shan't have to fight very hard for my honour.'

Then the zip moved. It flashed from one end of the course to the other in a fraction of a second.

'That's what I call a zip,' he said in an awed voice.

'Thank God that's done,' she said. 'Now take me in and give me a drink too. After that I feel there's no backing out.'

He turned her, to get the effect. 'I can see the escape hatch,' he commented.

She tugged at the dress, trying to conceal the top of her bra. 'There's too much of me,' she said helplessly.

'There's never too much of you, you look grand!'

'I wish we weren't going out!'

'Everything will be all right.'

'Do you really love me, Selwyn?'

'Try me! Cross that line on the carpet and you'll find out.'

'Oh, you're hopeless! Come on, then, if we're going. Put the light out in the bathroom, will you?'

'That reminds me. Better show it to *them*. Don't want them peeing in the airing cupboard.'

'They don't *sound* that sort.' But the anxiety was back in her voice.

'In a moment you'll see for yourself. Actually I think they're our sort.'

In fact a moment later she saw what he meant. There was a curious resemblance between themselves and the couple standing, each with a drink, on either side of the hearth. As the door opened they were talking quietly, seemingly into the fire, but now they turned and came forward, smiling, the man with his hand out. It was an odd, but not unpleasant sensation, taking his hand, as if she were being welcomed into her own lounge. Perhaps because he was of the same physical type as Selwyn she found the man very attractive. His handclasp was warm and dry. As his regard rested on her she felt that she looked nice.

'Good evening, Mrs. Chievely,' he said, 'you're our most glamorous mother this month.'

'Thank you! How long is your list of mothers this month?'

'Long enough to make it worth saying. Mothers get about these days.'

'And so you do as well? Where do you actually live?'

It was the woman who answered. 'On the telephone. It's our life these days, isn't it, darling?'

Her voice was thick, soupy, a fluid in which the consonants seemed merely to float. Muriel thought her overdressed for an occasion like baby-sitting, but she could see from Selwyn's face that he would think it a silly complaint to make. She felt a little embarrassed for him, staring in that fascinated way. She said briskly:

'Before we were married I felt like that. I was glad to get away from the blessed thing.'

'Well, you've nothing to worry about, Mrs. Chievely, we shall be right beside the blessed thing all evening, so call us whenever you feel like it. Some parents don't trust us. We've learnt to accept that.'

Muriel bridled at the satirical hint in her tone.

'We're not like that,' said Selwyn, 'once we're out of the house, we're out.'

The thick rich voice engulfed the idea: 'It's exactly what we want too.'

Selwyn was standing right over the woman.

'I want you to feel absolutely at home here.'

'The time will pass very quickly,' said the woman, 'we have lots to do.'

They all found themselves looking at a suitcase standing in one corner of the room.

'We take our gear around with us wherever we go,' explained the man, 'hoping for the right atmosphere to work in. Your beautiful house will suit us right down to the ground.'

'Right down to the basement, I hope,' exclaimed Selwyn.

'What work do you do, though?' asked Muriel, and felt her drink splash on her wrist as Selwyn nudged her.

'Correlating, linking, blending, cross-indexing, all that sort of stuff,' said the man. 'A thorough-going pest of a job. These moments before the parents depart are almost poignant for me, I enjoy them so much for their carefree feeling, in contrast with what has to follow.'

'Have a night off, on us,' babbled Selwyn, still looking idiotically at the woman, 'you can always come again and we'll blend a bit ourselves!'

'We can't afford to miss our opportunity,' said the woman, 'but isn't he nice, though?' she appealed to the man. Selwyn gave him no time to answer.

'Let me at least show you how our Hi-Fi stuff works. It's our great relaxation, isn't it, Moo? She's my moose, and it's her choice, all but the pops, so we call it moosic.'

'Hadn't you better shave?' asked Muriel.

While he was away she showed off the children. She had meant to list their peculiarities and forewarn the baby-sitters about their little foibles, grading them in the degree of their urgency, but after Selwyn's performance she was unable to mention them. It was doubtful, in any case, whether she could have lectured this woman, with her self-assurance and style, nor did she have the inclination to play the heavy mother before this charming, reassuring man.

'As soon as they're old enough I'm going back to work,' she told the man, as she quietly closed the bedroom door.

'They're beautiful children,' said the man with apparently genuine enthusiasm, 'an achievement in themselves. When you go back to work you must think of them, just as they are now, as something complete and perfect!'

The woman only said: 'I would like children like that. One could do anything with them.'

'Don't you believe it!' laughed Muriel.

Suddenly she was impatient to be away. She could think of nothing else to say, and somehow she felt in the way of this couple who wanted to get on with their work. She called to Selwyn:

'Do get a move on, darling, the invitation said seven-thirty, and it's miles!'

'Don't worry!' called back Selwyn, 'it's a party, not Grand Opera. They won't close the doors on us if we don't arrive on the dot.'

But to her relief he came out as soon as he had said that, and resisting the temptation to shake the hands of the baby-sitters, and thank them for putting up with them, Muriel took down her coat and let the man help her into it. She thought his hand stroked her hair as he did so, but she was not sure. Then they were ready, and Selwyn was chattering about the necessity of getting a little petrol on the way.

At the gate they looked back, and saw the baby-sitters standing in the doorway, the man with his arm around the woman's shoulders, watching them go. Muriel prayed that Selwyn would not crash the gears as they left. In the car as they pulled away (quite smoothly) she said:

'I'm sorry, Selwyn, that I carried on like that. They're certainly a perfectly reliable couple. I hadn't dreamed of anybody so mature and sophisticated when you talked about them. It was only, you see, that I anticipated some fearful teenagers trying to grub up some pocket money, and so naturally I was worried. I shan't worry any more now.'

'No? Well, all the same I shall give them a tinkle now and then.'

'Don't be so silly, darling, they're perfectly capable. If there were anything they could ring us. I left the number.'

'May be. But when I think of them absorbed in their tasks, blending and all that, I wonder if they would have any time to spare for anything bourgeois like our kids.'

'Oh, of course they will!' And then Muriel giggled. 'I know what it is! Selwyn, you transparent thing, you're jealous!'

'Jealous! You don't mean it! What have I to be jealous of?'

'I see it all. It's sweet! It's fantastic!'

'You're raving, Muriel! For God's sake!'

'You want to ring up because you want to interrupt.'

'Interrupt? Interrupt what?'

'Interrupt our baby-sitters making love.'

'You have sex on the brain! Just because they look so well equipped for it doesn't mean they have any such idea themselves. And personally I don't give a damn what they do if it doesn't interfere with their keeping a sharp eye out for the kids waking.'

'Funny,' said Muriel, leaning over so she could get some light from passing street-lamps to examine her make-up, 'because in fact that's true, isn't it? You don't think so much of their making love together, as making love with other people.'

'Well, the girl certainly gave me the eye. I felt pole-axed.'

'Darling, she did not! She was just there, and you were in the way of her rays. I don't blame you a bit, but I don't think you should call her a girl, she's almost as old as I am.'

'Old girl, you're all girls to me, until you positively chicken out.'

'I'm not going to think about them any more. I won't have my evening spoilt by being jealous of baby-sitters. It's bad enough spying on you at the party, where everybody's dolled up specifically to get at you.'

'Stop harping on jealousy. If there were to be any authentic jealousy in the air it would come from me, watching you melt before that bloke.'

'Melt! Oh, you liar! I did not *melt*! I thought he was a pleasing man, I admit. But *melt*, no fear!'

'Melt, get pleased, what does it matter so long as we're out for the evening together quarrelling about it?'

'We are *not* quarrelling. We are discussing the matter sensibly.'

'Quarrelling, discussing, what does it matter so long as we don't go on doing it?'

'Selwyn, I love you.'

'Moo, you are my queen.'

They felt at the party that it was the penalty for having been so long housebound that they knew nobody. But their hosts worked hard and soon they knew almost everybody. Muriel realised, when she had circulated a little, that the party was made up mainly of married couples, and found that few of them would have been there had it not been for baby-sitters. It was a lovely party; there was something in that punch which made everybody friends; she had the nicest shoulders in the room; it was like the party where she had met Selwyn but for the fact that she had been single then and worried about who was going to take her home; she made several contacts which she was sure would be a great help to Selwyn in his career—and it annoyed her to see him standing near that telephone and finally ask their host if he minded. She prodded him as he put the receiver down. He turned guiltily.

'All quiet on the Western Front,' he said.

'Who answered?'

'She did.'

'Oh.'

'Well, it was either him or her.'

'All right, all right.'

'You can make the next call if you like.'

'There's no need, not for either of us, to call.'

'As a father I feel it behoves me to keep in touch.'

'And as a rake you feel it behoves you to chat the female up.'

'Muriel, take that back.'

'Selwyn, I take it back.'

'Moo, you're the loveliest woman here.'

'Take me home, darling!'

'We only just got here!'

'Well, leave that bloody phone alone then.'

And for an hour or so he did. He made purposefully for the far corner of the room, and she was proud of him, seeing him tall against the wall, with a little semicircle of people laughing at everything he said. She could see that he was feeling like a genie let out of a bottle, and she felt guilty at having hemmed him in so long with house and kids. There was a young thing with a lot of blonde hair pouting and wriggling about in front of him, and affectionately and mentally wished them both the best of luck. Selwyn was really too indolent to be unfaithful, though he talked as if he were perpetually knocking them over. As long as she let him flirt she knew there would be no trouble. The exceptions in his behaviour were easy to spot, such as that self-conscious display before the baby-sitter. Momentarily Muriel's face darkened. She *would* make the next call.

'. . . so I have this need for an outside opinion,' said the stout planter-like man she'd been talking to, 'and it would just please me to act on a decision fallen from your fair lips.'

Muriel had no idea what he was talking about.

'I should,' she said quickly.

'Should? Should do what?'

'Go right ahead.' She could see Selwyn disengaging himself from his group.

'Christ!' exclaimed her interlocutor, 'that's a bit extreme, isn't it? This isn't China.'

'Will you excuse me?' asked Muriel, working her way round his bulk, and finding another group smiling her into their company. By the time she was free of them, Selwyn was on the phone and talking. In a pleased tone he was explaining the operation of the lighting system. Seeing her at his elbow he said:

'Trouble and strife at my side, wanting to pitch me back into the circus, so I'll sign off.'

He put the receiver down and Muriel said:

'What was all that about? What have you got to go into all those details for?'

'Oh,' said Selwyn casually, 'something to do with small print. They wanted to fix up the angle-poise in the lounge.'

'The angle-poise is in the study,' she said, 'and I locked that.'

'I know,' he said, 'I told them where the key is.'

'Who was them, this time?'

'The lady, as it happens.'

'The *girl*, the *woman* we hired, as it happens,' said Muriel, 'and as it happens I'm going to call right back and tell her not to touch that key.'

She reached out. Agitatedly Selwyn laid his hand on her arm.

'That would be very rude, Muriel.'

'I don't care. I'm not having them going through my private papers.'

'Don't be so silly. They're not interested in your private papers. I beg you to forget all about it.'

'You'll have to go on your knees. And if you do I promise I'll pour this drink right down your collar.'

'Well, I'm not going to stand here and listen to you make a fool of yourself.'

'Every two's a pair, they say,' commented Muriel, dialling.

She had not expected the man to answer. She instantly forgot the little speech she had formulated.

'Sorry to bother you,' she got out. 'I was just sort of thinking, you know how it is, wondering how everything was.'

'Splendid!' she heard. 'Have to congratulate you on the children. Answer to a baby-sitter's prayer. We have a little warm toddy ready in case any soothing needs to be done. Normally we're introduced to children, so we shouldn't be a shock if they wake up, but as you were in a hurry, we let it go. If they do wake up, I think we can get round them.'

'Our fault. We should have thought of that. In our old place we had lots of friends all round us among the neighbours, so, of course, it wasn't necessary.'

'Quite understandable. Hope you're having a good time.'

'Yes, it's a very nice party, thank you.'

'A woman with your style, Mrs. Chievely, has no right to stay in.'

'Thank you, kind sir.'

'Mustn't keep you from the gay throng. There's someone just behind you longing to make your acquaintance. Bye-bye.'

Behind her in fact stood Selwyn, smiling ironically.

'Did she confess all?' asked Selwyn.

Muriel flushed. 'It was him,' she said.

'Do you know, I thought it might be. You positively dandled that receiver.'

'You are a pig,' she said. 'Selwyn darling, introduce me to those people in the corner you were talking to.'

'Having fun?'

'I'm going to, from now on.'

The few words spoken by the baby-sitter acted on her with surprising strength. She thought that she had perhaps been seeing things out of proportion, and she realised that she was quite beautiful and clever enough to be enjoyable to talk to. She resolved not to watch Selwyn, and to make that elegant, smooth Pakistani mathematician, amongst others, remember that he had met her. She held her empty glass conspicuously before her, until, excellent-mannered man, he asked if he might fill it for her.

As they went everybody said it had been a lovely party, and meant what they said. Most of them said they would stay longer but for the necessity of getting home to relieve their babysitters. The Chievelys felt they could stay a little while more, each time the problem came up, because Selwyn was told, over the phone, that, if anything, the baby-sitters would welcome a late arrival, as they had not quite broken the back of their task, and a little extension of comfort and silence would help them vastly.

And, of course, when the party thinned out, and there was room to talk, and to talk about the things in life that really mattered, it was even better than it had been before. And in the end it was only because Muriel could see that their hosts plainly wanted to get off to bed now that she insisted they should go. She prised Selwyn away from the daughter of the house, who obviously had the stamina to go on relating to her parents' gorgeous guest until breakfast-time, and explained for the last time that now *they* would give a party, and they had the best babysitters in the world to recommend.

'I'm the only baby round here,' said the daughter, pertly, 'and I'm not going to be left at home with any baby-sitters.'

'Oh, you don't know,' said Muriel, welcoming the girl into a bond of man-relishing womanhood. 'If this one had been on his own you wouldn't have seen me, I don't suppose.'

Selwyn looked at the daughter. 'Would have suited me,' he said gallantly.

'Go on with you,' said the hostess, 'I think you're the best-suited couple we've had here tonight. In any trouble I know you'd be a team.'

'We get enough practice against each other,' said Selwyn, 'and now if I may I'll make one last call. Just to let them know we're coming. I'd better write you a cheque for the use of your phone. You've been most sympathetic, but I feel a little guilty over it.'

'Nonsense,' said the host, 'I know what it is. Help yourself.'

But there was no reply. Selwyn tried three times, the last time through the exchange.

'Funny,' he said, 'number unobtainable.'

'Some cross-up in the wires, probably,' said their host. 'Strange things happen at this time of night. I remember once I was trying to call . . .'

But his wife was offering coats, and the party was over.

In the car going home, Muriel said:

'I'm a bit sloshed, darling, we shouldn't have stayed so late, I wished it could have gone on longer, I was so enjoying myself, you were a terrific success, I was so proud of you, oh God, my head's spinning, are you sure this is the right way?'

'Damn right you're sloshed, darling. That was a hell of a sloshed sentence.'

'I just want to get home.'

'Soon be there.'

She dozed off while the car slipped along the empty streets, so it seemed quite soon after that she was watching him take out his door keys. She leant her head against his shoulder.

'Do hurry up, darling.'

'Hold up, Moo, you're leaning against the pocket. Drunken thing, you.'

She shook herself awake, and watched him trying to fit the key in the lock.

'Drunken thing, yourself,' she murmured; 'if I were going to be seduced by you I'd have had second thoughts by now.'

He straightened up, flicked his lighter on, and bent down again. She would never forget his face at that moment, as he stared back at her, still bent down, his black hair falling limp over his forehead. He said, with unbelieving astonishment in his voice which made it sound stupid to her:

'The key won't go in!'

'Nonsense, Selwyn, I'm far too tired for games. Come on, open the door, and let's get to bed.'

He fumbled with the key again.

'It's the wrong lock,' he announced in a queer voice.

She drew close and clutched his arm.

'What do you mean?'

He stabbed at the aperture with the key. He shrugged. 'Wrong lock,' he said again.

She snatched the key from him, and tried it herself.

'It's the wrong *key*, you idiot!' she said. Her voice was as strange as his.

'You know bloody well it isn't,' he replied, 'you use it every day of your life.'

'Well, don't just stand there holding that lighter like a torch-bearer. Ring the bell.'

'Yes, I'll ring the bell. I didn't want to wake the kids.'

'We'll just have to wake them. I'm not going to stand out here all night. You'll have to get the lock seen to in the morning. Can't you find out about these things before we go out? Honestly, Selwyn, I have to see to everything in this house.'

'That's bloody well not true!'

'I'm not going to argue about it now. Press the bell!'

'You press it. You may be tired, but you can raise your arm, I suppose. Talk about helpless femininity!'

Angrily she put her finger on the bellpush. She kept it there until he snatched her hand away.

'All right, all right, they're expecting us,' he muttered.

'This is so humiliating,' she said.

After a long wait the door opened a little. The man's face appeared. There was a dim roseate light in the hallway beyond him.

'What is it?' asked the man.

'Couldn't find the key, or something,' replied Selwyn. They both moved forward, but the door did not give before them.

'I don't understand,' said the man.

'Don't mess about, there's a good chap,' said Selwyn. 'I know we're a bit late, but you said you wanted to get on with it, so we took you at your word.'

'Hope the children behaved themselves,' added Muriel.

'This is a very strange time of night to call,' said the man. 'I think you must have the wrong house. There is nobody else in this building save my wife and myself.'

The door seemed to be closing, but Selwyn suddenly leaned forward and pushed against it. It gave a little, but not enough to allow him to insert himself.

He pushed his face within six inches of the baby-sitter's, and said:

'We're bloody tired, my good friend, and in no mood for fun and games, so if you'll just move to one side we'll take over.'

'Please,' said Muriel pathetically.

'No bloody please about it,' said Selwyn, 'we're coming in.'

'I should think not!' said the man. He put out a hand and seemed to lean it on Selwyn's shoulder. And suddenly Selwyn staggered back from it, as if there had been a spring in the man's forearm.

'What is it?' came the woman's voice from inside the house. 'What's all the commotion?'

The door opened and revealed her in the doorway to the bedroom. She was standing with one hand clutching together the neck of her dressing gown. Muriel recognised the garment for her own. Below the hem several inches of Muriel's favourite nightie, the scarlet one that she called her 'competitive nightie', fluttered in the draught flowing in from the cool outside.

'Those are mine!' shrieked Muriel.

'It's all right,' said the man, in that reassuring voice, 'don't worry, darling. It's only some drunken revellers.'

'It's all right,' repeated the woman, back into the darkness beyond her, 'it's only some bad people that Daddy will soon frighten away.'

'I want to see the bad people!' came the voice of a child, and as if plucked out of the darkness the woman suddenly had both the children, one on either side of her, holding on to her gown and staring at Muriel and Selwyn, with their arms around the woman's waist and their cheeks pressed against her hips. They stared accusingly, sullenly, darkly, as Muriel had never seen them stare at anything before.

She recoiled.

The door closed slowly. The man may have whispered 'Satisfied?' before it clicked to, or she may have made the syllables from the sound of dead leaves blowing along the pavement.

'I'll knock the door down!' raged Selwyn.

'You said yourself it couldn't be done,' said Muriel. 'Why did we have to have such a perfect house?'

She began to cry.

'They can't get away with this,' said Selwyn. 'I'll have this looked into straight away.'

'I'm scared,' said Muriel. 'They've thought it all out. Oh, did you see their faces?'

'To hell with their faces, we'll soon have a different look on their faces.'

'But what are we going to do?'

'It's incredible. You know what they're after, don't you? They want all that equipment I've bought. They think we're going off and then they're going to ship it all out.'

She backed away from him as if he had been one of them.

'Your equipment? Equipment!' she screamed. 'What are they doing to my *babies*?'

The line of light under the door vanished.

WHAT'S YOUR PROBLEM?

Mum and Dad knew what was meant by a mystery tour.

'It's just going to be a sort of a mystery tour,' Lorne had said defensively.

It was the one you went on when you had done all the others. It was much the same as all the others and getting your money's worth really depended on letting yourself be taken by surprise.

'Sort of a coach outing, is it, Lorne?' asked Dad, not very interested. He and Mum had turned it in, that kind of gallivanting. All right for young people of course.

Lorne hesitated, reluctant to tell the whole truth. 'There's not enough of us to fill a coach,' she said.

Mum looked alarmed. You never knew when Dad would tumble the truth, and Lorne had stretched it here, naughty girl, leaving her with all the worry. There were only two of them going on the outing, Lorne and Mr. Philip. If the boy was really going to marry Lorne, and stranger things had happened at sea, Dad would have to know, but . . .

'All in their own cars, I suppose,' grumbled Dad. 'I never had a car at that age. More money than sense today. Take some money with you and come back by train if there's too much drinking.'

'Lorne's not silly, Dad,' said Mum.

Dad just looked.

So the women thought it would be better if Mr. Philip did not come to the door. Lorne would walk up the street and wait for him at the junction, out of the way of prying eyes. As she was leaving, Dad appraised her appearance and said:

'You're wasted on them, my girl. You look good enough to be walking out with a fellow. Plan a little mystery tour of your own with a church at the end of it.'

Lorne was sorry then that she had kept him in the dark. If she had not been late already she would have told him all about it. As it was, she kissed him, and he blinked. 'Now don't start practising on me,' he said, and went back into the house.

Philip was waiting, kicking the tyres of his smart little sports job, when she arrived at the junction.

'Hello, kid,' he said, and held the door open for her. He went on kicking.

'Is something the matter?'

'No. Nothing. We've got a lot of mileage ahead of us, and I want to be sure.'

'Where are we going?'

'Rainbow's end.'

'Never been there.'

'You'll like it. They say there's money there.'

'Money isn't everything.'

'No,' he said, slipping in beside her, 'sometimes a chequebook's handier.'

The speed with which he fired the car into the traffic stream seemed to leave her reply behind.

She eased right down into the car, her feet probing forwards and her scarfed head comfortably backwards, and was overtaken by a sense of helplessness, the steady noise of the engine being only one of the many layers which enfolded her, remote from her own world. She had had the idea that she would be sitting up in this beautiful car, enjoying the envious glances, some from eyes which might perhaps have once thought her available. It would be cheerful and bright and she and Mr. Philip, *Philip*, would be ever so proud of each other.

Somehow it wasn't working out that way. The car went so *fast*. They were so alone together that they might almost have been sharing a bed. Well, not exactly, but at any rate sharing a common thrill. Was he thrilled, was she excited? She sneaked frequent glances at him and saw only an extension of the car. Men and their cars! He might at least say something!

'You're not very chatty this morning, Philip.'

'How's that, doll?'

'Aren't we speaking? Are you cross? Because I was a bit late?'

'Were you? Never noticed, sweetheart. Life goes on, women catch up.'

'What is it, then?'

'Don't give it a thought. It's nothing.'

'What are you showing off for, then?'

For a moment he took his eyes off the road. He looked at her as if he were judging the distance between her eyes, with a view to driving down that way.

'I never show off, Lorne, you know me better than that.'

'I'd like to.'

'What do you mean?'

'Like to know you better than that.'

'We've been out together quite a few times.'

'Always with other people. This is the first time just the two of us.'

'That's right, isn't it?' He sounded amazed at the realisation. He smiled, and there was a perceptible lightening in his voice as he took off into the language of flirtation: 'I expect I don't notice the others when you're with me, doll.'

She hesitated and decided to follow him up there: 'How do you know they aren't all with us now?'

He played up: 'All right, boys and girls, come on out and show yourselves, we know you're there.'

The car hummed down the sunlit road, which overnight rain had washed like a ribbon.

'They're embarrassed,' he said, and then, as a lay-by showed ahead: 'Let's let 'em out.'

He pulled the car in off the road, just ahead of a parked lorry. 'Once out, don't turn round,' he called to the imaginary stowaways. He grinned, that cheeky, boyish look came into his face which she and her mates at work knew when he dropped behind his old man for a chat, when they were making the rounds. 'What's your problem?' he asked in imitation of that sardonic question he always put to the girls.

'I want us to enjoy ourselves,' she said, trying to conquer the employee's nervousness which his manner had brought on. He put his arm round her, leant across and kissed her. She kept her hands on her skirt, choosing rather to have his hand on her breast, if he had to.

Apparently he had not, though, because he leaned back again after only a moment, and lit a cigarette. It was not a bit like the time he had kissed her after the Staff Dance. But that had been in the firm's car, bigger all round.

As he rested his hand on the wheel, and flicked his fresh cigarette at the wind, she felt she had been perhaps too cold. She did not feel a bit in the mood, at this time of the morning, but she wouldn't be a spoilsport, and she put her hand on his arm and said:

'Philip, Philip, please look at me?'

He turned his head towards her. She put her arm round his shoulder, she had to lever herself out of her seat to get there, and kissed him. Her lipstick stayed on the corner of his mouth, and smeared his cheek, where he had moved. She moistened her handkerchief and rubbed it off. She said, still apologetic: 'You took me by surprise, but I *do* like. It's all right, I like it when you kiss me. Only, it's you know, morning. I'm not accustomed.'

'You can get used to anything,' he replied, and she was not sure if this was forgiveness or not, so she said:

'I didn't tell anybody we were going out together today.'

'Are you ashamed of me, or something?'

She was outraged. 'But you asked me not to tell!'

'All the same, most girls would tell, in your position.'

'Really I didn't.'

'Truth, Lorne, no one?'

'No one, no one. Not even me dad. May I never get home in one piece, Philip. I did like you asked me.'

'Relax, sweetheart, it wasn't that important.'

'What you told me, you know, I did that. I was busting to tell, but then I thought it'd get back to you so if anybody started talking about you to me I just made out, you know, that we'd both had a bit too much to drink at the Staff Dance, and it was all good clean fun.'

He laughed, and started the engine.

'Bleedin' liar,' he mimicked the accent and stress of the canteen arguments.

'Bleedin' governor's man,' she dared.

Luckily he took it well. 'Man, not boy, anyway,' he laughed.

'We all know that,' she said casually, and apparently this was the wrong thing to say because he straight away flared:

'I've never laid a hand on any one of those girls but you!

Whatever you hear, discount what you don't know already.'

'I didn't mean anything, Philip. It was a manner of speaking, that's all. The girls know you're worth your job, regardless. Whether or not you were the old man's son. Honest!'

'I thought there was an implication.'

'It never come into my mind, Philip, to work in an implication.'

But he sulked.

'Yakking women,' he grumbled.

In a panic she tried to dissociate herself: 'I hate it meself, but you have to say something or the others think you're funny. Anyway, it's not only you that's the subject. It's everything under the sun!'

'Or who's to be next under the son?'

She hated that way of speaking, but she pretended it was nothing.

'Let them talk. You're big enough. You're not affected, really.'

'If it were me I'd put 'em all out, and bring in one man for every two women.'

By now she was losing patience: 'Just as well then your old man has a few years to go yet before you take over.'

Surprisingly, he now grinned: 'Just as well,' he replied, 'or I wouldn't have the time to be taking you out.'

She accepted the peace offering greedily:

'I've been looking forward to it all week, Philip, wondering what it was you meant to show me?'

'All sorts,' he said, 'but to begin with a little place down here on the left.'

The little place was enormous. It stood just off the main road, and was reached by a concealed drive, which was a bit overgrown and bumpy. The forecourt was full of puddles, and she could tell from the lack of curtains, as well, that nobody lived there. After the road it was very quiet. Philip jumped out and stood looking up at the long balcony which ran the length of the first floor. She waited, not knowing what was expected of her.

'Coming?' he called, turning after a minute.

She got out and followed as he walked towards the house.

'You're not going in?' she asked, as she caught up.

'What's stopping me!'

'Somebody might come.'

'It's been a long time empty.'

That was very evident as soon as they were inside.

'Oooh, Philip, it smells worse than crocodiles!'

'Yes,' he said, but he wasn't paying attention. He had his lighter out and walked forward.

'Mind how you go on the stairs,' he said, 'bloody wood's probably all rotten.'

She followed, thinking that if that were all it wouldn't be too big a problem. Dad knew a man, he was one of the group at the local, who was very keen to do jobs in wood.

Upstairs it was lighter, and you could see now *enormous*. Being empty it looked that way; probably with furniture in it, it would be a bit more homelike, but even so you'd have to gut two or three furniture shops and clear half the stock of John Lewis for fabrics before it could be made anything like cosy.

'This was the best bedroom,' said Philip, moving on again.

'How do you know?' she asked, standing beside him in the centre of a room the size of the packing room in the firm's basement. 'Have you been here before?'

'No, but it's obvious, isn't it?'

She did not see why, but she did not dare say so. He had turned away from her and was holding the lighter up to illuminate a picture set in the wall above the fireplace.

'Oooh, don't they look funny!' she exclaimed. 'He's only got one button on his coat!'

'Those coats only ever did have one button.'

'Saved sewing.'

In the picture the man stood over, but faced away from, the young woman seated in the chair. All the expression in the work was contained in the dress of the woman and the patterns on the curtain which held up the whole of one side: the faces of the pair, like the house they once lived in, no longer said anything.

'They were the Ainsleys,' said Philip.

'Did they live here? They don't look as if they knew one another very well.'

'They lived here. And died here.'

'Oh, I like that, don't you, Philip, when you hear people live and die in one home. And have their kids there and everything.' In the gloom she risked slipping her arm through his. She was reassured by the warmth of the physical contact in this spooky place.

'They had no kids,' said Philip; 'he didn't want her to have any kids.'

'What'd they get married for, then?' she said staring indignantly at the blank, passionless Ainsley, who had had all this house and had not wanted to populate it.

He laughed suddenly, a hideous vulgar sound which she welcomed, with its suggestion of a practical earthy presence, repelling the remote and eerie hopelessness of the olden-time couple who had had no issue. She laughed too, and looked up in his face questioningly.

'You'd want kids as well, I suppose,' he said.

'What girl wouldn't?'

'Mrs. Ainsley wanted somebody else's,' he replied.

'Poor thing.'

'He killed her for it, before she could.'

'Oh, Philip, no?'

'Oh, Philip, yes. Just about where we're standing.'

'What did you want to bring me here for? Let's get away.'

'As a result the place is going cheap.'

'I'm not surprised. I wouldn't give tuppence for it.'

'He wound a curtain rope round her neck. The house is quite handy for town.'

'Poor thing. I couldn't sleep for thinking of it, even if it was in Leicester Square.'

'She didn't even struggle. She knew she'd asked for it. The house is going for a song.'

'Let someone else sing. One little slip, poor thing!'

'He should have shot her, strangling wrecks property values.'

'Please let's go, Philip.'

'It would be a bit big for us, I suppose.'

'Ever so much too big, I couldn't agree more.'

'Such a pity,' he said regretfully. Once more his eyes caressed the image of the Ainsleys, and then he snapped the top back on to his lighter. She almost ran from the room, while he followed more sedately.

Back out in the car again, with the sun getting up high, making the beginnings of what looked to be a real scorcher, she felt a little silly, and hoped she had not spoiled her chances by giving way to hysteria. She forced herself to sound matter-of-fact and offhand:

'Don't you think that when anybody takes on one of these big old houses they always find that repairs turn out to be more expensive than they'd bargained for? That's what I was thinking of all the time, Philip.'

'You're right, Lorne. You're a shrewd girl. You'd make someone a capable, managing sort of wife.'

'Oh, I would, I would. You could rely on me. Mum always said I saved a shilling in every pound. I always compare prices, you know.'

'Enjoy shopping?'

'Yes, I do. It's a battle, I always say.'

'It's all a battle,' he replied, and the car was away again, whisking down the leaf-strewn drive like a knife through tissue paper.

This time he kept his foot down hard against the floorboards. Lorne was scared at going so fast and only saved herself from crying out against it by looking at objects a fair distance away: to watch the houses and posts and cows and things just over the hedges go racketing by was enough to make a person's head spin. She did not like to think of what Dad would say if he could see this mad race across the countryside. Once, over a little hump-backed bridge, she left her stomach behind.

'Whoooph! Philip, you'll get us both killed!'

'Nonsense,' he replied, 'that wouldn't give me any satisfaction.'

'London must be miles away now.'

'Forty or fifty.'

'Why do we have to go so fast? I don't get a chance to look about.'

'I want to see how long it would take me if I was in a hurry to get home to you, doll.'

'Philip, I don't know when you're being serious.'

'You'll learn.'

He almost missed the turning when it came, saw it just in time, and spun the wheel over, causing the gravel to spray out from under the wheels. The nettles fell as if scythed. He said, in the cool voice, deckle-edged with excitement, which the girls all knew when a new machine was showing signs of justifying the expense:

'Holds the road well, doesn't she?'

'I'm holding on to meself! My heart's ready to jump right out!' she protested.

'Give it to me, I'll look after it for you.'

'I've heard that before.' But she smiled. The next stop must be close by, after all.

It was, and what a surprise when it came! There was nothing. Well, hardly anything. Only a stupid old wood, with one stupid old telephone wire sagging almost to the field before it rose again to a stupid little grocer's, post office, and pub all rolled into one.

'There you are, doll, want to stretch your little fat legs?'

'There I am what? And my legs are not fat.'

'Let's see?' He put his hand on her skirt and began to raise it, and she slapped his hand and jumped out of the car.

'There's plenty for you to look at without that,' she said, but she was not really annoyed, because that was more in keeping with what she expected. She looked all round and went on:

'But what am I supposed to look at?'

'From the grotesque to the gorblimey,' he replied. 'How would you like to live in a caravan?'

'Very romantic, I bet,' she said, doubtfully, seeing the little cluster of caravans for the first time.

'If I were to marry you,' he said, 'it might take the old man a little while to get over it. We could do some penance in a caravan until he came round.'

She had been meaning to say that she had not actually said yes to the idea of marriage yet, not having been asked outright, but the notion of the formidable old man putting his only son into Coventry, more or less, for marrying one of the girls on the factory floor, was a new and terrifying one. She gulped unhappily and said:

'I'd put up with it if I had to, but it wasn't what I was expecting.'

'Life's full of surprises,' he said, 'and so are caravans. Come and have a look at one. Mind the barbed wire when you put those lovely legs through the fence.'

True enough what he said, the caravans were a surprise. The first one they looked at had everything: hot and cold running, Ascot heater, little stove, fold-up beds, radio and record-player, and whoever had it kept it lovely.

'Set us back about fourteen hundred quid,' said Philip. 'If you're going to be miserable you might as well enjoy it.'

'Are they all like this?'

'No, some are a little more debonair. This one faces west, so you don't get the sun in the morning, unless you turn over in bed and look the other way.'

'I'd face the way you was.'

'What are you, some sort of a sex maniac?'

'I know what's expected of me.'

'What a pity,' he said, taking her wrist in a painful hold, 'that Janet Smith did not. She put the brakes on just when she came to the downhill bit.'

'Oooh, you're hurting. Who's Janet Smith?'

'Had this caravan.'

'Don't, Philip, that hurts! I wouldn't like to be in a caravan neither at the top of the hill unless it had the brakes on.'

'I'm not talking about the caravan. I'm talking about the marriage.'

'That's different. I thought you was talking about the *caravan*.'

'No, the marriage.'

'What about the marriage?'

'It was only that in name.'

'That's silly. She deserved . . .'

'Deserved what?'

'Deserved to be, well, you know, unmarried again. Divorced, I suppose.'

'Or killed?'

'I don't say that.'

'She was a virgin when she died.'

'Poor thing!'

'He should have found out beforehand.'

'Don't look at me like that.'

'People spend such a lot of time thinking about houses and furniture and all that, they forget what they're getting married for. What do you say, Lorne?'

'I say you've got to, haven't you? Plenty of time for all that after.'

'Plenty of time now.'

'Philip, it's not our caravan. Someone might come!'

He laughed.

'Why are you laughing?'

'You can hire these places for the day, if you want.'

'Is that what you've done?'

'Yeah. I know you wouldn't like me to waste my money.'

'You might shut the door, then. Else with this draught I won't be too long in following Janet Smith.'

He let go of her wrist and kicked the narrow door to. She noticed that as he came towards her again the whole caravan swayed, and went on swaying as he bore her down. You couldn't be married in a place like that, there'd be no privacy. They'd know about it in the post office every time he came home and took a fancy to a bit of love. She had to wait till he was finished before she asked:

'What did Janet Smith die of? I bet there isn't a doctor for miles.'

Getting what he wanted seemed to make him a bit stupid, because he only stared at her.

'The girl you was telling me about, who had this caravan, what killed her?'

He shrugged. 'Her husband, of course. Cut her throat—she ran, but he ran faster.'

'Oh, Philip, don't!'

'Come on. Get dressed. I'm glad I only took this place for one day. It wouldn't do us. I should think it was the caravan that caused it all.'

'I thought it looked too small. But I didn't like to say.'

'Let's go and have a drink, eh? With a meal to follow, with lots of people all round us.'

'Oh yes, I'm hungry. I was thinking, however would I cook for a man like you in a tiny place like this? Because if you're like my dad you like to spread yourself when you have a meal. He always says that if you're really enjoying your tea you should be able to get right down on the carpet with it if you want to.'

He out his arm round her shoulder in a perfunctory gesture of commendation and said: 'To get the best of you I'd want a little space, too, doll.'

She smiled at him, but in case his imagination led him away again she pushed the door open and jumped out on the grass. As she did so she suddenly thought of Janet Smith jumping out of that same door and running, poor thing, with the footsteps of Mr. Smith, her husband, much too fast on the soft, silent grass, behind her. She ran to the car. Philip walked after her.

For the first time that day he drove at a reasonable rate. He seemed quite prepared to chat too, more like his true self, good-humoured and easy to have a laugh and a joke with, when he came round with the old man, making everyone wonder if the old man himself had once been like that, democratic and easy-going when he'd been young.

Lorne thought that it just showed that where men were concerned you had to cut your cloth, and what was dicey with one was just the recipe with another. Another girl might have made an awful fuss in the caravan, and spoilt herself as a result, but she had had the sense to see that he could go no further that day with the main business of the drive until she came across. As for that story of the girl who was killed there, that was all part of the fever. It took men different ways, and some had to build everything up a bit. It was best forgotten, now that he was in a good mood again.

They had their meal in a country inn, all beams and brass and men with jackets with flaps over their behinds. Philip let her sit at table with her face to the restaurant so she could see who else was there, so she knew that he was still pleased with her, for he was a great one for criticising other people's manners and behaviour.

It was an inn with a history, trust Philip for that!

But you couldn't talk to the staff about it, which was funny. Flags and shields and bits of armour and descriptions of people who had been a bit wild long ago, wherever you looked, but if you took them up on it, and asked about it, they just looked at you as if you were some sort of a museum curiosity yourself. So there was nobody to argue with Philip once he started to tell the tale himself.

Philip had fresh trout to begin with and she had just prawns in a cocktail glass, with one of them looking as if he were trying to jump out of the pink sauce. She wanted to save her appetite for what was to follow, which was duck and her favourite.

'Not that I've often had it,' she told Philip. 'There's not so much on it as on a chicken and my dad likes to get his teeth into his dinner.'

'I like to get my teeth into a bird too,' said Philip, which made her giggle. She could feel herself softening up, what with the wine, and the warmth of the restaurant after the fresh air, and the beautiful attentive way everybody looked after her on account of Philip being so sure of what he wanted, and Philip looking at her in that sort of way. She enjoyed comparing herself, too, with the other women there because she knew she had more style about her than any of them, for all their better chances in life.

'You don't listen to me,' Philip was saying.

'There's so much to look at. Philip, isn't it wonderful us being together and nobody knowing about us. I mean, to look at them they could all be just hired out for the day, couldn't they?'

'Go on, doll,' he urged, 'drink up and have a good time.'

'How do you know all these places, Philip? Why did you choose here?'

'Rolls-Royces and pretty girls you can't spoil by kind treatment,' he replied.

'Yes, but you do everything with a reason, so you must have had a reason for coming here,' said Lorne, wondering how she had come round to be saying anything so searching.

'I was telling you, but you weren't listening.'

'Oh,' she exclaimed, disappointed, 'something about highwaymen, wasn't it? I don't believe in all that, do you? I mean, if you come to look at men like that today they're nothing like what they're made out to be, are they?'

'Between work and play I haven't had the time to make a study of it,' he said.

'Oh, I didn't mean I was an expert. I don't mind, really. It's interesting. Only I don't always think that history was real, you know what I mean.'

'That beam's real,' said Philip, glancing upwards.

She looked up. The beam was dark, stained, pitted, cut, notched, uneven. It was wood, but it looked iron.

'That's real,' she acknowledged.

'From it Jack Pendleton swung,' said Philip.

She was mystified. 'What, he was fooling about? You wouldn't think it in a place like this!'

Philip roared. Neighbouring eyes took him in. Noses twitched in embarrassment.

'Fooling? No, it was for real! The beam here was the main staff of a gibbet, and Jolly Jack found out how serious it was to be a swinging sort of a chap!'

'They hanged him? What did he do?'

'His girl Bessie told the Excise about going out with him.'

'Perhaps she didn't know.'

'He soon filled her in!'

'Poor thing! But why was it so bad to tell them?'

'She went out with him when there was no moon.'

'Poor thing!'

'The only light was the gleam of gold.'

'Poor thing!'

'They surprised him, but he got away. But he returned and made her drink French brandy.'

'Poor thing. Oh, *poor* thing!'

'It's good stuff, in moderation. The amount she had that night killed her.'

'I hate brandy. I sometimes have a cherry brandy at Christmas, and then it's all right, but even then, you know, I feel a bit sick. Isn't it hot in here? Shouldn't we be going home soon?'

'Let me pay the bill first, Lorne, or they'll be after my blood.'

'How long will it take to get home?'

'What's your problem?'

'Nothing, Mr. Philip. Only my dad will worry if I'm home too late because he knows what the works outings are like and . . .'

'I've one more place to show you. *The* place. This one you'll like.'

'It's been so exciting today. I'll never forget it as long as I live.'

'Why call me Mr. Philip, then?'

'Well, it was the thought of going home, and then being back at the factory and all that, and we can't just go on like this with nothing settled.'

'When you see this next place you'll realise you'll never have anything more to worry about. You'll be off that factory floor, and I'll never have to stop by again to ask you what your problem is. Do you know, Lorne, every time I ask that question, and you're in the gang, my heart's in my mouth, wondering if you'll put your problem to me, right there in front of the old man and all the girls.'

'I wouldn't. Never.'

'Come on, kid, get your coat.'

'Yes, Philip.'

They had a brandy and a coffee in the lounge before they left, because at the last minute Philip suddenly decided he would like it. He taught her how to cuddle the glass to get the brandy warm. 'I always imagine the glass is a big round breast,' said Philip.

Lorne looked round the lounge to see who might be listening.

'Am I supposed to imagine that too?' she asked.

'Just imagine it's good brandy,' replied Philip, 'they haven't designed glasses to fire the imagination of women.'

They sat on either side of a very low table. She knew that men in the lounge were looking at her knees above it.

'Where are we going after here?' she asked.

'It won't go away,' he said. 'Drink your coffee, enjoy your brandy.'

'I could kill you,' she said. 'I'm longing to see this place you're talking about.'

'Kill time,' he said, 'look around, that's what you have to learn to kill.'

True enough, people just sat.

It was after three when they left. The sun was hot and high. The brandy responded even better to the sun than it had done to a cuddle. The road ran straight on up over the hill ahead like the metal binding on a suitcase. They had the road almost to themselves. It was as if people had deliberately got out of their way, left them be, so they could come to their decision.

But it was decided already. She felt that, she *knew* it.

She stopped thinking where they were going. She just let him drive. The reason why everybody thought men were better drivers was because they knew where everything was. The process of the day was as sure and settled now as the process governing her actions at the factory. Any moment now Philip would appear and say: 'What's your problem?'

The fields ran into one another as evenly as the *eau-de-nil* walls of the factory.

'I said: what's your problem?'

'Oh, sorry, Philip, I was miles away. Must be all that wine. I was, you know, nodding off.'

'Wake up then, doll, we're just coming up to it.'

It was marvellous how he just went to a place without any flap or flurry. Her dad would have had to ask at every crossroads and upset himself and a dozen others into the bargain. She could rely on a man like Philip once they were married and never ever have to worry about anything again. If he wanted to live out here that was all right with Lorne, even if it meant a caravan, or a haunted house, or a hotel where highwaymen were hung, so long as he was there.

But as they went over the little bridge, which had no pavement but had sort of lay-bys let into the wall so people walking could nip in before they got run over, she realised that up to now it had all been fooling, he'd only been showing her other places to make this one look even more marvellous. He'd been trying her out!

'Oh, I am glad . . . !' she started.

'Like it?'

'Isn't it just right, though?'

'That's what I thought,' he replied, bringing the car to a standstill alongside a well-trimmed lawn, a wide diamond in front of a grey stone house with mullioned windows. In the glass the reflection of the setting sun blazed like a fire at its strongest. Behind them, caged in the branches of a great wall of elms, the sun itself glowed like a fire at the end of an evening.

She took his arm, laid her head on his shoulder. She felt she had lived for a reason.

There was no one about. She wondered how they would get in, but she was not at all surprised when he said: 'I have a key. Rather naughty of me, since the occupants are only away for a week, but I think the end justifies the means.'

'But if it's someone else's house, how can it be ours?'

'Not to worry. It'll be more yours, Lorne, than anybody's.'

He led her into the hall, and she walked in after him.

'It's nice, people live here,' she murmured, overwhelmed by the richness of living which she saw in evidence all around them, 'not like the other places, where you remember who was killed there.'

'Can you light a fire, doll?'

She was startled.

'It's ever so hot!'

'Light a fire all the same.'

It was not difficult. The people had left Witch firelighters, and kindling wood in the hearth, and there was plenty of coal in the scuttle. She knelt in front of the fire, having first put down a golden cushion so that her stockings and dress would not get dirty. She wondered if it might not be better to get a newspaper to help the fire draw. One thing about coal fires, if they were more work, once you had got them going they were more loving than electric or gas. She looked up to ask Philip his opinion, and saw him standing over her with a sword in his hand.

It seemed to her for an instant that he had taken it down from the wall to look at it, being, like a man, interested in those sort of things. Her dad always kept a German bayonet hanging up in the hall from the war, and it was the only thing she and Mum did not have to take turns in cleaning.

But he wasn't even looking at it. He was looking at her.

'What's your problem?' whispered Philip.

'I don't know if the fire will go,' she murmured.

'It'll stay in now, doll,' he said gently, 'it'll keep you warm for a long time.'

'Poor thing, poor thing!' she muttered, as if she were someone else.

THE JINX

He was a man of medium height, clean-shaven, eyes blue, colour of hair brown, thinning and straight, skull broad at the forehead, narrowing quickly to long jaw, dimpled. Dominant features of figure included broad shoulders, reach above average, terminating in hairy spatulate fingers, trunk long in relation to length of leg, small feet. Irregular cicatrice stretched from knuckle of little finger of right hand to centre of wrist on right arm, consequence of industrial injury. Characteristic body carriage slightly stooping, steps short and rapid. Subject born in Dubrovnik, 1924.

This was Mihail Tilic, who took refuge in England in 1960. Sally Jayson, who fell in love with him, described him rather differently:

'Actually he has a face as pitted and lined as a desk at school, but it doesn't seem to worry him at all, and if it doesn't worry him I don't see why it should worry me. He has terrible trouble buying things off the peg because he's not a stock English shape and I think that's why you don't often catch him in a suit. He could wear a tie sometimes, though. He does for me, but then he gets interested in something and without thinking he unbuttons the collar and pulls the tie loose in no time, so I've rather desisted. He's terrifically strong. I've rather gone off Englishmen. They're so conceited, and you have to work so hard trying to find out what, if anything, they think important.'

'Englishmen' referred in fact to Martin Leroy, who had been getting around, gradually, to asking Sally to be his wife. To his married sister Martin complained bitterly:

'I don't know how it is that you try to put on a good show for a girl, sink half your funds on light-weight stuff, turn a fair number of pretty phrases, drop her the odd note which should make it clear that you're fairly serious, pick the job with deep draught instead of something more flash with quick returns, keep on the right side of her people and so forth, and all the value of it's gone as soon as some man like this Mihail comes along, who, to put it frankly, is little better than a salvage job. Then these columnists have the gall to say wait for marriage. Well, I thought so too, I thought Sally and I were on net, I thought it was understood, but now I've a good mind to drop by parachute into Bosnia or Carpathia, wherever this character sprang from, well the other side of waltzes, by all accounts, and say the capitalists were working me up and down a factory flue sixteen hours a day, and I'll bet I'd farm maidenheads by the cartload.'

'What a murky way to talk,' commented the sister, her mind chiefly occupied with suspicion of the thermostat on her iron.

'He's a murky chap,' rejoined Martin grimly, 'and the result is murk.'

'Take a holiday,' suggested the sister; 'when you come back it'll all seem different.'

'I took a holiday, and this is the consequence.'

'I think one day you'll look back on it and realise you were lucky to find out what she was like when you did.'

'I feel sick,' he said. 'I don't know whether to walk about or sit still, to go out or stay in, to live or die. When I found out I felt damned unlucky. It still feels unlucky.'

'That's because you're upset. I expect you were fond of her.'

'What a fatuous thing to say.'

She put the iron up and looked at him in surprise. 'You must have been,' she said.

'I was *in love* with her!'

'Did you tell her?'

'No, of course not.'

'Next time you'll know better, then, won't you?'

'There won't be a next time.'

'Nonsense!' she said firmly, resuming with the iron, 'there's bound to be somebody who thinks you're worth having.'

'I don't want anybody else,' he said, helping her to hold a shirt straight.

'Get her back from him, then,' she advised.

'I don't want her back,' he replied, subsiding exhausted into a chair.

'It'll wear off,' said his sister comfortably.

His head went back and he covered his eyes with his hands. He thought before asking:

'Do you think bad luck wears off, except on someone else?'

'I don't know what you mean. Why do you ask such a strange question?'

'Because the man's a jinx. He was my friend, you know, before he was Sally's lover.' He had her attention now. He rose to his feet and said farcically, out of his desperation: 'I befriended him because I thought he needed friends, but he's one of these wretched link-men who know everybody. I befriended him, but I bet he gets more Christmas cards than I do. Well, they'd better watch out, those people, when they send him Christmas cards!'

She said, bewildered: 'I don't think Christmas cards necessarily mean friendship, do they, not today?'

'I don't know what they mean,' he said, 'I'm feeling too miserable to think about them.'

'Meet some more girls,' she urged, 'and cheer yourself up.'

'My luck's so bad at the moment,' he answered, 'that I'd only have to see one across a room for her to go and see Father with a small bundle in her arms.'

It had been a coincidence, though, that Mihail met Sally.

Martin was unpleasant about it, described it in fact as a 'pick-up', but neither his friend nor his loved one accepted this term. They thought of it as a casual encounter. They had each gone to the coffee-bar to wait for Martin. He arrived very late to find them sitting at a table together. He was dining on her credit account. She was sipping an orange juice through a straw. The straw was bent because she was so interested in what Mihail had to say.

He stood over the low table.

'Hello, Martin, I'd given you up. This is Mihail Tilic.'

'I know. Good evening, Mihail. I didn't know you two knew one another.'

'We've just met. Isn't that extraordinary?'

'So you are Sally,' said Mihail, giving her a long look, which continued after he had closed his mouth on the contents of his momentarily arrested fork.

'Yes, I am Sally,' she said happily.

'Very good,' said Mihail, nodding, and abruptly swivelled to order coffee on Sally's account.

Martin was obliged to draw up a high stool from the counter

because all the small stools were taken. He was conscious of looking ridiculous. Then Sally attacked him:

'Do you talk about me to all your friends? Charming, I must say.'

'What he said *was* charming,' said Mihail for him.

'You all stick together,' she said to Mihail.

'Divided we fall,' he returned gallantly.

'I don't want to intrude on anything,' said Martin, 'but if we're going to dinner, Sally, we'd better make a start.'

'It's too late now,' she said, 'I've gone past it. I'm not hungry now.'

'I am not hungry,' said Mihail, 'I have eaten magnificently.'

'You're easily satisfied,' said Martin. 'I never eat here and I am hungry. Well, Sally, if you can drink orange juice watching Mihail eat, you can drink a coffee watching me.'

She cast Mihail a look begging forgiveness, shrugged her shoulders, and rose. Mihail seized her jacket and helped her on with it. She said over her shoulder:

'Don't worry about the bill. I just sign a chit.'

Martin overheard and said: 'And her father won't know that it was not Sally who ate it.'

Outside she said: 'How rude!'

Martin said: 'How cheap!'

'What a way to treat a friend!'

'Who else but friends can be treated like that?'

'Jokes like that just make it seem even more boorish.'

'After being hoofed out of one country after another I don't suppose he'll even notice it.'

'I noticed it. I've not been hoofed out of one country after another.'

'Stick around with Mihail and you will be.'

Next day she felt obliged to ring Mihail and apologise for Martin. She was fascinated to discover that he was talking to her from the landing stage whence pleasure steamers set off up and down the Thames. Apparently he worked on one. What an occupation life had dealt him! How unjust! But how well he carried it off! Sally was very impressed when he wangled a free trip for her (in exchange for the dinner) and he turned out to know such a lot about London. How amusing he was about Parliament! Not at all easy with a megaphone. It was a gorgeous sunny afternoon. Mihail was brown as a berry. Such a contrast with the insipid complexions of the men in her office. Two days later there was a man went overboard and got churned up by the paddles. Mihail felt awful about it and gave the job up. It was not his responsibility: it was up to people not to fall in, but, of course, after that the cheerful patter seemed to him a hollow mockery. Mihail was very sensitive.

The drowning was bad luck on Mihail. Martin said he was sorrier still for the drowned bloke, but Sally said he was a complete unknown. It is not so easy for an alien to find congenial jobs and that one had suited him down to the ground.

'Down to the bottom of the river, you mean?' said Martin cheerfully.

For a time Mihail was so upset that he seemed disinclined to go out and look for another job. Sally quite understood his pride and admired him for it. After having held jobs of considerable influence it must be a bit off to stand from dawn till after the powers-that-be have had their breakfast, hoping to land any sort of a job, just to keep going.

'The obvious answer seems to be to take your breakfast along with you and make a picnic of it,' said Martin unsympathetically; 'he might have got the job if he'd had breakfast. It would have toned down that intense look. I think these Poles rather fancy themselves with that behind-the-barbed-wire look.'

'Actually he got the job. And he's not a Pole.'

'No chance of a wooden baby, then.'

'How can you be so vile?'

'I'll mellow when I'm a director.'

'That won't be for a few years,' she said.

'Actually it will be in a few weeks. Dead men's shoes. I worried old Harvey so much he perforated an ulcer.'

'Martin, how marvellous!'

'That's a bit callous, isn't it? Sonya Harvey, for one, took it badly. Turned on the waterworks in the library. Poor old hag. Fearful to watch.'

'Oh, Martin, I meant marvellous for *you*, really!'

'That is the silver lining, undeniably.'

As Sally came to know Mihail better she decided that he was getting on rather well in his job at the Zoo.

'You see,' she explained to Martin, 'he meets so many people that I think he can forget how lonely he is really. It must be a great relief to turn his mind away from all those weird goings-on on the Continent to the people who come to the Zoo.'

'And the animals must be a great relief from them in their turn.'

'Oh, don't be so damned patronising!'

'Why not? Isn't he looking for patrons?'

A man in a strange country does not perhaps always know exactly what he is looking for, particularly if he has gone there only because he cannot stay in his own. But he is not looking for disturbances. Mihail had to leave this job too. There was a woman savaged. Some bystanders who saw her before the accident said she had been pretty. But nobody came forward who knew her well to describe how pretty.

'He won't talk about it,' reported Sally, 'he just shakes his head.'

'Time you began shaking yours.'

'Oh no, it was just rotten bad luck.'

'It strikes me,' said Martin, 'that your Mihail is bit of a jinx.'

'Our Mihail,' she corrected him, reluctant to burn her boats.

'I think I'll have a word with him,' said Martin, 'and see if I can find out who he does belong to.'

But it was impossible to find him. He should not have postponed the search until the weekend, but the duties of a junior director were too absorbing to allow him to take seriously the troubles of a spare-time acquaintance.

He called on Sally to tell her that Mihail had vanished. He was ready to tell her that he assumed he had moved on to yet another country. But he found that Sally had also left.

It was then that he perceived the degree of the jinx's attraction for Sally, and went to grumble about it to his sister. He did not go, of course, meaning to accept advice, but merely to hear himself say out loud to someone else that he thought Mihail was a jinx, and hear how it sounded. It sounded right. He knew something of the disasters which had followed Mihail across the Continent. Mihail had once said: 'On the Continent we have a sense of tragedy of life, which in Britain is not accepted.' Martin was annoyed by the impression this remark made on Sally. He thought himself it was just the kind of rationalisation that a jinx would make.

Mihail was a man of medium height, clean-shaven, eyes blue, colour of hair brown, thinning and straight, skull . . . etc., down to the cicatrice.

Martin gave the description to a private detective, who located the fugitive in an hotel near a railway terminus. Before he could put in a second report, in which should have appeared the promised meat of the situation, he suffered a serious accident. He was run over by a car advancing against the traffic stream in a one-way street. The agency declined to persevere with the commission. They told Martin that they thought he had not been straight with them; had not put all the facts he knew before them: this particular operative had never been run over before.

Martin went to the hotel himself, looking both ways twice every time he crossed the street. He also avoided men building and demolishing overhead, all animals, water, and unfamiliar food.

Mihail had been working in the kitchen. Sally was staying as a guest. The arrangement had not worked well. They had been discovered in her room together. He had been sacked. She had been asked to leave. Well, they were leaving anyway: it seems that even in Britain one is hounded, one is not left in peace, to work out one's own salvation.

'All my life,' said Mihail, 'I have stopped what I have been doing when I hear the knock at the door, and have wondered until the footsteps went by if they were coming for me.'

'They were generally coming for someone else you knew,' pointed out Martin.

'But still I stiffen in alarm,' said Mihail, 'the very next time I shall be in fear again.'

'The very next time they may be coming for Sally,' said Martin.

Mihail's eyes widened.

'You'd better vanish,' said Martin.

This conversation, which continued on a park bench, was not heard by Sally, who had gone back to the flat she had quitted, suffering from a sense of squalor. Mihail apparently accepted Martin's interpretation of his nature as being that of a jinx, because he wrote a letter to Sally saying that he saw now that he could bring nothing but evil fortune to those he loved, that he was tired beyond endurance of flight, and that he would make away with himself. Sally thought this meant suicide, Martin said that it only meant that he had decamped. Martin was astonished to learn that, either way, she still had no intention of returning to him, and asking forgiveness.

He had two men call on him, neither of whom, he was sure, was English, demanding Mihail's whereabouts. He passed them on to Sally. She would know, if anyone did.

When he read what the two men did to her he felt that he had been right in telling her that she did not know what she was getting into when she took up with Mihail, who had all the symptoms of being a jinx. Or something. It was too bad, and a great argument for not allowing girls to live on their own in bedsitters in a great city.

He told his sister that he would, after all, go on holiday.

'I shan't attempt any business there. It would be most impolitic while I've all this bad luck still adhering to me. I shall be compelled purely and simply to enjoy myself. I shall take my bad luck on the Continent, and waft it back where it came from.'

THE WORDS OF THE DUMB

Justin Thyme allowed the cornflakes to slide off his spoon back into the bowl, and emitted a series of tremulous whistles followed by a prolonged hoot.

His wife at the stove turned resignedly.

'And what was that supposed to be?' she asked.

'Polite request for the sugar, doll,' replied Justin.

'And who are we today?'

'Rock hyrax, native of the Cameroons, related to the elephant but only the size of a rabbit, no tail, lion's face . . .'

'Our flat's too small for the hyrax at breakfast,' she said firmly.

'The hyrax knows no breakfast-time,' he replied, rising to reach for the sugar himself. 'He simply lives down this hole and when he pops out, at any time of the day or night, the first you know of him is his opening salvo of remarks on the state of the nation. . . .'

The plump little man leaned back in his chair, and again the weird cry sounded in the kitchen.

'For God's sake!' she said, shutting her eyes. A thin dribble of tea ran from the spout of the pot she had uplifted from the stove.

'I think I do the hyrax rather well,' he said complacently, 'seeing that I've never heard one except on tape. Your coatimundi, your aardvark, is a doddle by comparison. You can get down to the Gardens and chat with them in person. I'd love,' he said wistfully, 'to pass the time of day with a hyrax. Two hyraxes, to take away the interview feeling.'

She sat down opposite him. She settled knives and fork squarely before her, waiting for him to get on with his first course. She put her face on praying hands, so that her nose pointed at him over the apex.

'Is it all right to ask when a hyrax was last written into a script?' she said. It was not certain whether she was intentionally muffling her speech, but those acute ears of Justin missed nothing.

'One is just a little,' he murmured reproachfully, 'an artist. One has one's little speciality. If writers elect to confine themselves to dogs under the moon, to cocks greeting the dawn, to cats mewing in the fog-bound castle, one does not necessarily let them dictate one's whole *idea*. One hopes for enlightenment. One plugs on.'

He balanced the phrases smoothly, lovingly. The beautiful voice, so dark and handsome on the radio before he had taken up with his 'little specialty', seemed to her suddenly fake and rotten. She dropped her hands on the table as a spurt of anger ran through her.

'Well, plug on with your flakes, will you?' she rasped, 'and don't make those bloody animal noises at me in the house all the time!'

'They pay the rent,' he said, and crunched his flakes.

She poured tea and said nothing more.

She was glad the children were at boarding school now. They would have sided with him. They would have thought it funny. Georgie had even tried one or two noises himself. He was not very convincing, and when Peter joined in they had found themselves ridiculous, and were in danger of choking from laughing. Justin should have seen that it was wrong to encourage them when they were already at the awkward stage, discipline-wise, and the Wilsons, across the landing, were so ready to complain at anything they did. But no use grumbling to Justin. Always a 'law unto himself', he would not mind the children's games. She suspected he might even be pleased if they provoked the Wilsons. He always called them 'the persons from Porthcawl', dating from the night they complained as he was just closing in on the correct pitch of the fighting male hippo. Remembering the incident, she flushed again with embarrassment: she had been unable to admit to the Wilsons that Justin was responsible. She had put the blame on Georgie, and he had seen his chance and conned her for hush money.

Hush money. As things were going, it looked as if she would have to dig deeper and deeper to quiet the echoes of Justin's feral music.

From breakfast Justin went into the lounge and closed the door behind him. She washed up the breakfast things, listening for sounds from the lounge, but Justin seemed to be keeping himself in check. Today she fed the cat, though it was normally Justin's job. It was understood that the creature 'liked a chat' first, and, of course, Justin was delighted, garrulously, to oblige it. She put down the bowl of scraps and watched it. It came and sat beside the bowl, looking straight ahead, paying no attention to her nor to the meal. 'Suit yourself,' she said to it impatiently, 'that's all you're getting.'

But doing the other household jobs seemed to work off the irritation, and when she was 'straight' she went through to tell Justin she was sorry.

He was standing in the sunlight by the open window, with his hands in his pockets. There was nothing he must do until rehearsals in the afternoon. He did not turn round when she came in. His elbows opened out briefly, and then subsided against his sides where they had been. It was like the motion of gills, and in fact he looked quite peaceful. From behind, his short squat figure, with his broad, well-covered shoulders, suggested a man of some physical power. She hesitated a moment. On occasions like this, when she had the sensation of intruding, she wondered if, after a dozen years of marriage, she really knew her husband very well.

She said: 'Isn't it lovely and sunny in here? Much brighter than in the other room.'

'It's the bright day that brings forth the adder,' said Justin.

'Darling, I do want you to know I didn't really mean it.'

'Mean what?'

'I'm sorry I got on to you about your silly old hyrax noise.'

'Hyrax words,' said Justin gently.

'All right, then, words. I don't know what came over me. We were up so late last night with all those night-owls from the programme——'

'Nocturnals,' interrupted Justin, 'not night-owls.'

'Darling, you are impossible. *Nocturnals*, then. We were up so late with all the nocturnals from the programme that I just wasn't ready for the fully fledged adult hyrax so early in the morning. Couldn't you,' she put her hand tentatively on his shoulder, 'arrange to practise just the *baby* hyrax at that time, and get around to the adult when we're all able to give as good as we get?'

He turned round and smiled at her. 'Think of the baby piglet when pulled away from the teat. Not all babies . . .'

He lapsed into chuckles. She smiled uncertainly, but she was glad that he seemed to have recovered his natural good humour.

She came forward by the window, and his arm went about her waist. 'Well, anyway, I didn't really mean you to be . . .' she murmured.

In answer he made the rolling burble of the dove.

'Perhaps I overdo it sometimes,' he acknowledged, and even while he was speaking, a pigeon, type ring-dove, landed on the window-sill and cocked an enquiring eye. They both laughed that he should arrive so pat. She felt happy. Justin approached his face to the bird and burbled further. It flew away.

'What were you saying to him?' she asked mockingly.

'Telling him that I was sorry to disappoint him,' replied Justin. He was entirely serious.

'Go on with you!' she said.

'It is difficult to communicate something like that with delicacy,' observed Justin, 'but I think I contrived not to ruffle the bird's feelings.'

Sceptically she looked at him out of the corner of her eye. Almost as the bird had done.

'Seeing it's so nice outside,' she suggested, 'instead of hanging about the house why don't you stroll down to the Gardens and see if you can't communicate some sentiments of great delicacy to some entirely new and extraordinary animal down there, and tell me all about it this evening?'

'I don't think there are any new arrivals,' he said, 'but I have to go down there anyway.'

'Have to go . . . ?'

'Even if it were raining like hell.'

'I don't understand.'

'Call it a duty. Now that I know.'

'Know what?' she asked anxiously. 'Darling, what are you talking about? *Have* to go down to the Gardens, even if it were teeming? I should hope you would do no such thing. I mean, all the animals are there for good, aren't they? There's no need to go down there in all weathers.'

'There's one won't be there for good. He's a caracal.'

'Is that the one with the big radar ears you were talking about?'

'Yes, he was born on the edge of the Kalahari Desert.'

'Are they going to ship him back, then?'

'No. They should do, but they won't have the chance. He's going to die first.'

'What's the matter? Is he sick, then? You saw him a couple of days ago, didn't you? I don't remember you saying he was sick.'

'He isn't sick. But he's going to die.'

'Of course he's not going to die! Unless . . . are the authorities going to have him put down?'

'No. None of that. He's just going to die. I know, because he told me so. Animals know. Some do, anyway. This one is quite sure.'

'Oh, Justin, you're letting this business of communicating with animals go a bit too far. This is absurd. Absolute nonsense.'

'I can speak their language, in some cases, can't I?' said Justin. 'Don't you think that they might find it exciting to tell me things? Animals don't want to learn. But they do enjoy telling. The things they tell me about, they're the things that matter most to them.'

'Well, while I can still communicate with you, can I tell you that the thing that matters most to me is that, apart from having your stroll down to see your caracal, you shouldn't be late for rehearsal? So get your script, and off you go now.'

In the hall she made him put on his raincoat.

'It's a long day, darling. You might not be home till late, and it's still very changeable. Remember yesterday was nice to start, and became quite overcast by tea-time.'

'I'll creep down between two stones,' he smiled.

'Send for me there,' she replied. 'I'll listen for the call, and, darling . . .'

'I haven't gone yet.'

'Have some lunch today. The one I packed for you last time you fed to the beasts, didn't you? Well, today I'm not giving you one, so you'll have to go into the cafeteria, and while you're there you can have at least a glance at that script. I know you haven't even opened it.'

'It'll only be a collection of cues. I'm a faithful dog again.'

'All the same, it's as well to be prepared.'

'Keep your fingers crossed for the caracal.'

She put up her hand with the fingers crossed for the caracal, and, though she didn't say so, for Justin as well.

He went out into the sunshine, and ambled along the road purring into the hedges like a tiger. Then he remembered that he might be startling small rodents, and switched to the rustle of that whispering witch the cicada, which would mean nothing to them.

He was still proceeding monotonously with this while waiting for his bus when a man who joined him at the stop asked nervously:

'Excuse me, sir, do you happen to have a transistor radio somewhere about your person? I've been hearing the most unusual sounds, and frankly they do seem to be coming from you . . . somehow. I hope you don't mind my question, but they sound rather frightening and horrible, and I don't mind admitting that I'm right on edge in consequence. . . . Sir, I am addressing you!'

Justin was obliged to turn round as the man tugged at his coat. He turned off the cicada's paean of praise to the sunlight. He considered the man without reply. Then the bus drew up and Justin mounted the platform. As the man who had pestered him seemed not to be interested in following him, Justin looked down at the closed face, and unreasonably he thought: 'What a dumb oaf!' As the bus pulled away he leaned out and gave him the full value of the cry of the frightened gorilla. The man at the stop was not to appreciate the fear in the cry: it sounded to him like rank aggression. He stepped back hastily against the iron pole, while the West Indian bus conductor grinned, shook his head, and charged Justin fourpence.

To begin with Justin sat down just inside the bus on the lower floor, but he was soon irritated by the female preponderance of passengers there, and, besides, the stairs looked to him as if they were there to be climbed, so he climbed, and the conductor watched him go suspiciously. It had occurred to him that the humour of his latest passenger might extend to trying to travel a considerable distance for the minimum fare.

But on the top deck Justin was equally unable to settle down. Every time the vehicle stopped, and some people got off and more got on, he was driven by an obscure impulse to change his seat. The other passengers had, he felt, relationships not only with one another but with himself. There were lines of attraction and repulsion between himself and all of them. He had vaguely noted this experience once or twice before, but on this occasion the desire to move in accordance with the strength of these forces had become compulsive. And yet the greatest surprise was that he alone in the bus was truly aware of it. One or two others registered these drives faintly, sufficiently to make them hesitate before choosing a seat, but Justin alone moved in obedience to an overall pattern.

He felt the claustrophobia of that moving truck, and wished now he had chosen to walk the short distance to the Gardens. It was so stuffy, with everybody smoking, and nobody willing to open a window, although the spring had been coming in grandly enough for optimism. He moved to the front of the bus and let down the window. He could sense the hostility behind him, but tried to ignore it and opened his script just to flick through it, in order to put the others in the bus out of his mind. But the hostility forced its way through, destroying his concentration, until he felt it as positively dangerous. In some agitation he snapped the script back into his pocket and rose to find a seat at the back of the bus. He was about to sit down in the very rear seat when he felt the conductor gently tapping him.

'You wishing to descend from the bus here, sir?' asked the West Indian.

From the window it was possible to look over the wall into the Zoological Gardens.

'That's perfectly correct,' said Justin, smiling enthusiastically, 'thank you very much. I was dreaming. I might have been carried on for miles.'

'No man dreams on for miles on my bus,' said the conductor in delighted appreciation of having won without fuss.

'No,' said Justin, 'we all need bringing back to the real world sometimes, don't we?' and almost without a pause he turned on an impatient man trying to bump him off the bus and directed at him the growl in crescendo of a wolf disturbed at his food. The other apparently then thought better of his desire to alight at that point, and sat down again to wait for the next stop. Justin stepped off by himself.

While watching the bus move on, he thought about his conduct during the journey, and the items of rudeness which had bracketed it, and the only expression he could give to his conclusion was to shake his head, as the conductor had done. At the turnstile an echo of his vulpine snarl recurred in his head. He stopped. 'I don't like it,' he grunted.

'Don't like what?' said the official, waiting to take his money.

'Having to give you a fiver for a two-bob admission,' replied Justin quickly.

'That's not a fiver,' said the official suspiciously, 'it's a oncer.'

'My mistake,' said Justin, 'they are easy to confuse though, aren't they?'

'Huh!' snorted the official, returning him a column of florins, and depressing the lever which would allow freedom to the turnstile.

And immediately he was inside the Gardens he perceived what the trouble was. It was this mad, metropolitan rat-race that was putting a strain on him. One should not cut oneself off so entirely from the country, from the relaxing greens of England's woodland, from the fresh winds that quickened the spirit, and the sly, secret rivers that slipped everywhere through it. Here inside these walled gardens, only beginning to bloom, it was plain to him how precarious was his chosen profession. Had he had someone else for a wife, someone less dug into her own nest, it might have still been possible to retrench, to go freelance, to sell to the radio his own interpretations of the intricate system of the animal world, which his speciality was opening up for him.

It was an exciting idea. It would at least bear thinking on! She was not adaptable. She might have to try to adapt herself. The male must continually be experimenting, whatever pressure the female brought against novelty.

At this time of the morning there were few visitors to the Gardens. The crowds would pour in after another hour, hoping to see the animals fed. They seemed to get an extraordinary satisfaction, while nibbling their own sandwiches, from watching the animals *devour* their food. It was as if the animals were giving rein to a talent which they themselves had lost. Justin stood in the centre of the large half-moon just within the gates and turned his head about, trying to pick out the particular messages from the general holocaust of signals.

Somewhere nearby a moose had calved. On no account was the young thing to stray another yard away from the speaker.

There was a certain hyena cast out from the group. The accusations were too thick in the air for Justin to understand, and the outcast had not yet protested.

There were some guinea-pigs nearby grumbling at a draught.

There was a puma pining over a loss.

There were two parrots who finished nothing they started to say. They were stupefied with boredom.

There was a baboon contemplating malice. Friends were encouraging it.

There were two boys laughing at the sexual activity of some monkeys.

There were hippos talking of different rivers.

There was an aguantibo still dissatisfied with yesterday's diet.

Having turned in, Justin moved slowly past the cages. The condor, enveloped in its own thoughts as closely as in its giant wings, never attempted to communicate, and Justin had given the condor up. But he struck up a sort of acquaintance with a peccary, who thought that the next run looked more interesting than his own enclosure and could not see why he should not be shifted, since that run had not been in use for a fortnight. Justin was able to say only that he agreed, his vocabulary not being extensive enough to promise the peccary that he would suggest it to the keepers. But the peccary was certainly pleased.

Justin without difficulty persuaded an otter to show off in the water, though the otter had begun by saying that the weather was not yet right for displays, and that he liked a larger public. And he had some trouble shaking off two sycophantic goats who assumed that they alone were the cause of his frequent visits. His most interesting exchange of the morning was with two tigers.

They had been recently separated and were now in adjoining cages. They were mother and son, and the son had become old enough to father a litter on his mother if the fancy took him, so now a powerful iron wall divided them. But simply they missed one another, and Justin was touched to watch them hopelessly working at the connecting gate between the cages. The simple mechanics of the gate were beyond their comprehension. Working in unison, the one shoving, and the other snouting up the catch, they could, of course, have managed it. . . .

Justin explained to them what they should do.

They listened attentively and then the female hurled herself at the gate, and pressed her great flank in the direction Justin had suggested. But the young male stared at him through narrowed eyelids, and suddenly turned about abruptly, and slunk almost on his belly into the farthest corner of the cage, whence he glared at Justin, until the man tired of trying to help them and walked on. Happening to look back when he had moved on a hundred yards, Justin saw the male wriggling in a narrow opening of the gate and leap triumphantly through.

Justin smiled and went to his dinner.

He found it difficult to eat. He kept thinking of the painful situation of his caracal, the meeting with whom he had left till last, since it would have lain on his conscience to have broken into an exchange with the caracal, now that he knew the animal felt he was living in the twilight of his life, without the excuse of pressing business. He pushed aside his pudding, untasted, and untied the packet of food he had brought for the caracal before putting it back in his raincoat pocket, where it would be easy of access. He had about an hour left before he must leave for the studio.

There were plenty of people in the Gardens now, but none around the caracal's cage. A notice near it, on an easel, read 'BLOCK CLOSED', but although Justin looked at the lettering, the two groups of symbols did not register in his mind. It was as if the arrangements of the management of the Zoo no longer bore any relation to his own arrangements with the animals in it. He walked up to the cage and looked for the caracal.

It was not in the forecourt. It must be asleep in its den at the back. He looked about him to see that no keepers were near, and called to the animal quietly. Nothing stirred. He called again, more loudly, though he had never before found it necessary to raise the pitch of the cry very much: the caracal picked up the faintest sounds.

But no keen face flicked around the doorway of the den. The cage remained deserted. There was no response from the caracal. Justin began to be afraid.

He hurled himself against the wire and cried loudly enough to reach the caracal had it been a mile away. But the only result was to alarm a keeper, who came hurrying over and took Justin by the arm.

'Excuse me, sir, but what is your business here, please? This block is closed. Surely the notice is plain enough?'

Justin wrinkled his brow. There was a lot he wanted to ask this man, but his fluency in human terms seemed just now to have deserted him. He only mouthed, and the single syllable 'Jack?' escaped his lips. Jack was the ridiculously inappropriate name by which the Zoo knew his caracal.

The keeper drew him up the path a few yards before letting go his arm.

'Yes,' he said, after a pause. 'Well, I was afraid that might be it. That's just the very one that snuffed it this morning.'

Justin was motionless, watching the keeper's lips move. He did not take in what the official was saying, but he knew what the substance was, without listening to the words.

'Jack's dead of something,' continued the keeper. 'Crying shame. Just as he was getting on so well. At least I thought so. But you never can tell with these creatures. Take them from their own country, their own part of the world, and it's as quick as that!' He snapped his fingers. 'Of course, until they find out the reason, the block has to be shut off. They're all in quarantine *pro tem*.'

Justin said: 'Dead. Jack.'

He walked away towards the gates of the Gardens, with the keeper following on after saying:

'I know how you feel, sir. Don't you worry, sir, we've all had a little bit of that in our time, here, any of us with a few years in the business. Surprising, isn't it, how it can get you? You wouldn't hardly credit that a dumb animal could upset you like that. Not as if it were one of your own, really, and yet . . . it's real enough, isn't it? I said to Kenny Roberts, who's been on this block, that it wouldn't be the last time he'd be upset, if he meant to stay with us, and the only consolation is that there'll be another to take his place. It was the suddenness that hit Kenny hard, same as yourself, sir. All yesterday, Kenny tells me, it was sitting here looking down the path, as if it was waiting, you know, but otherwise there was nothing unusual about him whatsoever. Nothing to give you any warning at all. But that's just the way it goes, I told Kenny, only those who've been with them every day for a long time sometimes get an inkling.'

Justin walked on without even waiting for the keeper to draw alongside. The sounds of the keeper rolled around him. They were friendly, but they had no meaning for him. He walked out of the Gardens without once looking round.

He could not take the bus to the studio. He could not have endured a repetition of the uncomfortable feelings which had overtaken him on his previous bus journey. He walked all the way, and found that his director was annoyed. Not only the director, but half the cast, repeatedly pointed at the clock.

'I told you it wasn't a rehearsal. We're doing a run-through, and then directly on to tape,' said the director. 'Anyway, even if it had been only rehearsal, I don't see why we should hang about for the blinking wolf, not for Siberia overrun with wolves, we don't. Come on, boys and girls, if we're all here now, let's get cracking!'

Justin merely looked at him, and strode by habit to his place, in the back of the studio, out of the way until he was called.

'Come on, Justin, for Chrissakes, wake up!' said the director, 'you know you're wanted immediately from the lead-in. All right, quiet everybody now. Ready, Justin?'

Justin felt himself prodded forward by his friend Talbot. He opened his script but the words were jumbled on the page. He could not, it seemed, focus them. They all, in the studio, were apparently waiting for him to speak.

Justin spoke. He said, in the language of the caracal, that he was sorry he had not been able to visit on the day he was expected.

At the end there was silence, then somebody tittered.

'All right, Justin,' said the director, 'that's very funny, but we're a bit pushed for time, and I can't go along with any more jokes today. So, wolf, man, do you mind, wolf away, will you? Do me a favour, scare me? Let's all try to get our thoughts centred on snowy wastes, shall we? Ready? Let's start again.'

Justin stared around at them all. They seemed to be expecting something from him, and he would have liked to comply with their wishes, but he was not absolutely sure what they wanted. There was this pause which came after the early music, and then they all looked at him.

He tried, tentatively, the honk of the homebound goose.

He stepped backward, as the director came forward. He felt the arm of his friend Talbot around his shoulder.

'I don't think Justin's very well,' said Talbot to the director.

'Bloody healthy goose, if only we wanted a goose,' said the director suspiciously.

'He's not hearing a word you're saying,' whispered Talbot.

'O.K.,' said the director resignedly, 'put him in a taxi, will you, Talbot, and try to get back right away. Unless anyone else wants to try, I suppose I'd better have a go at the wolf myself, just for the run-through.'

He imitated the sound of a wolf. It was faintly recognisable. It reminded Justin, in the doorway, of what he had come for. He turned about.

He drew his lips back and the studio echoed to the long rolling whine, followed by the staccato threats of the famished wolf. Justin meant every word he said, personally. He summed up his views of the entire cast, and backed away through the door before they could hunt him down.

'I'll have his head for mucking me about,' said the director. 'That was intentional, nobody can tell me different. That's the last time he works here, I swear it.'

Talbot put him in a taxi, and phoned Justin's wife. She met the taxi, and paid the fare.

Justin had the feeling that he knew of fantastic things that were to happen in the near future. There were magic things to expound, and warnings that he must give. He tried to convey it all to his wife.

He spoke in the words of a caracal. He tried the words of a hippo. He changed to the words of the great ape. He was fluent. The very words he was using made a new world plainer.

But only to himself. His wife understood nothing.

After an hour she mastered her fear and sat down opposite the chair in which her husband was gaily chattering. She began to perceive that he had retained nothing of human communication but the laughter.

She forced a laugh herself. She would have liked the lights on, but she suspected that he preferred to sit in darkness.

She made a monstrous effort, and mewed quietly. The family cat turned its head slowly, and watched with interest. Encouraged, she tried again.

ONLY A GAME

Jill pushed open the window and screamed at her waiting friends:

'Wait for *me*!'

They waited, as they were bound to, having come round to collect her. They kicked a ball in the street, and picked leaves off the hedge.

Jill kept looking, one knee on the window-seat, because she did not trust them not to leave her behind.

'Hurry *up*, Char!' she exclaimed to her little sister, but really meaning hurry up, Mum, who was swaddling Charlotte until she looked like a parcel on legs.

'Not my fault,' protested Charlotte, 'I'd be quicker'n you if Mummy didn't make me wear all these clothes.'

'There's a distinct chill,' said their mother, 'I'm not having you going out unless you're properly wrapped up.'

'Oh, do I have to take Char?' complained Jill. 'We're all ever so much older and nobody wants to play with a person if they're so much older than the person.'

'They do!' pouted Charlotte.

'Hold still,' said her mother.

'It's not fair on me,' insisted the elder girl.

'It's not fair on me either,' said Charlotte.

'Of course it's fair on you. You are silly! You're so small you're never going to grow up. All your life you're going to be younger and smaller'n me!'

'I am not small!'

'Stop bickering, the pair of you,' said their mother, 'you're worse than a pair of old women. You should be pleased to take your sister out, Jill, and you, Char, you must make an effort to join in, darling, when the others are playing games.'

'She *does*, Mummy, that's just the awful part. She joins in and gets knocked over, or she cheats or something, and whatever it is I get blamed, when it's her not me that's spoiled everything.'

'I don't,' said Charlotte obscurely.

'I expect she's just not sure of the rules, isn't that so, my pet?' said their mother, giving Charlotte's beret a final tug. 'Now run along and enjoy yourselves.'

Charlotte darted away to the door, but Jill was there before her, saying:

'*I'll* open the door. When you're with me, *I'll* do those things.'

Outside, Anthony had come right into the garden. He was swinging a conker on the end of a piece of string. He held it in front of him, pretending it was a propeller taking him to the front door.

Jill pulled Charlotte out of the way and said to Anthony:

'Mind you don't hit Char with that thing.'

'It's got eighteen victories,' said Anthony. 'It just beat Malcolm's, and his was a niner.'

'Malcolm's was a *red* conker,' supplied Charlotte.

'Brown,' contradicted Anthony, 'they're all brown.' He considered Charlotte. 'We're going up on the Downs so you can't come, Charlie.'

'Don't call her Charlie,' said Jill, taking her sister's hand, 'she's not a boy.'

'I'm not a boy,' said Charlotte.

'Just as well,' said Anthony, 'you'd make a rotten boy. Anyway, it's miles, so you can't come.'

'I can,' said Charlotte.

'Oh, let her come,' begged Jill; 'if she can't come I can't either.'

'Well, she'll have to be on your side in everything. Whoever picks you picks Charlie too. And that counts as two goes.'

'All right,' sighed Jill. They followed Anthony down to the gate, where he said to the others, flicking a thumb back without looking:

'Charlie's got to come too.'

'Hullo, Char,' said Molly kindly, 'what a nice new beret!'

'I've got new shoes,' said Charlotte, holding on to Jill and sticking out one leg, 'I'm too big for my blue shoes.'

'Come on,' said Malcolm, 'we've been waiting hours for you two. Unless we start we'll never get there.'

Charlotte clutched Molly's sleeve as she turned round with Malcolm.

'Mummy put my blue shoes in the cupboard,' she told her, 'for my hands later.'

'Why would——?' began Molly.

'She's got it all wrong,' interrupted Jill, 'she heard Mummy say they'd be *handy* later.'

'What for?' asked Molly. 'I still don't see.'

'Mummy's *pregnant*,' whispered Jill.

'Gosh!' said Molly, 'she's *always* pregnant.'

'I know,' said Jill, 'but she doesn't seem to mind. But it's bad luck on me because she has to rest in the afternoon and so I have to take out Char.'

'When I'm older I'm going out by myself,' said Charlotte.

'Char's a sweetie,' enthused Molly. 'I wish I had a sister but Mummy hasn't been pregnant for ages.'

'Shhh!' warned Jill.

'Doesn't *she* know?'

'She thinks it's going to be a present for her, and I jolly well hope she likes it when she takes it out for a walk in the afternoon because by then it will be her turn.'

'Mrs. Fishwick said she'd cut her throat if she had any more babies,' reported David.

'What do you know about it, nosy?' asked Jill, 'you're just a boy.'

'She cut her throat . . .' intoned Anthony, and they all picked up the tune, singing as they walked along the pavement:

'She cut her throat
On a ten-bob note
And this is what she said:
    I don't want no babies
    I don't want no kids
    I'd sooner have dogs with rabies
    And ears like dustbin lids.'

'We have a dog,' said Charlotte. She struggled. 'He has dog's ears,' she said finally.

For a moment they all looked at her, then all at once they were hooting with laughter.

Charlotte's eyes filled with tears, but she hung on. 'He's a nice dog,' she said, 'and he likes me best.'

'If he likes you best,' asked Anthony brutally, 'why doesn't he do anything you tell him to do?'

'Don't be such a beast, Anthony,' said Jill, 'you're the worst bully I've ever met.'

'Anthony can't talk,' said Malcolm, 'his dog doesn't like anybody. He even bit his *father*.'

'Who asked you?' said Anthony, 'just because you lost your conker.'

'I think that's really why I like big dogs,' said Philip quietly, 'they like babies best.'

'I am not a baby,' said Charlotte.

'Nobody said you were,' said Jill testily; 'now do shut up, or you'll spoil everything.'

'Can I see your conker,' said Charlotte, wriggling out of Jill's grasp and going over to Anthony.

The road the children took curled into the soft, cosy belly of the Downs like an umbilical cord. While the houses loomed over them, and the lights and the signs of the intersection threatened them, they walked warily, arguing and singing, but still under constraint. But when the warm folds of common land opened to them the tight little group broke up suddenly.

John and Michael and Dorothy, who had the ball at the head, gave up their subdued discussion of people who wore spectacles and ran up the hill after the ball when John kicked it. It was Dorothy who collected it because it bounced back and the boys overran it, while Dorothy, slower then they were, had time to see what would happen. She decided to kick it, but in fact ran most of the way to the top of the hill trying to co-ordinate herself for the final unusual effort. When she got her kick in, at last, it was rather a tame affair, going straight up in the air, but Michael got under it, and with great panache imitated the side flick of a good centre-forward.

The others, following, seemed to feel they were being left out of something, and rushed off the road and on to the grass verge and felt definitely the better for the transfer. At the top of the hill they all checked, meeting an onslaught of wind which pinned their ears back.

The water streamed from the corners of their eyes. Out ahead the down dipped, and rose, and beyond rose, and rose, and rose again. The branches of the trees swayed, and the heavy dried leaves rattled, fighting for a respite from the attentions of autumn. Charlotte just stood, with her face upward-pointing, and her jaw hanging open and her arms spread, finlike, behind her.

'Oh, Char!' called Jill, 'catch up!'

But Charlotte persisted in looking up. She thought of catching the clouds, flying free of the grasp of the stretching branches. Her eyes followed one then in particular, and her head went with her eyes, and her body went with her head, and she rolled somersaulting on the grass. She lay there giggling.

'Oh, Char!' said the exasperated Jill, yanking her to her feet. Charlotte hung limply, swaying from her sister's hold. 'Stand up properly, or they'll all think you're just a silly little girl who can't keep up.'

'I'm not a little girl,' said Charlotte automatically. But she jerked her gaze away from her sister to look for the others, and saw them, spread out, already halfway up the next hill. Against the Downs, and the bulk of the tree thrashing high above her, and the lots and lots of clouds and sky, they had suddenly became rather small. She did not like this idea, and she looked back apprehensively at the comforting bigness of Jill.

'Unless you come on and stop being such a spoilsport I'll leave you behind!' threatened Jill.

'I'm not a spoilsport,' said Charlotte, and rushed off down the hill. Somebody kicked the ball to her, or perhaps only kicked it and Charlotte's line intersected with its flight, but suddenly there it was, red and enormous, in front of her face. She struck out at it, and missed, and then she was sprawling all over it at the bottom of the hill. Her beret fell off, and she picked it up and held it clenched between her teeth, to have both hands free to hold the ball and run down the valley between the two low hills.

She heard the shouts of the others behind her. Then came the thumping of feet, made by one of the boys running after her. She felt fully part of the game, and did her utmost to escape with the ball. If she could just get away from the boy behind her she was going to turn round and kick it to one of them, preferably the one who was farthest up, right away on the top of the hill. And everyone would exclaim, 'I never knew a little girl could kick a ball so far!'

But she felt a hand grabbing her coat. She continued to run, but she was no longer making any progress. She felt despair as the boy's arm went round her waist so, before he could snatch the ball from her she flung it away, anywhere. It went softly over the bush just in front of them and disappeared. Seconds later Anthony overtook her, and Malcolm who was holding her, and called out:

'Charlie is a pest! She's thrown the ball in the pond. Well, I vote she fags it!'

Jill arrived and said that Char need not. It was an accident. And anyway it was only a game, wasn't it?

'She ought to get it out. She threw it in. If she doesn't, you can. She's your sister.'

Molly interjected: 'It's not a girl's job to go in water to get balls out.'

'Girls shouldn't throw them in,' said Anthony; 'if they do they can fag them. I won't.'

'Don't be so silly!' exclaimed Molly, 'she's only a *little* girl.'

'I'm *not* a little girl,' said Charlotte tragically.

'We could bomb the ball to the side,' said John with enthusiasm.

'No bombs,' said Malcolm. He watched the ball floating in the middle of the pond with mournful satisfaction. Somehow it eased the ache he felt at the loss of his conker.

Jill pushed the boys aside with contemptuous elbows. 'What babies you are! Boys! Scared of a little bit of water.'

She whipped off her shoes and socks and walked out into the pond. The bottom was horribly squelchy, but it was very shallow, and even at the centre scarcely came up to her calves. Picking up the ball to return she looked back to see that Charlotte had her shoes off and was about to follow.

'Don't let her get wet!' screamed Jill. She rushed back to the side, splashing them all, and nearly falling over in her haste. She arrived at the side just in time to prevent Charlotte from stepping into the water. She pushed the wet ball into Anthony's face with an impatient flick of her wrist, and with the other hand she smacked Charlotte.

Charlotte put her hand to her shoulder where Jill's hand had landed. They all held their breath, waiting for the tears. Charlotte went on looking at Jill's face and consoled her shoulder. Her small face became dark and reproachful. She went on looking at Jill while she pulled her beret back on, like a tea-cosy which came down over her eyebrows. Then she said:

'I hate you!'

She turned round and stumped off.

'Yes, well, I hate you too,' said Jill tranquilly, resuming her shoes and socks, 'and I'll hate you even more if you don't come back and put your shoes on. And,' she added inexorably, 'if I hate you more you can probably guess that I'll smack you a jolly sight harder.'

Charlotte came back and took her shoes. Molly wanted to help her put them on, but she turned her back petulantly and pushed out her bottom bad-temperedly.

'Let her sulk,' said Jill, 'she does that and then she forgets all about it. With her nothing lasts more than two minutes. I suppose she's going to grow up a bit barmy. I'm sure I wasn't like that when I was her age.'

'I expect that was because you were first,' said Molly.

'It's enough to break your heart,' confided Jill, unconsciously quoting her mother, 'to see her so contrary when everyone's trying to help her.'

But Anthony overheard and feeling he no longer led the action, he sang loudly:

'She broke her heart
Till it fell apart
And this is what she said
    Girls are rotten losers
    Girls are awful sports
    I'd rather wear some trousers
    Than a skirt inside my shorts.'

He ran forward and punted the ball far up the hill. Nobody ran after it. They all stood and watched it while it slowly trickled down and came to rest on the path in the hollow.

'Who's going to fag it this time?' asked Michael.

'You can,' said Anthony, 'it's your ball.'

'I won't ever bring it again,' said Michael, walking after it.

'I think this is silly,' said Philip, 'fighting all the time. Let's play something.'

'Let's play Handkerchief,' suggested Malcolm.

'No!' said Dorothy, 'you get cold when you're not in the middle.'

'Tig, then?'

'No,' said Anthony, 'Charlie's He all the time.'

'I'm not He all the time,' said Charlotte.

'Shut up, you are. No, I'll tell you what the game is . . .'

'Grandmother's Footsteps,' suggested Peggy, who was fat and favoured games which did not compel her to race anybody.

'Let Anthony think of the game,' said Molly.

'Hide-and-seek,' announced Anthony, 'but not here, there's nowhere to hide. We'll go over the other side of White Pig Down. I know some smashing places to hide there.'

It took them some while to reach and cross White Pig Down, and on the way they found a dog, which turned out not to be lost, a couple of bicycles entwined like their owners, and some conkers from which Malcolm selected one which eventually would challenge Anthony's (when it had some softer battles to gain experience). Peggy found a skeleton of a leaf and Philip found a twig with which he claimed it was possible to divine water. John climbed a tree and hooted like an owl, found a nest with no eggs in it, and grazed all the skin off his knee sliding down again. They played several games according to the terrain covered and held some races in which it turned out that Philip was fastest, Anthony second fastest, and Jill third fastest. Charlotte was allowed to compete and was given a start, but it was apparently not enough of a start, because she was last.

Across White Pig Down she marched contentedly beside Anthony, and put her hand in his. Anthony looked down with surprise and said:

'You're too big a girl to hold hands.'

'I'm not a big girl,' said Charlotte.

'Yes, you are,' said Anthony, disengaging his hand. He put his hands in his pockets in case she embarrassed him any more.

'I want to sit down,' said Charlotte.

'You can sit down when we play Hide-and-Seek,' Anthony told her.

Charlotte lagged until she was with Jill again.

'Anthony says I'm a big girl,' she reported.

'She thinks she gets bigger and smaller all through the day,' Jill said to Molly. 'I wish she would get bigger as fast as that. Wouldn't it be lovely if people grew as quickly as dogs?'

'I used to be smaller than my cousin,' replied Molly, 'but now I'm bigger. I grew two inches this year.'

Standing in the saddle of White Pig Down they could see immediately why Anthony had chosen to come there. The land which had been smooth and rolling, with only intermittent clusters of bushes and trees, became from now on much wilder. It was pitted at first with artificial workings, now disused, and beyond these the trees grew thickly, whilst here and there showed fragments from the living of the departed site-workers. Those who had begun to tire were freshened up again by the enthralling possibilities of this territory, and Malcolm perceived that Anthony would have a tremendous advantage, because he was the only one of them who had ever been there before.

Jill excitedly explained the game to Charlotte.

'All you have to do is find a place to hide. It's quite an easy game, really, and you can be as good as anybody else at it. Only you've got to stay absolutely quiet and not make any noise or you might be found, and if you are found you have to help the person who finds you find the others. Only it's not fair to let yourself be found, that spoils the game.'

'I want to sit down,' said Charlotte.

'Yes, *all right*, Char, you're going to sit down. If you find a really good place you can have a good long sit-down until you're found.'

John had to hide his eyes first. He went into the middle of one of the pits and stared at the chalk wall. He was to count a hundred.

'Count out loud,' commanded Anthony, 'so we can all hear you.'

Jill watched Anthony speed away. She watched the line of his running, knowing that he would already have the best places marked in his mind. Malcolm watched, too, thinking that as soon as he was caught he would make a point of seeing that Anthony was caught next.

Jill said: 'Come on, Char, I'll help you find a place, but hurry up because we've only got till he counts a hundred and I've got to find a place for myself.'

'Will you count for me, when I have to count?' asked Charlotte.

'I expect so,' said Jill, impatiently bustling her little sister across the suddenly unfamiliar ground. She could hear John dutifully counting at the top of his voice.

In a nice dry spot, screened by a low fringe of bushes, but which was quite high enough to conceal her when she sat down, she settled Charlotte.

'If you don't let anybody find you, you win,' she said; 'now be a good girl, Char, and don't spoil this game.' Charlotte nodded and shrank down among the leaves. She was very excited. She felt Jill had found her a lovely place, and she was sure to win, and everyone would say, 'Isn't it wonderful how clever Char is at hiding herself!'

But as soon as Jill had sped away she imagined John crashing in on her. She lay trembling, thinking that if he did everyone would be bound to say she had spoilt the game again.

'Coming!' called John.

Jill had not given herself enough time. She was still dithering over her place when John turned. In fact he caught a glimpse of her before she dived down into the space between two chopped-down trees. His conscience forced him to look elsewhere first, but somehow he was drawn to the spot, and once he had caught Jill's eye he knew his face showed that he had seen her. So Jill was the first found.

Charlotte watched this process with the fascination of alarm. It destroyed her confidence in her own place. If Jill was so bad at picking one for herself that she got caught first, then probably she was not very good at all.

The game lasted a long time, because all the places were new ones, and as each person was caught he or she had to explain what had made them pick it, and how near they had been several times to being discovered. Anthony was last, and as soon as he was found he wanted to begin another. Anthony was last, but for Charlotte, and Jill said it would be all right to begin another game because Charlotte was a bit tired, so she might as well stay where she was.

'That's right,' said Anthony, 'she said she wanted to sit down ages ago. It's your go, Jill, you got caught first. Hurry up, everybody, or we shan't get in another game. Just count fifty this time.'

Jill deliberately left Charlotte till last because she thought it would be cheating a bit to find her in the place where she had herself put her, and because she did not want her tumbling all over the bits of wire and so forth that littered the area, which was a bit rubbish-dumpy really, when you came to look at it properly, and because it would be rather a nice little thing for Char to boast of that she had not been found by anybody, either time.

She caught Anthony first. She had an instinct for the kind of place he would choose, a rain-water barrel with an outlet pipe he could spy through. A show-off sort of place, and not awfully difficult to find.

Anthony helped her find most of the others with almost contemptuous ease, so that the second game was much shorter than the first one.

All the same, Anthony did not think there was time for a third one. It was beginning to get dark and he had homework to do. Malcolm agreed. He meant to start treating his conker to harden it, before he went to bed. The two boys started walking up White Pig Down on the return journey.

The ball was retrieved from the chalk pit and lashed away homeward, into the dusk. Peggy walked after them, holding the skeleton of the leaf against the odd glow of the evening sky. She walked in a trance, guided only by the voices of the others.

Only Molly waited, irresolute, looking first at Jill, and then at the others climbing the hill.

'Go on,' said Jill, 'if you want, I'll just collect Char. I know where she is.'

She ran to the place where she had left her, but she could not at first see her.

'Char,' she said, peering into the leaves, 'we're going home now.'

There was no answer.

'Char?'

The wind rustled gently through the grass, and a clammy leaf pressed against her cheek for a moment, before sliding earthward.

'Char!' Jill made an effort to be calm. 'You're found. Come on. You've won, but you've got to come out now.'

But Charlotte had found herself another, a better, a winning, hiding place, and she was still in it.

Jill cried after the others: 'Wait! Wait!'

Anthony grumbled, 'That's all right for her to say wait. Her house is nearest. She'll be home first, anyway.'

The group of children walked on homeward, even hurrying a little, as they realised how far from home they had come.

Molly shouted back, 'Come on, Jill, it's late!' but she did not stop.

Jill ran from hiding place to hiding place. Each one looked different now, as it grew darker, and she found herself looking in the same ones twice over and only then realising she had been there before.

'Char,' she wailed, 'it's only a game! Come out!'

She felt she could shake Char and shake her and shake her.

'Char,' she shouted, and the bad temper broke into a sob.

A thin slime of rain mingled with the wind.

In the distance some people in their houses were putting on the lights.

DODENSRAUM

The law stood by the edge of the grave and pretended to look down into it. He didn't like it one bit. They none of them do. They don't mind a punch-up in a boozer, they'll get stuck in at a cup-tie when they're on a beating to nothing, they'll get up on the wet slates when some geezer wants to knock hisself off, but you stand one on the edge of a grave, when the padre's said his piece and the beloveds have helped one another off again and the tumult's off the boil, and the mist comes down the hill and the flowers begin to sulk on the wreaths, and I'm telling you, he won't like it. He'll push out his stomach and look at the buckle on his belt, and, if he must, at the tips of his boots, but there he'll leave it. He'll say it's all right without knowing if it is or it isn't, and he'll scapa. He'll run off on his little fat hairy legs and get in his motor, all subdued, and drag on a Weight till he gets his signal to blow. They're all the same, they've got no bottle at the last knockings of all, and by last knockings I mean in this instance the fall of the lumps of earth on the box in the grave. I can't say I blame them. I'd of been the same, before I went on grave-digging.

It was just as usual that afternoon. It was late on, on account of a close mate of the deceased hanging it out a bit with a lot of rabbit about his good judgement (which must have let him down one time or he wouldn't have been lying there shot twenty-five years ahead of his contract) and what a hole it would leave (as if there wouldn't be plenty to welcome his greengages, or the chance of goosing the little blondie he married) and who would have thought it, but there was a lesson in it for us in his death, as there had been so many in his life. A right load of old fanny. I could see it being seven o'clock again before I was indoors, and that would be three days on the trot: it was just at the start of the new year, always our peak period, and at home they'd be remarking on it, how irritable I was, and more than once I'd been on the point of turning the job in, which I would of, if it hadn't been for the beer money I'd been getting lately from the R.C.s. Night was coming down, black and as mouldy as the inside of my skyrocket, and I was glad at least I had a mate to help when the copper, tall thin lad, he was, with hands and feet sticking out of his uniform as if they was toothpaste coming out of a tube, takes a little shufti as per regulations and tells me to carry on, he has something to attend to.

My mate's a Paddy, not been on the job long. Come down from Liverpool, where he'd been in bother. A bird nicked his savings and had it off with a Pakistani as a reminder that money isn't everything. He thought about it too much, my opinion. But we was cheering him up and he was coming along quite nicely: only the day before, being cold enough to freeze the arse off you, we'd started a bit of a bundle down on the coffin, out of the wind. There we was wrestling, right tasty sod he was too, worth his weight, when an official of the Council come along and gave us a lot of old moody. It wasn't seemly, all this. If he could come along the following day, after that, I wonder if he would have spoken up in the same way? Or run for it, perhaps, emigrated probably.

Soon as the copper's had it away to his car I've shared out the loot with the Paddy. 'Here's a oncer,' I've told him, 'and here's half a dollar.' He's took it, and he's went: 'What's the half-dollar?' 'From the old lady,' I've told him; 'she come back with a dollar after she got in the motor.' The Paddy seems reluctant to take it, it brought on the miseries again from what I could see of his nose twisting about. 'Widow's mite,' he says, 'it'll be bad luck.' That upsets me, to hear men flying out against money people want to give them. 'You don't want help,' I say, 'you want shooting to be happy. And, secondly, it wasn't the widow, it was his old lady.' This only makes him worse. 'And she was a widow too, for her man lies underneath her son.' True enough, it was a family grave. I went: 'She came up before then, and she's thinking it'll be her turn next, and if I hadn't of took the dollar she'd of thought when that time came round she couldn't rely on fair treatment. Poor old cow, she's thinking that now her son's gone nobody might be at her graveside to attend to the trimmings. You're a hard sod, Patrick, I don't understand you.'

At this he gave me a bit of a smile. 'They'll put no more in here?' he said, half asking and half thinking to himself that since he's come on this game he's learnt a lot, and there may be more surprises round the corner. 'No more? They'd stack 'em together like empties in a brewer's crate, to keep the rates down, making certain only to have heads and toes alternate. She'll even be lucky, she'll know who's she's joining. Many are just consigned, mate, don't you worry yourself about that.' He looked at me, not knowing if I was serious. 'Getting crowded, is it, then?' he asked, and then, 'Give me the rake, and you take the shovel.'

Before I could stop him he's jumped into the grave. Well, I'd seen earlier on that they'd cut down a bit on the expense in the wood the coffin was made from, and, sure enough, dropping down like that with his heels first, eight feet if it was an inch, Patrick's gone straight through the lid of the coffin. Of course, our bloke sits up in his box, not having been warned he was to receive a couple of hundredweight of careless Paddy in his middle. Patrick didn't stop for an introduction, he's let out one wild shriek, then straight up the side like a cat going up a wall, and away down the hill he's rushed. No use me calling out to him. I tried, but I expect he thought it was our bloke wanted him back to ruck him, and ask him who was creating all the disturbance. I didn't like it much myself. An occurrence of that nature gets right into you, like being hooked in a barney when you've thought yourself only a bystander.

What I called that Patrick! And if I ever was to come up against him again, I'd say the same to his face. He could of come back. In his position I would of took a butcher's at a few people lined up at the nearest bus-stop, seen that the difference isn't all that much anyway, and gone back to give a mate a hand with refacing the side of the grave I'd mucked about during my inglorious exit, and repaired the coffin I'd smashed up. But he never. He left me to get on with it, and when I see that, I bloody near put my coat on and told them they knew what to do with their holes in the ground and all that fancy accommodation therein. But when I'd ate a pork pie, and drank a cup of the old hot tea from the thermos, I've appreciated that I couldn't leave the grave in such a two-and-eight without repercussions. So I've gone back to it. Nothing in life stays the same. Here's something you might not of thought of: nothing in death does either.

When I've set down the lamp again at the edge, and lit another to play on the narrow end where the feet lay, to be sure of distributing the earth evenly not to get a subsidence, I've seen that our bloke with the bullet in his heart is still sitting where Patrick's rude interruption left him, and at the other end, in an identical position, with his head leaning against the wall, and his hands resting on the side of the box, like twins in a bloody pram, is another dead man, the spitting image of the leading man in our recent drama. Naturally enough I've stepped back a pace or ten, to consider the action and whether one man on his tod isn't what you might call understaffed for a situation of this kind. I've looked all round me, slow and methodical, seeing that everything is in its place. I've noted the stone angel on the big tomb in the next row: still holding up aloft the stone wreath. Quite in order. A bit farther over there's the gate to the cemetery, the emergency exit or tradesman's entrance same thing, swinging on its broken hinge. Quite in order, well, it wanted mending but I hadn't got a motor up me bottle. At the bottom of the hill, where the road wound down into the High Street, a bus went by as if the driver thought he was on the M1, I expect he wanted his tea, if it was me on it he'd go to kip every two minutes. There was nothing different except the Z-car had gone, had it away to the nick, I don't doubt, directly he saw the Paddy running for his bus, thinking perhaps how will it tell best, the tale of this merchant with a bullet in his heart and the extra bird at the funeral who had to be held back from chucking herself in after him, while the little blondie he married stood up as straight and as quiet as a plastic flower. What I mean, the world of the living went on, not too extremely perfectly, but offering enough to tempt me. While I was lumbered with an additional dead bugger no one had mentioned.

It come to me then that they'd been trying to ring it on us, crafty teenucs, tried to work two in for the price of one. I was choked. Every grave's worth eight quid to the digger, basic, before the beer money enters into it, and I thought if the second one's trying to creep into paradise on a platform ticket he can think again, I'll expose him. I'll have him out on the grass to spoil, in full view of the cash customers. But if I'd done that the Council would have found fault. They're very exacting. Every grave is measured tight to the requirements of the individual, and that's the thought that's cut me short. The coffin for our bloke's been built round him nearly: it could of been tailored for him at Savile Row. There was no room for any stowaway. That turned me off a bit, I like to know what's going on. I walked a few rows away and leaned my head against an antique headstone for a Jimmy Riddle. No offence intended to the geezer down below, but that kind of marble asks for it. And then I went back to the grave determined to have a right go at the pair of them.

Pair? There was three.

She was picking bits of mud off herself. It was all in her hair and down her best party dress, but evidently what niggled her most was having her ears full. She kept hanging her head on one side and banging it with her palm. Like that I could see her face well, and if you don't mind it a funny greeny colour, like roast pork a bit on the nose, you could fancy lusting a sort like her. These days the birds paint themselves tomb colours, anyway. When I see them out I often think they've been absent-minded and left off with only the undercoat on. And the street lights make it worse, so it didn't affect me much either way. But she had a pair of Bristols on her, she had a figure, her dress was open like historical days, she was a little darling. The two blokes are still sitting back making a hobby of doing nothin', but all at once she sits up all businesslike and says:

'It's the last straw, James. We can't fit you in down here, and that's all about it. There isn't room.' Her voice was thick and slow, like smoke in winter.

The old geezer nods, and goes on nodding like it was easier to go on nodding once he'd started than leave off. James is our boy, with the bullet in his heart, and his eyes come open, steady, and my first impression from those eyes was that that bullet was inevitable. And the way they fixed on her elevations was more to be expected than polite. Well, there'd been two columns of James in the *News of the World* and in his life he'd been all the characters barring ginger beer. Then he's smiled like some villain who's been given eighteen-and-six change for a ten-bob note.

'Heather,' said James, 'I know you. The painting of you fetched a ransom!'

'Great-Aunt Heather, if you please,' says she.

'Death is a great leveller,' said James. All slimy, the way he said that. It was like the leeches going through the mud.

'You have a great deal to learn, my boy.'

Now the old fellow's opened his eyes. 'A great deal, Jim. But time is on your side. You will learn that we have our distinctions.'

'Don't tell me, Father!' says James. 'What am I now? Died on the wrong side of the blanket, I suppose?'

This caused the old man a lot of amusement. 'The wrong side of the cerement, perhaps, huh, huh, huh, huh! If you're not careful, huh, huh, huh.'

'Don't be tiresome, Gerald,' she says, 'that isn't in the least important now. There's going to be a great deal of trouble unless James makes up his mind quickly to a change of accommodation. You know what the general feeling is, and to sit there making jokes is utterly irresponsible. You're his father. Speak to him. Tell him that he must go. Conditions are appalling as they are. We are simply unable to welcome him. His reputation is that of a man of considerable ingenuity and, I have heard, chicanery. I can think of no man better able to find other premises than a property speculator who made a fortune.'

I have to admire that James. He stood it well. 'In all my life I never evicted a relative, Great-Aunt,' says he.

'Don't take it personally, Jimmy,' said the old man, 'we have one slot left, and everyone is agreed that your mother should have it.'

'She may prefer to lie alongside my real father,' said James, 'had you thought of that?'

'Ah,' says the old chap, lowering his head, 'that is possible. In which case I would prefer it to remain vacant for ever.'

So Heather sees that it's up to her. The boy's too sharp for his old man. Of course, he's in recent practice.

'It is naturally distasteful to us to reject you,' she said, 'but there is no alternative. When the site of this cemetery was settled it was apparently not taken into account that it had been one already centuries ago. From each separate period there are several generations now installed. Relations between the two groups are amicable, but the tolerance of our forbears is conditional upon severe limitation of the new entry. We must respect their generosity and hospitality. James, I am asking you to do the same. Begin your new condition well. Leave them be. Choose again.'

'Poof,' said James, 'squatters.'

'Everything dies but the dead, James,' said Heather; 'insults no longer touch us.'

I can see they're all mates; but me, I don't feel I'm getting enough attention. And that last remark of Heather's was a nasty dig. It's a thought I've had since I was a kid, that there's some kind of a big leak going on everywhere. I don't know where I picked it up, it was never at school, that you can rely on. Whatever you have, wears out, see what I mean? Without any reason that I can see. If it's boots, or a motor, or a watch, it's the same. From the moment you get them, they become less boots, motor, and watch than they was at the kick-off. My old man was always on about razor-blades: if you use only the one edge, its opposite number gets blunt contemporaneous. Even the mightiest river runs finally down to the sea. All that. I can't see why it should. Say you have a puppy. You look after him and he gets bigger and bigger until a certain age. Then he begins to go downhill when he's perhaps ten, perhaps older, but he'll definitely turn it in before he's twenty, whatever you do. If he has minced steak for his tea, you still can't hold him. Whatever it is, it goes. The snow melts, you can understand that, but the heat of summer, that goes likewise. The colour of your curtains goes with it, and if you drink beer or champagne it don't make no difference, you piss it up against the wall. You can see why people do their nut over diamonds, but it's a fallacy, if you was to live long enough you'd see them turn to sand. I listened to a talk one afternoon on the transistor. I had a soft number making a little three-footer for a kiddy run over coming out of school, and he was an educated geezer talking about the centre of the earth, and that interested me, because I never dig deeper than fifteen feet, there's no sense in it, the water comes back at you, and the strength of his message was that the earth gets colder each year. I didn't like to think of it. I put my overcoat on, although it was already May.

'Oi!' I've shouted down to them, 'what's the bleeding game?'

They've all three turned their greeny boats up to look at me. They give me the sensation I was the bloke upstairs woken by the all-night party.

'Why don't you all settle down?' I've went. 'Don't you know it's a right liberty you're taking with me?'

Old Gerald sighed. Like you sometimes hear come from inside

the box when cack-handed bearers don't carry it evenly. But he's a real gentleman, he knows how to speak nice. If he'd have had a titfer on when he was put away he'd have took it off. That sort. 'I'm sorry, my boy, for your trouble, but we shan't keep you long.'

Heather reached up and stroked the side wall. Where her fingers touched it shone. 'If this is your work, it's beautifully done.'

'Thank you, miss, it is a bit of an art.'

'For which he's well enough paid,' said James. I was beginning to think him and me might fall out soon. Only I wasn't certain a belt on the hooter would make much odds to him now.

'You're all mouth, you are,' I've told him. 'If you can't behave properly I'll have you straight out of there and see how you get on elsewhere. In the Corporation rubbish-tip, perhaps, or down by the railway line with the trains to stop you sleeping.'

'You wouldn't dare!'

'I might, though,' I've answered, 'for the novelty's sake.'

'He might decide,' said Heather, 'to move you again and again, from place to place, so that you never had rest.'

'Stop putting ideas in his head,' said James, 'he couldn't carry such a project out.' All the same, I've seen that that one was as good as if she'd hooked him. I liked her spirit. She was a good 'un.

'All the same,' said she, 'another home for you must be found, James, only it can't be done without your co-operation. Perhaps if this young man would help, a place could be found for you which would be acceptable, and you can see from this sample there'd be nothing lacking in the craftsmanship.'

James shrugged his shoulders. I could see like many of these tycoons you read about he had a weak character once you called his bluff. 'I don't care a monkey's,' he said. 'I don't want to stay where I'm not wanted. Only it's a bit hard to be for ever with strangers, or all by myself. I get on all right with people, you know, but there's got to be a bit of give and take. Tell you what,' says James, 'I'll give up my claim here if you'll come along and double up with me, Heather.'

With all the crumpet he'd had! All the same, I've thought, now we're getting somewhere.

But even while she's thinking it over there's a kind of heaving at the bottom of the box. Into the middle of them, like a log oozing straight of the water, another geezer emerges into the company, big enough for two, like a flaming gorilla, and not wearing as much. He wipes the mud from his face with the inside of his arm, and shakes it so the water flies off like a wrestler's sweat coming off after a long bout. He puts his hand on James and James shrinks away. I don't blame him.

'Is this him?' asks this newcomer to the gathering.

'Don't be impatient, Ben,' said Heather.

'Get out!' went Ben.

'He's going, Ben, it's all right, darling.'

'They're coming to see him go.' Old Ben's all agitated. He keeps looking down. He's bald as a blinking brick, and the top of his bonce is the only part of him without wrinkles.

'Go back and tell them to wait, there's a good fellow,' she's pleading with him, resting her fingers on his shoulder.

Ben's looked once more at James, then he's slid away. The last was the shiny top of his bonce like a dumpling going down in the stew.

We've all stopped, to reflect on this very tricky situation. Then Heather's made it trickier. My opinion, she could of held herself in another five minutes. But there you are, women have to have jam on it. 'He may want to come too,' says Heather. That's it! James has used up all his talent for compromise.

'I should flicking coco,' says James. 'What do you take me for, some sort of a pansy on a pendulum? I've made my terms. It's a simple contract. You're all the nineteenth century I've got time for. Take it or leave it. If you don't accept my proposition I'm not putting myself to further trouble.'

'Please, James, try to understand——'

But he won't let her finish. He's got his wild up now. He looks up at me.

'Come on, you,' he says, 'don't sit about all day. Get on with it. Get this grave filled in and leave us to it. You'd no business delaying in the first place. I've had this all my life, delays in the building on account of the layabouts I've been obliged to employ. I know what it is with you: you want to hang it out for overtime. Well, I'm not indulging it.'

And he drops down in the box flat as a haddock on a slab.

'No, no, no!' the other two are yelling. What a carry-on! After all you hear about all your troubles being over. I'm undecided what to do. Just to let them know I'm impatient with it, I've heaved a couple of knobs of clay down. The bird's up on her feet, and I can't stop myself thinking that if I'd lived in her day I'd have filled her cradle for her. Better than filling her grave. Though probably speaking we'd not have met.

'I'll go, then!' she says.

'Madness!' shouts old Gerald.

'You make my arse ache,' says James. Nice! To his old man!

'Where do you want to go to?' This is me. I can see that unless I'm careful I'm going to be lumbered. It's occurred to me that if I'm found at night burying a half-naked girl in some quiet spot I'll finish up shortly afterwards in one of those graves with lime in them.

'Away from here,' she replies, 'anywhere so long as I can fulfil my promise to all the good people in this cemetery. I undertook that our numbers shall remain the same. I will fulfil the undertaking. Help me out of this grave.' She reaches out her arms, and her Bristols are pushing at her dress as if they wanted helping out too.

'I happen to know,' says James, from where he is lying down, 'that a great many of my friends have their names down for this cemetery. Mostly members of my golf club. Besides,' says James, 'from what you say all places are going to be crowded sooner or later.'

'Young man,' says Heather, 'help me out!'

I've taken her cold hands and she's come like a nail being drawn from a plank, straight up, and I've put my arms round her waist and sat her down beside me.

'I feel weak outside,' she whispers, and lays her head on my shoulder. 'You are so nice,' she says, 'tell me your name?'

'Parvin,' I said, 'Georgie Parvin.'

'Georgie. What a *helpful* name that is, Georgie. I never had anyone called Georgie before. Wasn't that silly of me? Georgies are obviously rather special.'

Her face is right next to mine and her breath is like the draught under a door. But I look into her eyes, and was I talking about the centre of the earth? They give me the sensation that I could see through them right down to it. Her lips are very close to mine, but she twists them away suddenly and she says softly, 'No, Georgie, that would be dangerous for you.' That's what birds are inclined to say, so I believe she has not lost any of her old instincts, not understanding at that moment what she really meant by it.

Now it's the old geezer's turn. 'You may wander for ever, Heather, come back!'

'No, my Georgie will look after me.'

I'm beginning to see that if I put myself about a bit, and dig her in somewhere comfortable, where they won't build a house or a road over the top of her, I may be all right for a bit of spare and no comebacks, so I say:

'Yes, of course, it'll be dead easy to fix you up. I'm always noticing places that are going to waste that would be ideal for eternal rest. Sometimes for a codgel, sometimes for a score, sometimes only one or two. You'll be all right with me.'

'You people don't realise how many men and women there are today,' says James, 'how many living are going to be dead and places will have to be found for them. I've racked my brains fitting people in to live with one another. I've got some idea of it. You make me laugh!'

But James has his eyes closed. *He* doesn't realise that others around him aren't laughing. They're all coming up now to be present at his departure and they don't like what they see. Short and tall, fat and thin, dressed in all sorts, they're creeping out of the mud. Whenever anyone speaks all the heads move slowly. They're helping one another out of the grave. Heather's shaking her head against my shoulder. 'It's a shame!' she cries. 'It's what I hoped would not happen.'

And an old geezer in a blue waistcoat takes it on hisself to speak for them all.

'It would happen sooner or later, Heather. We have decided that we should march. We must take our opportunity now that it has presented itself. We will all seek new homes elsewhere. Unscheduled, unplanned, unmapped, we may lie in peace.'

'Good luck!' went James. 'I'm stopping where I am. It cost me a bomb to get an entry here. I'm not shifting now.'

'You will be on your own, then,' says the old boy.

But something is worrying Heather. She twists about in my arms. 'But it sometimes takes centuries for one of the dead to slip into a proper grave unobserved,' she tells him, 'so many of you would only torment the living with their search.'

The old geezer's looking at us both. 'I wish I knew your young friend's name,' he says.

'Oh,' says Heather, 'that wouldn't be fair!' Then she leans away and looks at me.

'Do you like me, Georgie?' she says at last.

'I like you, yes, to say I like you, you're all right.'

'Others have found me beautiful.'

'If it's beautiful, you're beautiful, I don't deny it.'

'Others have loved me, Georgie.'

'I could understand that, Heather.'

'What do *you* think of me, Georgie?'

'Well, I can't talk with so many around, can I?'

'I've been quite fair with you, Georgie. You can see how we're placed. We need a nice boy to dig graves for us all, and we have no way of paying you for it, Georgie. Only if you thought I would be a fair price for it, that's the only payment we could make. You wanted just now to kiss me, and I wouldn't let you, would I? That was because after a kiss from me your time amongst the living would not be long. But, Georgie, that day will come, anyway. What do you say?'

It's not often I've not been able to give an answer. The longer I wait, the more of them there are sitting round the grave. I had to feel sorry for them. They was like people standing on a station they don't know in the middle of the night when their train's packed up on them and they don't know when there'll be another one. They're all looking at me for a decision.

I've stood up. 'If that's all of you,' I've said, 'and you've all got your minds made up, I suppose it would be favourite if we covered our old china, James, in underground here. All right, brothers?' James gives me one last wink, and then he's rigid. There's a little cheer goes round the mob, like a cold wind it felt, and the lamp goes out, and it's black as Newgate knocker. Even then I reckoned to see a couple who missed the workmen's hop out before I shovelled the clay down. As I worked I could see their shapes moving about me. None of them offered to give me a touch, but that was expected, they was dependent on me for the physical side of things from then on. Even so, I didn't do so bad. I filled it in almost without getting up a sweat, and then I was stood there at the end of a long day, with more work ahead of me than I've ever believed in contracting for.

I don't mind. I'll do it. I agreed to it, and I won't swallow. It's dodgy, I can only do a little bit at a time. But I've worked in a fair number already. Nice little allotments where you'd never expect to find a corpse. And I don't say they're not grateful. Straight, I don't know where some of them find the energy to make their last little speeches to me. 'Shall I get in now? Shall I wait till a cloud comes over the moon? Please accept this medallion, it come from the neck of an officer at Waterloo. I couldn't wish you better fortune than a similar grave.' And lots more like it. Very nice, a real experience.

But, of course, they have to take their turn. And some of those farther down on the list don't half nag. Each one I put away makes the others get more on the hurry-up. They want to hear all about it. I've had to put the block on them coming round to my house for a report on the latest. If my old lady was to see just one of them she'd never be the same again. It's her nature to see them even without their being there. It's enough just explaining why I'm out so much at night without their showing theirselves. I've been obliged to invent a bird I'm courting so she don't worry I'm not in my bed. If she was to know I'm out digging graves she'd either think I'm off my twist or she'd straight round to the Council and tell them we can do without that kind of overtime.

And I can see it's a worse difficulty each time finding a new place for them. Sometimes it's been a real risk and I've put some away where if ever they're disturbed it won't leave off being a sensation for years. I've even got one at the bottom of the Mayor's garden! Gardens are good, but you have to be careful of those back bedrooms.

Sometimes a window goes up, when my shovel's struck stone and some geezer pokes his head out and watches while I lie in a bush waiting for him to go back to bed. One time when that happened I had a right lary bugger to bury and he gets impatient and wanted to shock the geezer back and keep his head under the blanket for a twelvemonth. Sailor he was, should of been buried at sea, thick as pig shit, not fit for a nice little garden like the one I'd selected for him.

Sometimes a copper stops on his beat, when he sees me on public ground, and asks me if I'm all right. I tell him I couldn't sleep. It don't affect my conscience to say that: it's near enough true. But when I do go to kip I'll surprise them, the way I mean to kip.

Sometimes some old slag, out on the game, wants to have a little go with me down an alley, but I can't leave my shovel, not while a man from the time of Edward, in his Teddy whistle, leans on the fence, doing his pieces at every interruption.

Sometimes I hear from an upstairs window a new baby crying and I think: 'That's one more to find a grave for, one more to add to the millions overcrowded down below. Why don't they leave off making so many babies?' But they'll not be my worry. Someone else can work them out, I'll dig in those I've agreed to.

I say that, and I'm doing all I can. But some of them right down the end of the list are scared I won't have the opportunity. They know how I fancy that Heather, and I'm certain sure we was observed one night, down amongst the diggings of the new Victoria line, having a little cuddle.

LAST RESOURCE

She had thought to wake at first light, but she slept until the sun found her in her cover, and fired directly into her eyes.

Instantly she sprang into a crouching position, half expecting to find death in mid-bound towards her. In fact she raised her forearm as if to ward off a blow, but with the habit of being hunted she avoided disturbing the low palms with it. The crisis of awaking straight into the consciousness of vulnerability being quickly over, she peered between the fronds at the steep slope which separated her from the sea.

For several minutes she kept up her scrutiny before she was satisfied that nothing larger than a pig was hidden in the short vegetation. Three buzzards wheeled in slowly diminishing, descending circles over a point on the headland, with the inevitability of flotsam coming down a whirlpool. Something there was dying. But all the other birds she could see were happily preoccupied with domestic matters. The woman in the hide was satisfied that as yet nothing was approaching.

The steepness of the slope looked to become less acute as it passed beyond the shoreline, but she knew from experience that the water was deep in the bay, and that the deception was caused by the refraction of light. On either side of a fiery hedge of reflections which grew up from the sea in the direct line between her and the sun she could see the water as placid and undisturbed, and on the bed the outline of each stone, each terrapin, each waiting clam, the enormous head of a jewfish watching from his cave like a dog in a kennel, the drifting shoals of coral fish. She wasted little time admiring them: she looked straight out to the reef, and judged from the violence of the spume rising above it that the passage through it from the ocean side would be too dangerous to cause her to fear any threat from that side. For the same reason, plus the certainty of giving her position away, she could not attempt to get out that way.

She made a quick job of plaiting her hair, without once taking her eyes from the scene outside. She tied the ragged ends with strips of creeper. She had thought several times of cutting it off, alarmed as her imagination presented to her the idea of it in the clutch of a strong brown hand, of it winding round a muscular forearm, of her head coming back and her throat exposed to the knife. But she kept at it, as a symbol of her refusal to give in to such fancies, and because it was reliable as a protection for her neck from the sun.

The unpleasant fantasy now recurred, however, and she reached for the knife to put an end to the conflict. But her hand came down on bare stone where she expected to touch the handle. She scrabbled frantically and did not find it. The knife was no longer where she had laid it before going to sleep! A hideous prickling of panic attacked her, like a rash on her back. Bitterly she reproached herself for not having driven it firmly into the ground. She had not wanted to mar the fine edge she had put on it in the slightest degree, and now, leaping to the rock, she found that it had been dislodged perhaps by some rodent, or by herself moving in her sleep, and had fallen down a fissure in the rock. She could just see the gleam. She grazed the soft flesh of her forearm probing down for it, but she could not extricate it. One finger just touched the handle, and with a tiny chink it dropped a further few inches out of reach. She had to have it!

She heaved on one half of the stone, which seemed to be split all the way down, but it would not budge. Then she sweated over the other half without a better result. It was too firmly embedded. The only solution was to dig it out. It took her about quarter of an hour of frantic shovelling and gouging and wrenching at roots to ease the pressure of earth about the base sufficiently to enable her to prise one half loose with a stick for lever. When it moved at last it toppled over suddenly and crashed down the slope, with ever-increasing leaps down to the shore. The birds screamed with annoyance. She snatched up the knife and kissed it. She had forgotten about her hair: she was only glad to have the knife.

She laid it where it could not get away again, and sat down to attach her sandals. She had slept on her tunic: she shook it out and dropped it over her shoulders. She hesitated a moment before putting on the belt: she wondered whether to leave the tunic off altogether. Like an idiot she had dyed the leather crimson, and it must show up at a great distance. Then she thought of injury to her breast, took the tunic off, and put it on again after having reversed it. It was not so comfortable, and the slots for the belt did not work so well, but there were thorns on the island, and insects, and malignant juices in certain plants whose names she would never know but whose powers were familiar enough: she could not go naked on this day.

She cached her few treasures, the comb made from a fish-spine, her handful of boar's tusks, the empty perfume bottle with the jewelled top, the key to the flat in Knightsbridge, and the Dutch coins she always carried about with her on the cruise because she felt that her husband was stingy with his tips.

For a moment she remembered Edwin as he had been. She saw him endlessly active, pacing the deck, joining in every sport, begging a turn on the drums at the dance, bullying a heavy industrialist at the captain's table with the heavy artillery of his huge arsenal of facts. Then she thought of him as he must be at this moment, somewhere on the island. Knowing himself hunted he would not have waited so late in the day before moving. His hair might be matted and heavy, the clarity of his features spoilt by the beard he detested, but he would still be trying to improve his relations with the world about him, all the time. Edwin would not give up easily. He would take some killing.

And so would she herself. She was faintly amused contemplating the power in her own thighs and calves. She clenched her fist and watched the muscles in her forearm rise. Then she slid the knife into her belt and, after one last look at the western approach to the slope, moved off at an easy lope in the other direction. It was beginning to be hot.

Edwin felt good. He was sure he could reach the summit of the lesser of two small peaks without being observed. The greater was no good for his purpose because a bare escarpment led up to a final sharp rock where concealment would be impossible. The one he had chosen was shaped like a hollow molar, and once inside he could see a good third of the island without himself being seen.

At the outset he had been very shaky. He had had a terrible night, disturbed first by a swarm of flying ants with an agonising, if local, stinging power; and then later by his own nausea. He attributed this to his meal of salt fish, and blamed himself bitterly for having relied on his store instead of finding fresh. On most of that side of the island the fishing was poor as well as dangerous: the Pacific squeezed itself incessantly between a long rank of thin sharp rocks which from a height slightly resembled, set against the foam, the black keys on a piano keyboard. But there was one spot he might have tried: the mouth of the little river, where the water was more still and shallow, sometimes attracted a few species. But he had not wanted to leave any traces whatever of his occupation, and a fire particularly would have given him away. Supposing, that is, that the quarter of the island in which he had chosen to hide himself away had been guessed at.

As soon as he believed that the salt fish was responsible for the outrage to his stomach he had prowled about searching for an emetic. Only his faith in his phenomenally retentive memory for the details of the island kept him going as he blundered about in the dark, feeling and peering at the bark of different trees. But eventually he had come upon the one he wanted, and he chewed on it until it took effect, and cleared him.

When he laid himself down again to rest, dreams so ugly wailed through his sleeping mind that the discomforts and upsets of his waking experience seemed trivial by comparison. He dreamed, naturally, that he was being hunted, but the actual enemy of the day to come made no appearance. The replacements were mortifyingly unexpected. His pursuers, in this hideous indigo sleep, were his friends, lovers, and colleagues. In turn he was trapped by those he had lain with, teamed with, fought alongside, comforted. His school friends had followed him over the tryline as he ran with the ball, and beyond the deadball line and then through the crowd, which wrapped itself stickily about him until he suffocated. His first mistress had taken him on the edge of the Isis, and bitten him through to the bone. His mates from the days of his international track triumphs had hounded him with javelins, removed the landing pad as he pole-vaulted, tamped down either end of the tarpaulin tunnel as soon as he entered it during the obstacle race. The cup he had won he bore home to his parents, who mocked the inscription

'FOR MARRIAGE', and put in it an ostrich egg which, when cracked, emitted a choking miasma of hydrogen sulphide. His regiment had bound him and offered him as a hostage for their own safety.

He was glad of the day. He was glad of the chance of action. He put his chances of survival no higher than fifty-fifty, nevertheless he welcomed the sunlight which would bring the enemy.

He moved as soon as it was light, and was almost immediately miserably hungry, having jettisoned everything he had eaten the day before. But he was able to make a good meal of fruit, choosing those which had had no chance to ferment through direct exposure to the sun. To husband his strength he confined himself to a steady walk and, gradually, warmth returned to his body. As his mind focussed on the problems of survival, the grim images of the night were forgotten, the tone seemed to return to his muscles, and his confidence was renewed. In his fantasy the betting came in a bit, at six to four.

He was climbing all the time. It was the first principle of his tactical thinking that in a small territory a man gains a psychological as well as a physical advantage by being that much nearer to the heavens than his enemy. He wondered if a similar idea might have occurred to Catherine, but thought it unlikely. Knowing her so completely, after one year's marriage in England plus twelve on the island, he would have staked the island against the coral reef that she would think first of the water. The idea would derive from the days when she had herself ridden to hounds. He was inclined to pity her for basing her feeling of safety on such a primitive superstition. Here on the island, since there was only one river, one would always in a sense be on the same side as the pursuer.

The vegetation around him thinned. Before him were the beginnings of a flattish expanse of igneous rock, mossed over here and there, but otherwise sporting no heavy fauna except where a few breaks and fissures had permitted a few small thickets to establish themselves. He halted at the edge of the cover and fixed his eyes on one of these. Between him and his target the hot air above the rock was visible, as if compressed into horizontal iron bars floating free of the laws of physics. The sweat was running down inside his beard, and a light breeze momentarily made him aware of the moisture in the small of his back.

He remembered suddenly an occasion in their first year on the island when he had waited in the thicket for Catherine, who was looking for him and calling. He had been after a bird, and her shouts had driven it away and in irritation he had waited there till she was close, then pounced on her to frighten her in her turn. She had been very shaken and he had been obliged to reason with her for some time, pointing out that an instant's reflection would have told her that it must be he, Edwin, who was pouncing. But at that time she still was not used to their being alone on the island and she had wept a little, and exclaimed pettishly that when someone jumps out on you you don't have an instant for reflection. The curious sequel had been that he had made love to her there in the thicket. It was a long time since they had been as close together as that. In fact now, feeling that she at that moment was sharing with him the stretched sensitivity of the hunted, he felt a slight pain, something indeed exquisite in its novelty. To think of an albeit strange bond existing between them again was a factor to appreciate. He hoped almost that she had perceived it as well. It was the most lively idea, which he wished he could have that instant communicated to her, since the day three years before when they had sat together watching some two-funnelled merchantmen pass along their horizon and off it again, after which a kind of numbness had struck them both.

He shook his head. He could not now afford any sentimental speculations. He must get himself unobserved into his eyrie before worrying over Catherine's putative change of attitude. To do that he must cross exposed terrain and immerse himself in the thicket, at maximum speed. He had once covered a hundred yards at the White City in ten three, and the hundred had not even been his distance. Here the ground was uneven, to such a degree that he calculated a slight arc would be an improvement on the straight line, but he reckoned nevertheless that he could accomplish the dash in about the time that it took a shock wave to travel from the coral reef to the shore when one of the big rollers came pounding in from the imprisoning sea.

He ran, counting to keep his purpose steady. The sun was in his eyes, suddenly, and his goal seemed unattainable. He would be running for ever. And yet the sprinter's 'float' came to him at the mid-distance. '. . . five and, six and, seven and, eight and . . .' He cracked on the pace for the tape. '. . . nine and, ten and, eleven and, twelve . . .'

'And a bit!' he gasped aloud, flinging himself into the shade of the thicket. He stumbled at the same moment that the sun was hidden. His ankle was snapping a creeper, and an arrow was piercing his shoulder.

Catherine crossed Sussex in about twenty minutes. The lightly mossed rolling granite hills offered an easy foothold once she had taken off her sandals which made the descents slippery.

It was her idea to go down Wookey Hole, but when she reached it, and looked at the tiny, evil-looking aperture in the rock, she was put off. She forced herself in as far as the waist and felt cold moist earth clinging about her thighs, and a reluctance to leave the world of open sky and prodigal sunlight checked her.

'I would rather die running!' she thought, and yanked herself clear again. She squatted on the edge of the hole, trembling. She said to herself that though she had probably not yet been seen, the chance was there. And the probability then was that she would simply be imprisoned underground: the entrance would be blocked up, and she would die without fighting back at all.

Edwin had always said that in the event of attack they should climb. Her instinct was for the bolt-hole, imitating the fox and the hare, or to get in snug by the river bank, like the otter. But, with the consciousness of hounds and ferrets, she could not follow it. She looked despairingly down at the Hole. It would not do. When it came to the bit her idea was inadequate: she had let herself down. She must think again.

Above her towered Schiehallion. Edwin had been up it a dozen times, but she had never thought it worth while. She could see from most points on the island that there was nothing to be gained there. Now she wished that she had made the climb at least once. Then at least she would have been sure. She was tempted to make it now, but the risk was too great. If Schiehallion afforded no eyrie she would be as vulnerable as a snail on a garden wall.

Beyond was Skiddaw, out of sight. Edwin by now would almost certainly be ensconced within the crater. She wished now that she had gone directly to Skiddaw. She could have laid there and waited, and made a sacrifice to the sun.

A small rodent whisked along the lip of the hole, as if summoned by the idea in her mind of sacrifice. Her hand flashed across. She held it. The other went to her belt for the knife. She cut the creature's throat and held the still-twitching carcass aloft. Then she cast it from her, for the insects to pick and the sun to dry.

It was something she had never done before.

She thought it strange that the closer to death she came, the more alive her mind should become. Her tunic was a barrier now. She flung it off and opened her armpits to the sun. She turned about, and took in the sun, like an access of power.

Then soberly she reassumed the garment, and trotted off in the direction of the Wye Valley. The sun was where it belonged, in the centre, the spearpoint of heaven, and she was still alive.

For Edwin it was a slow, and a baffling, return to consciousness. Peaceably, only a few inches away from his nose, leaf-cutter ants went by in procession, like little red-hulled yachts with an enormous spread of green canvas. Intermittently two or three would be hit by a squall and would stagger out of line, doggedly to rejoin it within seconds.

He tried to understand the evenly spaced gusts of wind which picked out only a few. Then he realised that they were caused by his own breathing. He was lying on his side in a thicket. It was the thicket under Skiddaw. It was the thicket which in the game of nomenclature Catherine had called the Tulgey Wood. He tried to remember how he had come to be there. Was he on his way down from Skiddaw? Had he rested there and slept? It was the heat of the day, so that could not be the case. He tried to raise himself, but there was no strength in his arm.

He felt the limp arm with his free hand. He felt the arrow, projecting. Then he remembered it all. He rolled over hastily and pushed himself into a sitting position. The sun was high. He must have been the victim of a faint which had converted into sleep. How strange that the enemy had not moved in to finish him off, having once struck him down.

Then he perceived the mechanism of the trap. It was the standard thing, with a very simple rig. The trip-wire across the path went round two trees and knocked loose the peg on which the bowstring was held. Running his hand over the creeper which had served as trip-wire he noticed that it had dried and was slacker than it would have been when first the trap was set up. For this reason perhaps the velocity of the shaft had not been enough to be lethal. He smiled: it was something which he, as a setter of traps, would have calculated. And then as he went on thinking about it, a sense of outrage, mixed with fear, clouded over his view of the incident. This was a trap designed to get him, based on an understanding of his habits. He snatched the arrow out and the wound exuded. It had not gone deep, and it was unbarbed, but he did not like the appearance of the injury, as far as he was able to see it.

He must get back down to the sea, and clean it out. He must rethink it all, but the paramount necessity was to get the wound clean. If he merely went on up into the crater of Skiddaw, and let it cook all day in the sun, it would go off like an unbled pig.

He heaved himself to his feet and ran out of the Tulgey Wood. His progress back, across the clearing he had last covered sprinting, was more like that of an exhausted marathon runner.

As he willed himself on, he was sustained by the memory of that autumn of convalescence, in the fifth year of their stay on the island, when the leg had been poisoned and Catherine had built him the shack at Fowey, and hunted for him, nursed him, entertained him. She had come into her own in that time.

But inevitably there had been an overdrain on their capital. When he had come through she told him one day that she was spent. He saw her swimming, the even pull of her powerful strokes broken only for an instant as she waved to him, watching from the shore, and then she had not looked back again. He saw her, in his mind's eye, forge through the narrow gap of the Needles, and disappear round the headland. He had made one hundred and two notches on the pole at Greenwich before he saw her again.

Catherine came down through the Wye Valley very cautiously. One of the best stocked of the areas on the island for game, it was also one of the trickiest to hunt because of the heavy undergrowth and the thousand twists and hides and turnings available to the beasts. For the same reason it would conceal the enemy very comfortably. And the constant roar of the surf was a distraction to ears stretched for the sound of a footfall.

Almost now she wished for a confrontation. She was beginning to suffer. The enemy was proving unexpectedly over-subtle. The sun was striking now obliquely through the branches, but a long time remained yet till nightfall. She realised that some of her fretfulness was caused by increasing hunger, and the insects which settled on her sweating back and probed the interstices of her skin were an additional irritation. She slapped at them impatiently, but her presence was continually exciting new swarms to venture.

She found the salt fish where she expected it to be, noticed the signs that Edwin had used it, raised it to her lips and immediately knew it was rotting. . . .

She felt a hopeless, helpless anger towards Edwin for not having looked after the matter properly. She would have liked to cram the whole lot down his throat. He was probably snug, well fed, fully armed, ensconced in Skiddaw. If he could see her, and he probably could, he would be smiling that indolent sarcastic smile which her intimate friends had said was the lure with which he had originally hooked her. But if he were watching from some closer vantage point, hereabouts, still in Wye? She whirled about, the fish falling as she moved.

But there was nothing. The intolerable tranquillity continued. The surf boomed, protesting still at the presence of the island after thousands of years, as it would do till it had boomed the island away. In the underbrush the insects sang to each other or perhaps, as Edwin maintained, mostly threatened one another. The birds merely hopped about, from one patch of shade to another. Understood, in this context, that the enemy only waited, while she ran herself dizzy.

She came to a decision. She would go to Skiddaw. She would not take Edwin's usual route, the easier ascent, because on the far side there would at least be shade. She would make for the Tulgey Wood, but then work round via Epping Forest to Camp Six. After that there would be a direct frontal assault.

Having decided, her spirits rose again. As she went she noticed here and there the signs of Edwin's journey. It helped keep her mind concentrated, looking for them. The time seemed to pass quickly, but in fact an hour and a half passed before she stood on the fringe of the lowland trees, looking out at Tulgey Wood.

She sprinted as Edwin had taught her, and counted as well, as if she had taken over a part of his mind. The knife slapped on her thigh at a much faster tempo. She had a better action than Edwin, but she had never achieved the 'float'. It was an easy run, in comparison with those she had made earlier in the day. It was the first time she had come out, flagrantly, in the open. 'Six and, seven and, eight and, nine and, ten and, eleven . . .'

'And a tiny bit!' she exclaimed, avoiding the trip-wire. When she sat down to rest she saw that the trap had been sprung. There was blood on the ground, and the arrow, broken in half, lying beside it.

She looked up Skiddaw, and at last saw the enemy. The declining sun showed him on a ledge perhaps a hundred yards from the summit, motionless. She watched for several minutes, but he made no effort to climb higher. His brown body seemed now to be on fire with the last of the sun.

She stepped out of the Tulgey Wood and walked towards Skiddaw.

Up on the ledge Edwin saw her moving steadily towards the middle slope. He looked desperately across at the sun, whose disappearance would bring the end of the game. She had time to reach him: he clutched the boulder to his chest, and poised it to roll.

He saw her discard her tunic and sandals.

He cried out: 'You cheated, you cheated!'

The cry echoed across the island, but there was no other answer.

'You set that trap two days ago!'

She stooped over the tunic and picked out the knife.

The sun was half hidden in the sea as he gathered himself about the rock. He still had the mountain on his side.

A GLUTTON FOR PUNISHMENT

Writing to his sister, Lady Caroline, in England, Caspar Henry sat in a profoundly easy chair, his back to long high windows, with light galore flooding all over him. Some of the windows were open, and a light, delicious breeze reached him at the end of a suave association with the Mediterranean. For the trouble of turning his head Caspar could instantly take in a fine view of the leisured elements in the port, and the Arabic citadel-cathedral in all its fantastic show-off brilliance. The restful olive of the wall beyond his desk, however, held nothing flamboyant but a single painting, executed by some anonymous American expatriate, which Caspar had picked up himself and hung on the wall as a test, before making up his mind whether to take or leave it when he returned home. In the picture long shadows thrown by many high black rocks reached hungrily for a solitary nude reclining on a beach. The girl, whose face was hidden in her arms, was a nasty copper colour and the sun which had done all the damage, now abandoning the wretched creature, was one of those small ill-tempered painting suns who seem to usurp their position in the sky. Caspar liked the scene because he thought it contained a small truth about the way people on holiday overdid it.

Caspar sat and smoked his cigar and wrote his letter and looked at the picture and thought how his sister would hate it. He decided for the time being not to tell her about it. He had plenty with which to fill his letter. It was easy to write: he poured a continuous flow of chat into it, bearing on its surface a bright sprinkle of descriptions of trips to spectacular places and quaint customs observed. They had often bored him, except where he had detected the stirrings of some property development, but he wrote as if he shared her view that unkempt countryside abroad refreshed the eye and with it the soul. Caspar was most accommodating always. Once on a journey in Cornwall his sister had exclaimed: 'Isn't it amazing how blue the sky is, and how green the grass is!' and he had wanted to remark that green sky and blue grass would have surprised him more, but because he was always polite to women he had only murmured: 'Fantastic! Heart-warming', without irony. But he was finding it hard to keep out of his comments a certain note of contempt for his luxurious surroundings, and for himself that he had allowed himself to be persuaded to immerse himself in them.

It was not the fault of the huge hotel that he was sad. But he was writing of the hotel in a faintly disparaging way:

. . . a bit of a Puritan, I suppose you'll think me, when I say that I think it a little absurd and tasteless of them to have built a hotel on this scale and of such pretensions on an island like this where no one works. I could see the point of it in Berlin, or London, where a man wants a battery of people to organise les petits soins, *to keep the small provocations of life at bay while his mind is free to rest on his major projects, impress guests, and all that sort of thing, but here the greater the niceness, the greater the grossness, if you see what I mean. We are blessed, for instance, with three swimming pools, and not one rectangular. All three have undulating, 'natural' shapes supposed to be restful. But the whole island is already restful. Everything has a soft shape. It is absurd to contrive more. There is nothing to rest from. And that feeling, my dear, proves that you were wrong. I did not* need *a holiday. I was in no danger. It is the very indolence of this holiday world, the sloppiness, which I find enervating. But like everybody else I am lost in it. When I write to you I realise it, but generally I have my faculties dulled too. If I lived here long I should lose all idea of myself. I would tolerate everything. It is just as well that I have a firm idea of who I am when I am at home. I think of your own astringent outlook, and some bone returns to my thinking. I look forward to seeing you again, and that will be soon. . . .*

The floor waiter, without being summoned, appeared at seven with a long drink in a short-stemmed glass. On the first day of his stay a long-stemmed glass had been knocked over by the carriage of his typewriter. This one fitted snugly underneath. From the third time of giving the order the matter had obviously been entered in his hotel dossier, and a kind of *perpetuum mobile* set up. It was the kind of hotel which not only indulged caprices but sanctified them. Looking across the flat roof, on the other side of a low wall which defined the area of his verandah, he could see at exactly the same time each evening the barman begin to check his stock preparatory to opening the hotel nightclub at eight. It was exclusive to the residents and their guests. One night, unable to sleep for sunburn, he had lain in bed, propped on an elbow and reading. He had looked up and caught the eye of the torch singer who was standing in the window with a drink in her hand. She had looked very dark and young and lovely and had seemed to want him to go over and dance, or something. But before he could think that this was what she meant, by looking at him so steadily, a smooth young fellow had drawn her away. Caspar had promptly thought how painful it was even to wear a light pyjama jacket: he winced at the idea of her putatively long nails tearing down his inflamed back, and put the light out. She had not come to the window again.

The boy who brought the drink laid the menu for dinner beside him, and begged to be of further service. Caspar tipped, and declined the offer. He scanned the menu, printed with polyglot vulgarity. He picked out some items he had never tried before. Like everything else which went to table he knew they would be dealt with by the kitchen with textbook efficiency. He came to *calamar, bläckfisk, inkfish, poulpe*, and plumped. Having decided, he straight away informed his sister.

. . . tonight I shall have octopus. Alla romana, *I have opted for. I watched the article being sold this morning, very early, when the fishermen brought in the catch. I slipped out of the hotel especially early to watch, and thoroughly enjoyed a Dutch auction. It was beautiful fish they were selling, at give-away prices. Rich and full of meat. Fish must be good when to look at it raw makes one hungry. Lovely colours . . .*

Another person had come down to the quay with the same idea. A young English girl, perhaps twenty or so years old. Slacks and slippers and no socks. Loose blouse and a glimpse once or twice of a white thingummybob underneath. She was staying at a pension up on the green but dusty hill, and it was, she affirmed, in the process of being a most gorgeous holiday which she would never forget. Only, her friends were terrible! They did make her annoyed. She wanted to get the absolute maximum, and here they had promised to get up with her, and when the time had come it had been impossible to *kick* them awake, lazy pigs! So she had thought: 'Dammit, stop there, then, in all your brutish wallowing! But I'm going!' and here she was, and awfully glad. They would be wildly jealous when she went back and told them all about it and, by the way, thanks for explaining everything, which just made the adventure perfect! She was a nurse. He had inferred that they were all nurses.

He had walked around with her, saving her more than once in all the bustle from sitting down in a box of lush, dripping mullet, or from the waving claws in a basket of lobsters. He had explained pricing mechanisms to her, and she had shown herself to be possessed of a lively, receptive mind. He had been about to suggest breakfast in some open-air café under the shadow of the palms, and under the aegis of a statue to one of the island's many distinguished philanthropists, when she had declared an insuperable urge to stroll along the quay and look at all the boats. Caspar had examined the boats earlier, but he had complaisantly strolled. Sometimes it was nearer running than strolling. Some of the boats would never be put to sea again, Caspar explained: they were showpieces. The gear in those which were still seaworthy was being stowed away: in some the cycle was complete and the crew were lolling about amidships. From one of these a boy had called to her. A short, dark, broad boy he was, and Caspar thought his expression one of levantine malice. The girl stopped, while Caspar walked on. In a moment she was pattering after him. 'Could we, please?' she enquired. 'I think he's inviting us on board.' Of course he was. Boys of his type were everywhere, appraising the foreign girls. Grudgingly he escorted her aboard, stiffly declining the proffered arm which would have helped him from the narrow gangplank on to the deck. Caspar was the only one who spoke both languages. He acted as interpreter for the two handsome children. In his own country he would have used the term 'go-between'. When he excused himself and went ashore alone he could hear behind him, nevertheless, a form of communication maintained. It was only laughter, as the fisher boy made a meal for them both, with insalubrious equipment, but it was enough. Look for them tomorrow, and they would know each other well.

Caspar took a sheet from the typewriter and inserted another.

The sun had the cathedral nearly on fire. Even the houses in shadow were glaringly white. Caspar complained to his sister that people on the island took dinner too late in the day to suit his digestion. He sat back and lit another cigar. He never relighted one which had died. His letter done, he would have his bath and a drink in the American bar, before going in to dinner. Afterwards he would go for a little walk in to town, and sit in a chair in the avenue, perhaps visit one or two of the quieter bars where he was known, and come back a leisurely stroll and read in the lounge before going to bed. To retire too early was pointless until the night-club simmered down. He would look in at the Bar Barossa, if Pepe the Catalan was on duty, and perch up on a high stool while the flamboyant buccaneer told his clientele how he could handle them, in New York, Manila, or London. Visitors from other countries, usually rich, young beautiful women, to hear Pepe tell it, almost cried for Pepe to serve them, to go overseas and be majordomo. It was credible: he was a *figaro*. Caspar could have hired him himself, had he not always been content to rely on his sister. The occasion of their meeting had been Caspar's wish to know a couple of young girls. He had passed the Barossa one hot forenoon and seen a couple of Danes, lovely blonde girls in the otherwise deserted bar. The little one was an elfin creature who could have worn his signet ring round her waist, while her plump friend looked as if she lived on butter. He liked the look of one as much as the other. The little one was as fine as a spring chicken. The bones of her delicate limbs could scarcely have hardened from cartilage. The plump one had a bottom as cosy-looking as an eiderdown, and a bosom whose birth was visible even from the street, white, glistening with health, enormous. In the terrible vulnerability of this holiday Caspar found no common factor in the girls that attracted him except, certainly, youth. It was a catholic taste.

The girls talked to him politely. His hopes alternated from one to the other. They were dependent on chance for entertainment, on just such a chance as his passing by and being attracted. They seemed merely to be passing the time away. At his invitation they drank. They chose sometimes wine, sometimes orange juice, sometimes coffee. Occasionally they ate something instead, a salt fish, an olive, a cake. Caspar spent hours in the bar trying to devise some means of separating them, so that he might be able to bear one away. But he was unable to break their neutrality. When it became at last obvious that the Catalan behind the bar had a hold on the little one, he concentrated on the plump one, and then it turned out that she too was a rival for the little one. He had in fact been drawn into a struggle for dominance, and was welcome because he provided a relief. So he gave up and listened to Pepe. Pepe was more glad to see him than the girls. He was able to talk to them by talking to Caspar. He told Caspar terrible, insulting things about the girls, and they appeared to love it. They protested and sulked, and then laughed to the point of dissolution. He was plainly the master. Caspar wondered how it was done.

On later occasions he looked in first for the girls, and only went in if they were not there. When they came he left. Pepe and Caspar talked about the northern invasion. The women came south from Sweden and Denmark and England and Germany and Switzerland, with or without money but on their own, independent, at least superficially free. It had taken a season or two for the local boys to appreciate what was happening as their island became more popular, and the 'amenities' were hurriedly constructed. But they fully understood now: Pepe claimed that many of them saved up their money and their strength through the winter months in order to be at maximum potential during the summer. It was an international scandal, it was not of their making. It was necessary to be philosophical, and with philosophy a young man might see that it was patriotic as well as polite to look on these young ladies as a kind of bonus. The situation was accepted now: the scandal was dimmed: it was a sport, with rules. The boys who swarmed on the beaches and in the *avenidas* on the hunt were known as the '*picadores*', after the man in the bullring whose function it was to tame the bull in readiness for the kill. Certain hotels encouraged the *picadores* to attend their dances by allowing them to enter free, subject to inspection by the doorkeeper, while the most beautifully dressed northern ladies had to pay cash to come in. In this sport Pepe was an obvious *matador*. Caspar was horrified by Pepe's contemptuous assessment, but he was also thrilled. He was jealous of Pepe, but he could not dislike him. The Catalan was ever ready to acknowledge his wickedness; to admit that had he been a greater man, a wiser man, a nobler man, a gentler man, a richer man, a better-educated man, he would have been, well – with a helpless gesture – another man altogether.

On the night following the great festival display of fireworks, which had for hours teased and challenged the stateliness of the stars over the bay, Pepe told Caspar that he had himself seen very little of it. He hoped Caspar would describe it, for he himself had danced all the while with his face in a warm, sweetly scented stomach, and the two northern breasts which had rested comfortably on the top of his head had obscured the spectacle for him as effectively as a double eclipse. He had at the last been obliged to take his partner to bed in order to be able, for a little while at least, to look her in the eye and find out who she was. Caspar was fascinated by the account. It was painful. There was no pretending it was not true. Pepe did not care enough about him to invent. He was appalled by the vulgarity of this island, but he was drawn to know more. Out of the many thousands he would have liked just one young woman for himself. He was, as a man, efficient, polite, healthy, tall, and so forth, but that one amongst the thousands always went with one of these small, slick locals instead.

. . . the typical Iberian is very small in stature, but into the small package a great deal of charm and vitality are packed . . .

But he could not write all his thoughts about the small men, because he feared to shock his sister. He left the sentence standing on its own. It looked odd. But it would look odder still scratched out. He sat back again. Time to draw to a close.

He looked up to find the chambermaid standing near him. She was wanting to turn the beds down. She was apologetic. She had not known there was anybody. Sir could not have heard her knock. She could assure him she had knocked. He realised that it was almost dark now in the room. He switched on the small table lamp. By its soft roseate light he thought he could see surprise in her heart-shaped face. He perceived that she was embarrassed to have come upon him in an unlit room, closed in with his own thoughts. She asked if she should come back later.

No. He shook his head. He would be taking his bath now.

She would run it for him?

No. He would take a shower. For the novelty. There were no showers in England, not indoors, anyway.

The peasant stared in astonishment. It came to him that she thought he was being sarcastic.

He pushed back his chair and rose as she approached the beds.

She drew down the first counterpane, and then stood with her back to him, bent over while she folded it. He looked morosely down at the heart shape of her behind. He put his hands in his pockets. He thought wistfully: 'If I were a younger man, if I were somehow different at least, she would not take any chances, she would make sure that there was always a piece of furniture between me and her.' But she knew she was safe.

As she went to the other bed, he told her that one bed would be sufficient. She looked at him uncertainly. The second bed was never slept in, and yet on each night she had turned it down, and remade it in the morning. It was her routine. He wondered if she supposed that he had somewhere on the island a wife who was consistently unfaithful to him, and, if so, whether she was sympathetic. Probably indifferent. He had seen the girl once on her night off, in the company of three others, in the fashion of the island girls, linked in line abreast across the pavement, walking up the central avenue. Pure, honourable girls all, with a different idea of conduct. Their untouchability accounted for the kinetic violence of the desires of the males.

One evening after the bullfight he had sat in a café in the company of a petty official he had met at the performance. He had something to do with the prison. He had begged Caspar for introductions to any foreign girls he might know. Tears had stood in his eyes. His position was one of extreme delicacy. In eighteen months of engagement he had not yet been permitted a kiss by his fiancée. At the same time his public status made it impossible for him to frequent the 'mouth-watering' whores from the mainland who worked the islands in the season. Caspar was revolted. He saw his own inefficacy reflected in this pathetic, clumsy appeal.

The maid was turning down the second bed. He told her sharply to leave it alone. Seeing her stiffen at the tone of his voice, he was tempted to explain to her that quite simply he had made a sudden decision to come to this hotel, of necessity, as a relief from strain, and that only double rooms were available. But he felt altogether hollow and defeated. The effort was too great. He watched her march out of the room without a word.

He went into the bathroom, and thought that if he really wanted to bring her back he could summon her by pulling on the tassel over the bath. He undressed and looked at himself in the long mirror, and ran his nail along the line of his tan. He had fallen asleep one afternoon by the side of one of the pools, with his towel round his neck, and the consequence was a piebald appearance.

In the next apartment the American girl was taking her shower. It had been explained to him that she was a starlet of some kind. The cinema, he supposed. Yes, that was it, because someone had told him she had got into it via the beauty-competition circuit. His informant had told him that they put their breasts in ice shingle to make them stand up firm just before each heat. She would never have a piebald tan. He wished he could walk just once across the lobby with this lovely creature on his arm.

He turned out the light in the bathroom and softly mounted on to the lid of the lavatory. He peered through the slats of the Venetian blind. A ventilator shaft separated his bathroom from hers. He could see her, striped by the slats of her Venetians. She was not more than ten feet from him, as he pressed against the cold tiles, holding his breath. Her breasts were not as large as he had expected, but she was such a tall girl that they may only have seemed . . .

He hurriedly stepped down and let his breath out in a long sigh. For a moment it seemed to him that he had seen somebody else in there with her. It could only have been the flower-patterned shower-curtain billowing out. It could equally well have been the flower-patterned bathrobe of the muscle boy, from the apartment beyond the American's, being thrown casually over a rail. Caspar would rather not know for certain. This was the girl who had pretensions to the official status of most beautiful girl on the coast, who came trailing clouds of crisp, virginal titles behind her – Miss Egg-Whisk, Miss Paper-doily, Girl Sundae, The Mousse Mouse, Ruffles Royal and Miss Terry (of the Terry Teevee Teasy Time) were only a few. And this symbol of dainty, dimity things, this pot-hunter, this girl who was herself a trophy, was apparently ready to leave her glass case and frolic with an oaf. Caspar took his shower in the dark, unable to look at himself in the mirror. He was outraged by his own behaviour.

As he towelled himself down, he said to himself that in another man he would regard such a carry-on as symptoms of the frankly neurotic. He must turn his back on it all, behave like the gentleman his sister thought him, and where he could not ignore these young women, see them as a father might, or where their conduct might seem to invite reproach, as a tolerant uncle. It was a serious matter: the perfect courtesy for which he was famous was dependent on his respect for himself.

He dressed smartly, but quietly, and went downstairs.

He was sitting in the American bar with the airmail edition of *The Times*, a bowl of pecans, a tray of pretzels, olives and twisps, and a very dry martini clustered about his shin when he chanced to notice that someone was looking at him. He read through the Law Reports and then noticed that she was still looking at him. Lest it be a coincidence he cracked the crossword and then let her come into focus again.

She was still looking at him.

She sat under an amber light, motionless, staring at him steadily. She looked as if she might be able to maintain the attitude for hours. She had not touched her drink for so long that the sediment had settled in a darker patch at the bottom of the glass. Smoke from a cigarette in a holder rose in a thin unwavering line. The curled fingers which held the toy were encased in elbow-length gloves the colour of jasmine. A small, golden evening bag hung on a filigree chain from her wrist. The bag went with her dress, of gold lace mounted on white silk, Empire line. A chinchilla wrap hung casually about her shoulders. It might have been the fur cape Caspar had given his sister on the day he became senior partner. Briefly, at the instant he first was aware of her, she had been exactly like his sister. The hair, in a French pleat, the sharp features, the small bones, the rigid carriage, even the fashion this woman had of crossing her legs without seeming relaxed, were all like her. But as he now returned her fiercely inquisitive stare with a mild, surprised appraisal of his own, he found points which combated the identification. The eyes themselves were deep-sunken, so that he could not have described their colour: perhaps, he thought, topaz, perhaps the amber of the lamp, certainly not the cool grey he knew so well from his sister's frank scrutiny. And then she had freckles. The hips were wider, the bosom higher and fuller: probably all wire and foam rubber: when he got away from the face he got away from his sister.

'Ugly old devil,' thought Caspar, deciding after all not to have another aperitif.

He was obliged to pass her table on his way from the bar, and as he came up to it she rose and barred the way. He recoiled a step: he could see this time that the eyes were bloodshot.

'It is very early for dinner, Sir Henry,' she said. Her English was good, but the accent was there, either French or Belgian. She had spoken to him as naturally as if she were accosting the only other human being in some desert place.

'Sir Caspar,' he corrected her, 'Henry is my family name.'

'It is an experience to encounter a true knight,' she said.

'I don't know about a true one, but certainly a real one,' he smiled.

For the first time her expression changed as her lips tried to smile. They bent at each end. The heavy muddy flesh of her face resisted its spread.

'If you are a knight I shall request a favour. As a solitary woman.'

'I am flattered,' replied Caspar.

'The food in this hotel is insupportable. I have not eaten properly for a long time. It is hard for a woman to voyage about the town unaccompanied. Would you lend to me your escorting powers?'

Caspar thought of the dinner he had marked down in his mind. He felt saddened at the idea of losing it. These rich old women liked steak and chips, and left the chips. He had watched them.

'You must be very hungry,' he said.

'I could eat a horse,' she said.

'I should be pleased to help you find an adequate substitute, supposing that a horse is not available.'

'It is possible to find everything on this island if one knows how to look,' she replied.

'Everything?' murmured Caspar.

'Everything has a price,' she said, 'but in this hotel they believe the price is money.'

'Yes, well, money is very expensive,' said Caspar.

'But you need not look so worried,' she continued, putting her holder in the evening bag and snapping it shut with a small definite click, 'you are rich enough. I shall only eat – what you have.'

'My horses and dogs for a start, then,' said Caspar, with a fair imitation of gaiety, offering her his arm. She settled her wrap firmly about her withered shoulders, and took it.

In the lobby they passed the American girl, tapping briskly towards the dining-room on the arm of a powerfully built youth. Not the oaf, but another oaf. Caspar darted at them a look of defiance, which the American girl failed to notice. He turned it then on the staff ranged behind the great semi-circular desk in Reception, who returned it with perfect impassivity.

Free of the many familiar eyes in the hotel, Caspar felt better. He was hungry himself, and he took her to a cellar restaurant well known for its helpings. She did not eat a horse, nor yet did she content herself with a steak, with or without the chips. She made her way, at times with ferocity, right through the menu. She had, for instance, a chicken off the spit, for herself, and Caspar shuddered as she not only dealt with flesh and skin, but broke the bones and siphoned out the marrow as well.

He complimented her on her enjoyment of it all.

'You make invigorating company,' she replied, pointing a greasy talon at the list of savouries on the card. The *tortilla* she had chosen to finish with would have been, thought Caspar with repulsion, a meal in itself. He stoked a midget cup of coffee and watched her eating with sombre satisfaction. He had stopped trying to make conversation: evidently eating was to be literally the main business of the evening.

But at the end, wiping her fingers with gusto on the tablecloth, she laughed at him. 'My Sir Caspar,' she said, 'you look as if you would rather be with those other idiots in the hotel, and be talking of the price of shoes in Spain, and the price of hats in England, and the taxes on land in Austria, and the cost of alimony in America, and the charge for——'

'It is at least a conversation,' he broke in defensively.

'But it is not!' she cried. 'It is a display. On the side of the *piscina*, in the *salle à manger*, in the bar, on the beach, in the bath, and in the bed, there is the flash of money from a fire without heat.'

'It is just as well,' said Caspar, 'when people content themselves to speak about the subject they know best.'

'*En tout cas, mon cher Caspar*, I have warned you. I was hungry. *J'avais faim. Por Dios, que hambre!*'

'You are not hungry now, at least?'

She laughed, screechingly. People looked round at her.

'No, Sir Caspar, but I am thirsty!'

'I thought the *entremets* looked a little salt,' said Caspar, magnificently.

'You will take me elsewhere for a drink?'

'I was about to suggest it myself.'

Again she emitted that wild, chilling screech of laughter. Caspar gave her the benefit of the doubt and assumed that it was not intentional, but the result of some accident, or a defect of some kind, or a nervous spasm. And yet, after the extravagantly predatory fashion of her onslaught on her dinner, and the general abandon of her manners, she was composed and statuesque as she left the cellar, particularly as they passed through the restaurant on the ground floor where the modish people dined. The manner in which she received her wrap, without even looking at the hat-check girl who had looked after it, reminded him very much of his sister.

Then they went out on the town to slake her thirst. They went drinking. Caspar marvelled at the way this woman could drink. In his life he had never witnessed anything like it. She drank like a busload of rugger men. She drank like a *bierstube* full of German students. She drank to match a gathering of Scandinavian woodcutters. She put it away like a crew just back from the tropics. She soaked it up like a ton of sponges. He could not believe that any woman could eat and drink like this one and remain so thin and haggard. She had a loose throat, which seemingly was a great help technically, meaning that she could clamour for more wine when he was still sipping his way through a cognac, and he had seen that asset in others, but in the matter of intake he appreciated that he had a phenomenon for company.

Almost in the manner of an expiation he took her to his favourite bars. More than once they were asked to leave by the management. Always people began by welcoming them, seeing in her loud greeting and hoarse chanting enjoyment of her entertainment only the boisterous goodwill of holiday licence, and always they finished by withdrawing quietly into their separate groups, leaving her alone at the bar with Caspar. In the Barossa, Caspar was obliged to restrain her forcibly from putting on a private striptease, and hurling her Dior creations in the dust at the feet of the guitar player and his patrons. Pepe began by sardonically complimenting Caspar on a 'bull who would not need to have the *banderillas de fuego* implanted to make her full of fight', but he soon withdrew when he saw the braveness of the creature. Caspar's last sight of the place, as he bore her struggling into the street, still wrenching at her zips, included the little cameo of the two Danes bent in embarrassment over their *apfelstrudels*, in unspeaking communion with the appalled Pepe, who rearranged unnecessarily all his little plates of food along the counter until her shrill voice could no longer be heard.

At the bottom of the hill, in a quiet, dark, side-street, she leant against a wall. Nearby, a large wrought-iron gate kept the world out of a pretty little *patio* in which the fountain flowed. She rolled about the wall, laughing and mouthing obscene insults at those who had criticised her, while Caspar stood away from her in the middle of the street, aghast at such a display. He felt pity too for such a lonely being. He asked himself in fear if his sister, in her cups, could ever have given way like this. Gradually the outpourings of the hellion he had undertaken subsided, until there were not more than hiccups. Then she said, in the tone of a naughty young girl who is not sure if she will be punished, but wishes to test the power of her charm:

'Well, I did tell you I was thirsty.'

'I have lost everything that was of any importance to me here,' he said solemnly.

'You still have me,' she replied.

'Yes,' he said, 'I still have you. The question now arises: what am I to do with you now that I have you.'

For answer she suddenly shivered and drew her wrap around her. She turned away and walked towards the road which ran round the port. When he caught up with her she said:

'I am cold and tired now. Will you find me a bed now, Sir Henry, where I shall not be disturbed by my friends who haunt me in the mornings?'

He walked with her along the coast road, and often was obliged to support her, until they reached the hotel. Then he danced her through the crowd of young beauties and their *picadores*, and across the empty gardens where on marble courts the herons stood in a sapphire light, as if in natural pools, until they passed through the opened crystal doors. Then he led her up the stairs to the night-club. There the young torch singer sang a number which he felt was directed to him alone, but he had given up all idea of her, and walked his old crone on to the verandah, and helped her over the low parapet and across the flat roof, and then again over the parapet and into his own apartment.

He drew the curtains and switched on a single lamp. The voice of the night-club singer was muffled now, but he heard it as plainly as ever, because he had heard the words so often:

'Cuando calienta el sol allí en la playa
Siento tu cuerpo, vibrando cerca de mi . . .'

But no one was ardent on the beaches, the sun was too much, like the presence of a king, for men and women to turn to one another. It was only later, when darkness fell, that the heat they had absorbed returned to concentrate their brains on the persons of others.

The maid had, after all, come back in his absence and turned down the bed. He was sorry he had been rude to her. It was his only slip. He would apologise in the morning.

The old woman was lying across it, plucking her jewels away, and rubbing her bangles off her arms to go where they might, rolling silently across the floor. She had abandoned herself, as his sister had never once done, not in a lifetime.

She said, with her eyes closed: 'Take off your clothes, Sir Henry, and lie down beside me.'

'God forbid,' he said, 'that ever I should lie down beside a fiend who carries Hell about with her!'

He doubted if she heard him. She was naked, and her arms were outstretched to receive him. He turned out the light and drew the curtains back again. The music of the night-club throbbed on, remotely, privately. He turned away from it to join her.

The reflections of great day awoke him and looking at it, confidently enveloping the cathedral, he felt it promised to be golden. His mind was clear and fresh, and he was inspired to think that he must make the most of the short time that remained to him. But when he made the first move to bound out of bed he found that an arm about his chest restrained him, and he remembered.

He twisted quietly and slowly round. There moved forward, in sleep, protestingly, into his arms, the most beautiful girl he ever remembered seeing.

He lay still, and looked about him. Her gown and her underclothes were still where she had thrown them. One shoe was hooked by the heel on the edge of the table, the other was in the wastepaper basket. He caught the glint of one of her bangles by the wardrobe. He turned back from the sight of these things and admired her. He gently curled aside the covers and thought that, while the prestige of showing her off on his arm to all his friends, and to jealous strangers, would be tremendous, this vision would be reserved for himself alone.

She opened her eyes and looked at him. They were clear, and innocent of all struggles. She lowered her head and laid it against his chest.

He said, into her golden hair: 'How long will this last?'

She replied: 'While we are on the island together.'

'I see no reason why I should not extend my stay,' he said reflectively.

'I am glad there is some time still to the end of the season,' she said confidently.

He said, hesitantly: 'You are astonishingly beautiful this morning, more beautiful than I would have thought anyone could be.'

She answered, very seriously: 'I have been coming to the island since I was a little girl, and many men have taken me out, but never have I met before with one who gave me all I asked.'

When the chambermaid answered the bell, Caspar ordered large breakfasts for two. The chambermaid smiled at him conspiratorially, as if she had known all along that he would eventually find something which he seemed to have lost, right at the beginning.

TO START A HARE

Bambrough had firmly assumed charge of the alarm clock. Privately he suspected that Croucher and Tilley would funk it when the hour came round. The last time anyone ran away from the school they'd been whacked with the dog's lead for it (you could hear it even in Matron's room) and stopped all half-holidays for a month.

Bambrough was not running away himself because he was going in at number three against Wiggett's Junior Colts that afternoon and after that term he would be going on to Wiggett's senior school himself, so there was not much point in it. But Croucher and Tilley had another two years still at the prep before they went anywhere. They knew that it was decent of Bambrough to help at all, considering that he might not play if it was discovered that he had helped.

It was Morbey's clock, which his mother gave him. He did not like to lend it, because his mother told him not to lend it to anybody, and he was afraid that it might get confiscated when its part in the escape was known.

'Don't be a dog in the manger,' said Bambrough, 'you never ever use the alarm.'

'I tell the time by it,' said Morbey.

'You can tell the time by any old clock. If you want to know the time ask me.'

'You don't know how to work it,' protested Morbey, 'there's a special button you have to know.'

'You can show me, can't you? And if you show me wrong I'll lam you.'

Several other voices in the dormitory guaranteed Morbey a lamming if he compromised the venture in any way. Croucher and Tilley sat on the ends of their beds and listened self-consciously to Perrott and Dickson praising their decision to run away.

Mr. Harbord suddenly appeared in the doorway to put the lights out and caught Morbey standing by Bambrough's bed with the clock still in his hands.

'Into bed all of you,' ordered Mr. Harbord. 'Morbey, what are you doing standing there without slippers or dressing gown?'

Morbey turned guiltily. Bambrough reached out and took the clock from him.

'My fault, sir. I asked him to give me back my clock.'

The whole dormitory admired Bambrough for owning up.

'You should think of these things earlier,' said Mr. Harbord, 'not wait till time for lights out. And it's no excuse for you, Morbey. I've told you about running about half naked before. Look at you, with your trousers hanging off and your jacket all unbuttoned. Pull yourself together, boy, and get back to bed. Next time I catch you I'll give you an imposition that'll last you for days.'

Morbey surrendered the clock and ran back to his bed. He resolved that moment to join Tilley and Croucher when they did their bunk.

'Watch those springs, for heaven's sakes, boy!' exclaimed Mr. Harbord. 'Is everybody settled now?'

'I didn't clean my teeth, sir,' said Johnson, who was a bit M.D.

Mr. Harbord lingered by the switch. He looked at his watch impatiently. 'Hurry up, then, but you are a confounded little nuisance, Johnson!'

'He did clean his teeth, sir, he did!' cried several voices. Everybody wanted Mr. Harbord out of the way so that they could go on discussing what Croucher and Tilley were going to do.

'Up to your old tricks, are you?' asked Mr. Harbord.

'Can't I go?' asked Johnson.

'Can't I go what?' prompted Mr. Harbord, expecting sir at the end of the sentence.

'Can't I go to the lavatory?' said Johnson, tossing his head uncomfortably.

There was a subdued chorus of laughter. Mr. Harbord flushed.

'Yes, you can go,' he said, 'and you can write me out fifty times: "I must not be insolent".'

'Oh, sir! How do you spell insolent?'

'Look it up, Johnson! It's a word you're going to need to know.' As Johnson wriggled past him, running to the washroom, where a moment later he could be heard brushing his teeth for a second time, Mr. Harbord said genially to Bambrough: 'I should get a good night's sleep, Bambrough. You'll find you'll have to play yourself in tomorrow before you risk any stroke-making. I hear Wiggett's are sending down a strong side, particularly where their bowling's concerned.'

'Yes, sir,' replied Bambrough. 'I had quite a good net today, sir. Mr. Adams was putting them on the spot, sir.'

'Yes,' said Mr. Harbord. 'I heard about it. Mr. Adams said you were flashing a bit outside the off stump. Try to keep your head down more, I should. And that applies to you all at this moment. Good night, boys.'

'Good night, sir.'

The lights went out. Johnson squirmed back past Mr. Harbord. Mr. Harbord reached out and took the toothbrush from him, sighed heavily, and closed the door. As soon as the sound of his receding footsteps had diminished, Denby whispered loudly:

'You are a fool, Johnson! If you hadn't asked him how to spell it he would have let you off tomorrow. You won't get out of it now.'

'I don't care,' said Johnson, 'if you don't clean your teeth they all drop out.'

'Not next morning, you idiot! You can miss once. Anyway, you'd already done it once. You'll brush them so often they'll drop out anyway.'

'He wouldn't have let him off,' said Croucher. 'I had to write out two pages of Latin just for knocking Bell's cap off, when I said it wasn't fair he made me go on to the end of the chapter and that was a whole extra page.'

'I don't care,' said Johnson, 'I've already got *I must not* written a hundred times so old Hard Board can teach his grandmother to suck eggs.'

'He'll see the difference, you fool,' said Lister, 'old ink goes all black.'

'I did pencil,' said Johnson triumphantly.

'You're not *allowed* pencil,' several voices told him.

'I think he's a bloody swine to everybody,' said Tilley in a high-pitched voice, 'and when I've run away from this rotten dump I'm never coming back!'

'Have you got everything ready?' asked Bambrough.

'We've got our games clothes in our lockers,' said Croucher.

'We brought them up when we were carrying up the clean sheets for Matron. Old Tillers asked if we could and she said O.K., but at the last minute it was almost mucked up because Wilson wanted to help too. But she wouldn't let him, ever since he dressed up in her clothes.'

'That was jolly lucky,' said Bambrough, 'because Wilson would have blabbed everything.'

'But if you wear games clothes,' said Denby, 'they won't allow you on the train.'

'Of course they will,' said Bambrough.

'I've never seen anybody in games clothes on a train,' said Denby.

'That just shows how much you know about it. I suppose you've never been on a football special? They're all in games clothes there.'

'Yes, but they won't be catching a football special,' persisted Denby. 'I think it's silly to be running away in games clothes.'

'What do you know about it?' said Croucher. 'You haven't got the guts to run away and you haven't thought anything about it. In games clothes you can move much more quickly. That's what people wear games clothes for.'

'Well, I've thought about it,' said Morbey, 'and I'll come with you. I'm sick of being here. It's the most unfair place in the world.'

'You can't,' said Vernon, 'you haven't saved up for the train ticket.'

'My mother gave me two pounds for my birthday,' said Morbey, 'and I kept it.'

'Have you got it with you?' asked Bambrough.

'Yes,' replied Morbey.

'Give one pound to Croucher and one to Tilley.'

'No,' said Morbey, 'it's mine.'

'We don't want his money,' said Croucher, 'and we don't want him either.'

'It's my clock,' said Morbey, 'why can't I come?'

'Because you haven't got any games clothes up here,' said Tilley.

'But I hate this place more than you do,' complained Morbey.

'Make your own plan, then,' said Tilley, 'you can run away by yourself. But this is our idea and we don't want anybody else.'

'Morbey's just a copycat,' said Bambrough, contemptuously. 'I votes we put him in Coventry.'

'Don't wake me up, then,' said Morbey, 'when the clock goes off. Don't expect me to help you. It's my clock.'

'I promise you,' said Bambrough, 'that unless you help I'll lam you.'

'All right,' said Morbey, 'but I'm scorer for us against Wiggett's tomorrow. And if you make any runs tomorrow you won't get them unless I put them in the book.'

'You couldn't do that. You'd be expelled.'

'That's what you think. Anyway, if I was expelled I'd still be getting out of here. You don't have to run away to get out of here, you know.'

'Morbey, you're just stupid. Everybody knows you're stupid so you don't have to prove it. If you get expelled you can never go to any other school, and then if you go in the Army you can't be an officer, and if you want a good job you can only be a doorman or something like that, or break stones in a chain-gang, and you get left out of everything because nobody wants you, so if you want to be expelled you know what's going to happen to you.'

'My father has more money than yours, so it's more likely you'll have to ask me for a job, and that's how much you know about work, and if you did get given a job by my father you couldn't get any higher unless I was on your side, which I wouldn't ever be, so . . .'

'It wouldn't matter to me if your father had all the money in the whole world, because I'm going in the Army, and that isn't a job, that's the Army, and in the Army you don't get higher by sucking up to anybody like your fat father, you get *promoted*, and when I get promoted high enough I'll just come to your father's business and make him surrender it all to me. I'd probably have you both shot.'

'You couldn't do that, Bambrough, because this isn't——'

The door swung suddenly wide open.

Mr. Harbord stood in the opening. 'Who's talking?'

Silence.

'I'm waiting.'

There was no answer.

'Was it you, Vernon?'

'No, sir, it wasn't me.'

'Denby?'

'No, sir.'

'Podmore, I thought I heard your voice.'

'No, really you didn't, sir.'

'Well, if I'm not going to be told I shall have to punish the whole dormitory. Harris?'

'No, sir.'

'It was me talking,' said Croucher.

'Ah, so at last someone has the guts to own up. Were you talking to yourself, then, Croucher?'

Silence.

'You know what they say? Only people with a screw loose talk to themselves. But I think if there's anyone in here with a screw loose it's the chap who's letting Croucher take all the blame himself. I don't suppose you'll want to talk to that chap again, will you, Croucher? Not if it's going to mean six of the best, when three apiece would have been the answer otherwise?'

'I was talking to Croucher, sir,' said Tilley.

'Ah!' said Mr. Harbord, and the whole dormitory, internally, released a corresponding 'Ah!' as they appreciated that Croucher and Tilley had done a very clever thing. Because everybody knew that old Hard Board believed in letting chaps stew in the thought of what was going to happen next day, and never visited summary punishment. If it had been old Adams he would have whisked them straight out to the washroom and let fly with the first slipper he picked up. But Croucher and Tilley would not be there on the next day. Everybody grew more excited as they realised this meant that Croucher and Tilley were really going through with their plan to run away.

'Well, Croucher, Tilley, shall we have a little business straight after prayers tomorrow morning? Yes, that would be the best time. Then we can all go off to breakfast thinking of making a fresh start to the day. Good night!' Mr. Harbord closed the door.

No one spoke again, but after a minute the noise came from Bambrough's bed of the alarm clock being wound.

Bambrough had been oiling his bat. It stood by his bed. Before settling down he stroked it, for luck, and to make sure it was still there. He went to sleep quickly.

Morbey lay with his hands behind his head. He thought of waiting till Bambrough was asleep and then sneaking the clock back. But he fell asleep before he could put the idea into practice.

Johnson lay thinking of what would happen to Croucher and Tilley when they got caught. He wondered if they would be beaten twice, for running away, *and* for talking after lights out, and if so which would take place first, and whether they would be consecutive beatings. He was not sure that in the end it would come to anything. It was all a big fake, he surmised. He had, after all, run away himself once or twice, and nothing much had ever been said. He had not even been beaten. But Croucher was one of the boys who did get beaten: he had been beaten often, everybody knew that. And this time it would be bound to be a hell of a whacking, everybody said so. His excitement increased until he was dying to do number one. He realised now that he really should have gone to the lavatory instead of brushing his teeth, but it was too late now. Mr. Harbord was probably waiting just outside the door for a chance to hit him. He pulled the bedclothes over his head, and then, for a minute fighting against it, and at last just giving in, he relieved himself in the bed. The tension released itself simultaneously, and cautiously he pulled himself upward until his head was clear of the sheets. He looked anxiously around in the darkness, wondering if anybody had somehow perceived what he had just done. But the dormitory was silent. The lights of a car passing in the road moved in a lovely succession of expanding and contracting rhomboids across the ceiling and he watched them breathlessly until the darkness was deeper than before, and he himself slid on towards his own personal darkness. He hoped that the alarm would not wake him up. He hated to be awake in the middle of the night. But if he stole the clock so that this would not happen, then Bambrough would lam him, and besides Croucher and Tilley would not be able to run away, and then they would not be whacked, which they ought to be, for being so famous about it. Why had he never become famous for running away? Perplexed, he sucked a peppermint and slept with it still half melted on his tongue.

Denby was almost asleep when he sensed some boy near his bed. He quickly pulled his arms free of the sheets ready to defend himself. But then he realised that whoever it was was going to Croucher's bed next to his. Then he heard Tilley's voice, a whisper:

'I say, Crouch! Are you awake?'

'What is it?' from Croucher.

'I can't sleep.'

'You've jolly well got to.'

'I can't!'

'Pretend you're not going. It's the best way.'

'But, Crouch, I know I am.'

'Well, then, just think you're going home. Your whole family will be there and everything.'

'I know. That's what scares me. I didn't write home or anything.'

'I didn't write either. It's no use writing. They read all your letters here in case you say anything about the school.'

'But I don't know what my father will say.'

'I do. My father will beat me. But I don't care. Because I know that at least he won't send me back. He's quite a good chap, my father.'

'My father, you never know what he's thinking. He's a bit funny about money. And if he thinks that he's paid all that for me to come here he'll be bloody wild with me for not sticking it out. Honest, he'll kill me.'

'Well, you can't not go now, Tillers, you promised me.'

'Oh, I'm glad I'm going. It's for your sake I'm going, really it is.'

'Oh, don't be silly,' said Croucher awkwardly, 'they're beastlier to you even than they are to me. Look how the Drain is always picking on you to do all the worst jobs. He hates you.'

'I hate him, so we're even.'

'I wonder if we'll be together at our next school, eh, Till?'

'I don't expect so. Will you ask your father if you can, though, and I'll ask my father if I can.'

'I promise.'

'I like you ever so much, Crouch. I'm going back to bed now.'

'All right. Don't forget the torch.'

'I won't. I've tied it with a bit of string to my belt. Have you got the sandwiches?'

'Yes. There's two jam and two corn beef.'

'Suppose they don't let us buy tickets?'

'I think they have to if you've got enough money. Besides, if they don't, we can always pretend we're engine-spotting and then just get in at the last minute.'

'I wish it was over, Crouch.'

'If you go to sleep now the time will come much quicker.'

'I'm going to concentrate like mad on my dog at home, and I bet I go to sleep in one minute.'

'Good man. Where's your hand?'

'Here. On the sheet.'

Croucher and Tilley shook hands. Tilley felt his way back to his own bed. He sat on the edge and went through all his pockets, feeling that everything agreed upon was there. He told himself that he did not care what happened as long as he did not let Croucher down. He felt how lucky they were to be in Sainsbury dormitory where the others would all be on their side. If they had been in Rattray dorm it would have been impossible, because of all the sneaks and wets there. And, anyway, there was no window on the street in Rattray dorm. He looked at the windows through which he and Croucher would soon be climbing. A moon, the thick sweet yellow of butterscotch, was beginning to show, and a faint breeze lifted the curtains above Bambrough's bed. Tilley could see most of the beds at that end of the dorm now, and the shapes of the chaps asleep. If he didn't know exactly where each of them slept he would not recognise them at all. He wished he was one of them, who did not have to run away. With stiff arms he laid his clothes back on the chair and crawled into bed. It must be hell's late. He tried to think of his dog, and he could only think of the dog being taken away and put to sleep, because he had only had the dog given to him as a reward for passing his exams and getting into the school. How rotten unfair it would be on the dog if he was sent away to be put to sleep just because he could not stick it at school. The tears for his dog ran down out of the corners of Tilley's eyes and into his ears. He wished he was one of the other boys. He wished he was grown up. He wished he didn't have a dog. He wished he was like Croucher who knew what he was going to be one day. He wished he had been top of the form, or good at games like Bambrough. He wished he had a sister, he wished his father would *understand*. He wished, above all, that he was asleep and not thinking all these things which he did not usually think about. But his cousin was to be married next week, and she had specially asked that he should come to the reception afterwards to pass the snacks round. In the icy waste of his unhappiness Tilley found this snowdrift to shelter in, and there sleep found him.

Croucher thought of Tilley. Had it not been for Tilley he would never have decided to make a bolt for it. He could have let them do what they liked to him: he was used to it. But when they began picking on Tilley all the time it reminded him of the way he had been upset at the start of his own series of punishments. In this school getting punished was rather like a chap having a bad cut which every time it was knocked started to bleed again. If you hadn't been punished before you wouldn't get punished this time, but once it had started there wasn't any way of stopping it. And they certainly hated Tilley: whatever he did he got caught, which showed they must be *deliberately* trying to catch him, because nobody gets caught every time. Some chaps never got caught doing anything. Someone like Denby even cut a maths lesson once and it wasn't noticed. Mr. Anstruther came in late and didn't have time to take roll-call. It was the only time that ever happened, but if Tilley was just late he would have to stay in afterwards, and if he forgot one of his books he wouldn't be allowed to share. Anybody could see that Tilley was not that bad, except the masters. 'In this school,' thought Croucher, 'they want to *make* some people bad.' He was glad to be friends with Tilley. It just showed, now they were friends, that some people you thought were wet when they first came turned out to be as good as anybody else. The best bit about Tilley was that he was only friends with people he really liked. And once he was friends he never took umbrage, because he thought that being friends was more important. And in a thing like running away he was the best man to have, because if he wasn't very clever at lessons he was very clever about other people and he was a genius about plans. It had been his idea to go in games clothes because he said then anybody who sees two boys running across the fields won't think it's anything except two boys told by the school to practise their running. 'One day,' thought Croucher, turning his pillow to get the cool side against his cheek, 'I'm going to teach old Tilley to fight so well he could even lam somebody like Bambrough, who's always siding about threatening to lam people. Still, Bambrough must be O.K. really, or he wouldn't be helping.' A man could rely on Bambrough. Croucher adjusted his pyjamas comfortably about his burly little body and stretched out for sleep confidently, and dived in as carelessly as he would have entered the swimming pool.

Bambrough did his bit exactly as promised. At the first twinge of the alarm he came awake, snapped it off, and jumped out of bed. He raced across the dormitory and shook Croucher.

Croucher looked up at him in bewilderment.

'Time to hit the trail,' said Bambrough, coolly watching.

'Oh yeah,' said Croucher, slowly pulling himself up on one elbow. He hated getting up on any day.

'Aren't you going?' asked Bambrough after a few moments of silent scrutiny.

'Yeah,' muttered Croucher.

'I'll wake everybody, then,' said Bambrough.

Tilley woke before he was shaken. He was horrified to find that it was quite light. They'd forgotten that in the summer it got light so early. His fingers were so stiff with the excitement that he tore a button off trying to get out of his pyjama jacket.

He stood by his bed, naked, motionless, unable to think what he should do next. All round him chaps were awake and stripping their beds. They were tying the sheets together so he and Crouch could climb down from the window to the road. All except Johnson were contributing. Johnson said it was only five o'clock, so he didn't see why he should make his bed yet. Vernon and Denby started to explain, but Bambrough said there was no time to go all over that again for one chap, and the three of them simply upended Johnson's bed. Johnson slid right down on his head, squeezed between springs and the wall, but he still tried to wrap his cocoon of bedclothes round him, until Wakefield came over too and they dragged him out and left him on the floor.

Suddenly Vernon exclaimed:

'Gosh, Johnson, you are a smelly monkey! Look what Johnson's done. This sheet's all wet.'

'Leave him,' commanded Bambrough. 'If that's what he likes we'll all piddle on his sheets for him. We've got enough sheets without his.'

The rope of sheets was soon ready. Croucher tested all the knots to make sure that chaps hadn't done grannies. Anybody who couldn't do a proper reef knot had to stand aside. Corlett went quietly on to the landing and came back with the hook from the fire-escape rope. You couldn't get the whole rope without breaking the cord which attached it to the wall, and that in turn would set all the fire alarms going. The hook was attached, and fixed to the window-sash. Then they threw out the rope of sheets and waited for five minutes. The danger was that Mr. Harbord would see the sheets going past his window.

During this time Tilley and Croucher stood by the window in silence, looking out across the fields. A faint ground mist crept across the green and nothing else moved. Tilley had the funny feeling that everybody outside the dormitory was dead. He wished he could see just one person somewhere walking about, or a dog or something. But all that happened was that a light wind shook the tops of some trees, and the rustle of their leaves sounded to him impatient and also forbidding.

'It's all right,' said Bambrough, 'old Hard Board's still asleep or he would have come up by now.'

Tilley felt a wave of nausea suddenly build up in his throat as he looked down at the road below. The last sheet was swaying about loose on the pavement. Whoever's sheet it was was going to get it in the neck because it would be bound to get dirty like that. Tilley felt a light jab in the small of his back. He turned and saw Morbey.

Morbey said nothing. He only pushed a pound note into Tilley's hand. Tilley shook his head.

'Please!' said Morbey, 'please. I don't want it back, honest.'

'You'll starve,' said Tilley cruelly, 'if you don't get enough cake.'

'All right,' said Morbey, 'I don't mind what happens to you. When you get halfway down I'm going to take the hook off and you'll be smashed to smithereens.'

'Oh, listen to old Morbey,' said Vernon, 'always trying to be different from everybody else.'

Bambrough turned round. He said sharply:

'I thought I told you to keep cave, Morbey?'

Before Morbey could reply, Denby thrust eagerly between them. 'Shall I keep cave, Bambrough?'

'I was to keep cave,' said Morbey. 'That was the plan. You can't change your mind.'

'Yes, he can,' retorted Denby, 'when he's got somebody so dumb as you to keep cave.'

'Both of you keep cave,' decided Bambrough, 'Denby on the Private side and Morbey on the Rattray dorm. We don't want any of them coming in and being nosy.'

Those looking through the windows saw at that instant a sudden twinkle of light flash over the top of a hill in the direction of the station, as the windows of an oncoming car met the first rays of the sun. It acted like a signal.

'I don't think we'd better hang about any more,' said Croucher. 'Shall I go first, Till?'

His face looked very white to his friend, and his eyes were wide and bulging in the way that had once inspired Wilson to call him Froggy until Croucher had made his nose bleed for him.

Tilley nodded. He could not believe now that he was going to do this dreadful thing, run away from school and cut himself off from all the other chaps. Perhaps any moment now somebody would interrupt, Morbey or Denby come crashing in calling: 'Cave, cave!' but the room was still, the chaps moved into a semicircle round them.

Bambrough said: 'What are you taking a torch for, Tillers?'

Tilley looked down at it, and felt stupid. He fumbled at it. He shrugged.

'It's too late to take it off now,' he said, 'it's tied on firmly.'

Croucher had his leg over the window-sill. Bambrough smiled approvingly. He was going down exactly as Mr. Adams had taught them all in cliff-climbing. As the hook suddenly swung, and the sheet went taut with the strain, Tilley thought he would be sick. But he forced himself to look over to see how Croucher was doing it. Briefly Croucher looked up at him, with an intense concentration, as if he had never seen him before in his life, then averted his eyes again, back to the rope of sheets. Tilley wished he'd gone first, because if he had he would now be almost down.

Croucher, down, seemed to bound once, and wave both arms above his head. He looked up and down the road and then made beckoning motions.

Tilley threw down first Croucher's bundle, then his own, which Croucher laid neatly on the grass verge, as if it were important that they should stay as clean as possible, then returned to the bottom of the sheet rope. Tilley could see that there was much more loose sheet trailing about at the bottom, now that Croucher had stretched it. He stepped back into the dormitory and took a deep breath. Everything round became frighteningly tiny as he reacted against the whole wild scheme and the window he was supposed to go through looked so small a pocket diary would have blocked it.

'You're next,' prompted Vernon.

He looked round at them all, urging him, forcing him out. He would have liked, as he had done a hundred times before, to have run, in a quick exhilarating scamper when a foot was heard on the stairs, back to his bed. But every bed was pulled down, with a sheet off. Except for Johnson's. He had made his again, and was getting back into it. Tilley wished that he too was M.D. and nobody caring.

'Go on, Tillers,' said someone. 'Crouch is waving. Quick, before somebody comes.'

As Tilley went through the window the last image that impressed itself on his mind of the school he was leaving was Bambrough's face, close up to his, the eyes fierce and shining and a funny sort of sideways pull on his long jaw.

He was glad of the knots on the rope to hold on to. With them it made it much easier to climb down than the ropes in the gym, and not so burny either, but on the other hand his feet kept forgetting that there was another one, and another one below, and several times he was hanging on only by his arms with his legs swinging loose. On one occasion, as he was just outside Mr. Harbord's room, he thought he was going to swing right through the glass and he had a momentary vision of Mr. Harbord's face as he would look as the boy landed on his bed in the midst of a rain of glass fragments. But just as the window came so close that he could see into the gloom beyond, well enough to pick out the shape of one of Mr. Harbord's pictures on the wall, the rope went firm, as

Croucher down below steadied it. He was pulled up in time. But, even so, the torch suspended from his belt touched the glass with a faint clink.

His feet rested on the ledge or he might have fallen. For five seconds he did not move at all, waiting for Mr Harbord's face to appear, to puff him with a cold, sarcastic word to his death. But Mr. Harbord, seemingly, slept well. Slowly, moving his hands with short, convulsive movements, he began to descend. Once his head was below the parapet he felt easier again, and the farther he went down, the more his confidence rose. He went down the last couple of sheets at a rush, and collapsed on his bottom finally at Croucher's feet.

Croucher helped him up.

'Good man, Till,' he said, and Tilley felt it had been worth while. The rope of sheets flashed away from them. They looked up and saw the faces of the boys of Sainsbury dormitory, white against burning brick. They raised their arms and trotted off, so absorbed in their flight that a speeding lorry missed them only by feet.

It was agreed that as soon as they were into the first field they would work right the way along to the left under the hedge, so that they could look back and see if anything was happening in the school. If any masters' heads did appear, or Matron's (who had frightened them only the day before by mentioning at breakfast that she always got up hours earlier than anybody else at the school because of all the extra work their carelessness subjected her to), then they were going to make straight for the trees at the corner and collect some eggs from a nest there. That would not be quite so bad as running away.

Under the hedge, squatting, Tilley asked:

'What do you think they're doing now in Sainsbury?'

'Making the beds, double-quick.'

'Do you think they'll go back to sleep? I wouldn't.'

'Bambrough will. He has to go in number three today. If he makes a score he'll get his colours. I heard Mr. Adams talking about it with Parvis.'

'I'm sorry about Mr. Adams, aren't you, Crouch? He never did anything to me.'

'No,' said Croucher, 'he was fair. If I was him I wouldn't work at a school like this. I'd go to sea, or something.'

'You could probably play sports for money.'

'Not somebody like Mr. Adams,' said Croucher, 'he's not that sort of chap.'

'He was the only one who wasn't a swine.'

'If we ever come back when we're grown-up and bomb this place we'll give him a chance to get out first.'

'And nobody else.'

'Nobody!' affirmed Croucher. 'Now let's get as far as we can away from it.'

They rose and jogged along, stooping, beside the hedgerow, crossed a stile into another smaller field which was so steep that the grass and weeds were left uncut. They went up this hill pressing on each knee to help themselves up. The undergrowth was wet and slushy and their tennis shoes were soaking when they reached the top. But they were encouraged by the sight of so much sun in the valley beyond, spreading its golden dominions, the dew coming off the grass in a thin vapour, with the effect of surrender.

Tilley clutched his friend by the arm. He was going to tell Croucher about Bambrough's face as he had last seen it, but he could not put his presentiment into words. He wanted to suggest an alternative route to the station, but there was the station ahead of them, only about two miles away.

'What?' said Croucher, wondering.

'Nothing,' said Tilley.

'Last in London's a big drip,' said Croucher.

Side by side they raced down the hill towards the station.

'Right,' said Bambrough, as their silhouettes disappeared off the horizon, 'I think we've given them enough of a start by now. Morbey, go and wake up Mr. Harbord and tell him what's happened.'

'Why me?' said Morbey.

'If you don't, I'll tell him you wanted to go too.'

'All right,' said Morbey, 'but I'll tell Croucher it was you who sneaked.'

'Who cares about Croucher? He's just a show-off.'

'Anyway,' said Vernon, 'if we don't report it we'll all get blamed.'

'You can't run away from school,' said Denby, 'nobody can.'

'I did,' said Johnson, 'I ran away.'

'Oh, you're always running away, you don't count,' said Denby. 'Anyway you're still here, aren't you?'

'Yes,' said Johnson, 'but next time I run away I won't tell anybody.'

'Don't pay any attention to Johnson,' commanded Bambrough, 'he can stay in bed.'

'Where are you all going?' asked Johnson, sitting up in bed and looking about him in a panic, as all the boys started to dress.

'We're going to help catch Tilley and Croucher,' replied Morbey, at the doorway.

'Mr. Harbord doesn't want you to help,' said Johnson, dressing all the same; 'he always comes after anybody who runs away, in his car.'

'Yes,' said Bambrough, '*you* get caught in a car because *you're* just a stupid fool. But Tilley smashed up his car last night. Tilley and Croucher aren't like you. They know how to run away.'

'Gosh!' said Denby, 'Mr. Harbord will kill them.'

'But if they get to London they'll go about saying we're all cowards,' said Bambrough. 'Now do you see why we've got to stop them?'

Mr. Harbord was dressing hurriedly. He said to the boy in the doorway:

'I don't care for informers, Morbey.'

'No, sir.'

'Tell Bambrough and Denby I want the garage opened. Here are the keys.'

'Yes, sir.'

'I'll deal with you when we come back, Morbey. But I should just like to know one thing.'

'What, sir?'

'What did Croucher and Tilley ever do to you?'

'Nothing, sir.'

'It's despicable, Morbey. Sometimes I don't understand you boys at all.'

'No, sir.'

'Well, don't just stand there, boy. While you're gawking those wretched people are running.'

Morbey vanished. Mr. Harbord turned to the window and looked out through his binoculars. Far up the valley he could see a train.

'I say,' panted Croucher, 'the train's coming! We won't get there in time.'

'It's all right,' said Tilley, 'that's the wrong direction. It's the down train.'

'Gosh, Till, you're marvellous.'

'So are you, Crouch.'

'Shall we stop for a sandwich now?'

'No,' said Tilley, 'whatever we do, we mustn't stop.'

'Whatever happens now, I'm glad we did it.'

'So am I.'

'I'll bet from now on lots of chaps run away.'

'I say, Crouch, look! In front of the station, isn't that Mr. Adams' car?'

They stood side by side, motionless, looking.

Uncertainly Tilley suggested:

'He must have got off the down train. He must be coming back from London.'

'Why doesn't he drive off, then?'

'I don't know, Crouch. I don't know why he doesn't drive off. You can never be sure what masters will do.'

'We can't wait.'

'I know, Crouch. I'm thinking. Honestly I am.'

In a pincer movement, spreading across the fields behind, Mr. Harbord and the boys of Sainsbury dormitory raced along. Bambrough had a whistle.

'We could go by road,' said Croucher at last.

'Get a lift? Gosh, we might go anywhere that way!'

'Anywhere would be better than staying here.'

They ran down to the road. A car almost immediately came along. They waved their thumbs wildly. The man at the wheel waved cheerily at them and smiled as he flashed by. Then there was nothing. The road lay bare and empty for three or four minutes.

'Here's another one! Let's stand in the middle of the road,' said Croucher.

But it was Mr. Adams' car. They turned back and ran, leaping the ditch and cutting back into the fields. They heard the car pull up beside them as they tore along the grass. Up on their left a whistle sounded.

'We can't!' panted Tilley.

'I'm going to run until I die!' replied Croucher.

The top of the hill was dotted with running figures.

'I've got such a stitch!' said Tilley, slowing down.

'Charge!' cried Bambrough.

Mr. Harbord watched the semicircle rapidly tighten on the hunted pair.

'Bizarre!' he murmured. His fingers twitched convulsively.

THE ATTIC EXPRESS

In the evenings they climbed the steep narrow stairway to the big room under the roof. Hector Coley went up eagerly and alertly. The boy followed his father draggingly. In the family it had always been called 'Brian's room,' but to Brian it seemed that his father's presence filled it.

It was a long room, with low side-walls and a ceiling like the lower half of an A. There was a large water-tank at one end: the rest of the space was 'Brian's'.

Coley ran the trains. The boy looked on.

Sometimes, when his father was absorbed, attending to midget couplings, rearranging a length of track, wiring up a tiny house so that it could be fit from inside, he looked away, and merely watched the single square of attic window gently darken.

Coley hated Brian to lose interest. He would say irritably: 'I can't understand you, Brian, beggared if I can! You know something? Some boys would give an arm to have the run of a playroom like this one I've built for you.'

The boy would shift his gaze and rub his hands together nervously. He would stoop forward hastily and peer at all parts of the track. 'Make it go through the crossing,' he would say, to appease his father. But even before the magnificent little Fleischmann engine challenged the gradient to the crossing – which would involve the delicious manœuvre of braking two or three small cars – his eye would be away again, after a moth on the wall, or a cloud veiling the moon.

'It defeats me,' Coley would say later to his wife, 'he shows no interest in anything. Sometimes I don't get a word out of him all evening unless I drag it out of him.'

'Perhaps he's not old enough yet,' she would reply diffidently. 'You know, I think I'd find it a little difficult to manage myself – all those signals and control switches and lights going on and off and trains going this way and that way. I'm glad I'm never asked to work out anything more complicated than a Fair Isle knitting pattern.'

'You miss the point,' said Coley impatiently. 'I'm not expecting him to synchronise the running times of ten trains, and keep them all safely on the move, but I would like a spark of enthusiasm to show now and again. I mean, I give up hours of my time, not to speak of money running into thousands, to give him a layout which I'm willing to wager a couple of bob can't be matched in any home in Britain, and he can't even do me the courtesy of listening to me when I explain something. It's not good enough.'

'I know, dear, how you feel, but at ten I do feel it's a little——'

'Oh, rubbish,' exclaimed Coley, 'ten's a helluvan age. At ten I could dismantle a good watch and put it together again better than new.'

'You are exceptional, dear. Not everyone has your mechanical bent. I expect Brian's will show itself in time.'

'There again, will it? His reports all read the same: "Could do much better if he applied himself more . . . doesn't get his teeth into it . . ." and so on till I could give him a jolly good hiding. No, Meg, say what you like, it's plain to me that the boy simply won't try.'

'In some subjects he's probably a little better than in others.'

'Nonsense,' said Coley energetically, 'anybody can do anything, if they want to enough.'

One evening, after listening to his complaints meekly for a while, she suddenly interrupted him:

'Where is he now?'

'Where I left him. I've given him the new express in its box. I want to see whether he's got enough gumption to set it out on the track with the right load. If I find it's still in the box when I get back——'

'Yes, dear,' she said, surprising him with her vehemence, 'why don't you bring the matter to a head? It's getting on my nerves a bit, you know, to be down here reading and watching television, and to imagine you struggling. If he's not really interested, then could we have an end to all this? I know the railways are your pride, but honestly I'd rather see them scrapped than listen to any more of this.'

He was astonished. He went back upstairs without a word.

The boy was squatting, with his face cupped in one hand, elbow on knee. His straight brown hair fell forward and half obscured his face. The other arm dangled loosely, and the forefinger of his hand moved an empty light truck to and fro a few inches on the floor.

The express was on the rails. Brian had it at the head of an extraordinary miscellaneous collection of waggons: Pullmans, goods trucks, restaurant cars, breakdown waggons, timber trucks, oil canisters – anything, obviously, which had come to hand.

'Sit down at the control panel, Brian,' snapped Coley.

The boy did not reply, but he did what he was told.

'I want you to run this express tonight,' said Coley, 'and I'm not going to lift a finger to help. But I'll be fair, too, I won't criticise. I'll stay right out of it. In fact for all you know I might as well be on the train itself. Think of me being on it, that's it, and run it accordingly. . . .'

He was trying to keep the anger and disappointment out of his voice. The boy half turned a moment, and looked at him steadily, then he resumed his scrutiny of the control panel.

'. . . take your time . . . think it all out . . . don't do anything hastily . . . keep your wits about you . . . remember all I've taught you . . . that's a gorgeous little model I've got there for you . . . I'm on board . . . up on the footplate if you like . . . we'll have a gala and just have it lit with the illuminations of the set itself . . . give me time to get aboard . . . I'm in your hands, son . . .'

Coley stood on the railway line. The giant express faced him, quiet, just off the main line. He started to walk along the track towards it.

He felt no astonishment at finding himself in scale with the models. *Anyone can do anything, if they want to enough*. He'd wished to drive a model, from the footplate, and here he was walking towards it.

But at the first step he took he sank almost up to his knees in the ballast below the track. It was, after all, only foam rubber. He grinned. 'I'll have to remember things like that,' he told himself.

He stopped by the engine and looked up at the boiler. He whistled softly between his teeth, excited by so much beauty. What a lovely job these Germans made of anything they tackled. Not a plate out of line. A really sumptuous, genuine, top-of-the-form job! He wished the maker a ton of good dinners. The thing was real, not a doubt.

He stepped on through tiny, incisive pebbles of sand, treading cautiously. One or two had threatened to cut into his shoes. Looking down, he noticed a right-angled bar of metal, gleaming at his feet. He realised in a moment that it must be one of the staples which had held the engine's box together. Chuckling over his own drollness at playing the game to the full, he picked up the bar and with an effort almost succeeded in straightening it right out. Then he advanced on the wheel and tapped it. The wheel was, of course, sound. He ran his hand over the virgin wheel. He lifted his arm and placed his hand against the smooth gloss of the boiler. He could do that because it was quite cold. He smiled again: that took away a bit of the realism, to think of a steam engine run on electricity. When you were down to scale it seemed you noticed these things.

Then he frowned as he noticed something else. The coupling of the first carriage, a Pullman, could not have been properly made up by Brian. The first wheels were well clear of the rails. He ran past the tender to have a look. Sure enough. Damn careless of him! He was about to call out to Brian when he remembered his promise to say nothing, and thought he'd make the correction himself. It was just a matter of sliding the arm across until the spoke fell into the slot in the rear of the tender. The remainder of the fastening was simple. He jabbed the lever in under the arm and strained to shift the carriage.

After a minute, during which the carriage swayed a bit but did not move, he stopped and took off his coat. He was still in his office suit. He wished he were in his old flannels and lumberjack shirt, but at least he hadn't changed into slippers. Sweat trickled down his back. He hadn't had much time for exercise lately, though his usual practice was conditioning on the links, alternate fifteen yards running and walking, for eighteen holes. Without clubs of course.

He hurled himself at it again, bracing his full weight against the lever. Suddenly the arm shifted, and skidded over the new surface on which it rested. The spoke found the slot, and the whole carriage crashed into position on the rails. The lever flicked off with rending force, and one spinning end struck him under the arm, just near the shoulder.

He thought he would be sick with pain. All feeling went out of his arm, except at the point of impact. There was plenty of feeling, all vividly unpleasant. Almost mechanically he leant down and picked up his jacket. Trailing it, he tottered back to the engine, and slowly hoisted himself into the cab. There he leant over one of the immobile levers until he had partially recovered.

He was still palpating his startled flesh, and establishing that no bone was broken, when, without any preliminary warning, the train suddenly jerked into motion. Wheeling round, he managed to save himself from falling by hooking himself into the window of the cab. He looked for his son, to signal he was not quite ready yet. Even without the blow he had just sustained he would have liked a few more minutes to adjust himself to the idea of being part of a model world before the journey began.

But he couldn't at first see where he was. In this fantastic landscape, lit but not warmed by three suns, all the familiar features had undergone a change. The sensation resembled in some way that which comes to a man who visits a district he knows well by daylight for the first time after dark.

In the direct light of those three suns, an overhead monster and two wall brackets, everything glittered. Plain to Coley, but less noticeable to the boy at the table on which was spread the control panel, were separate shadows of differing intensity radiating from every upright object. But the objects themselves sparkled. Light came flashing and twinkling and glancing from the walls and roofs of the houses, from the foliage of the trees, from the heaps of coal by the sidings, from the clothes and faces of the men and women. The lines of the railway themselves shone, twisting and turning a hundred times amongst windmills and farms and garages and fields and stations, all throwing back this aggressive, stupefying brilliance of light. Coley screwed up his eyes and tried to work it out. The train slipped forward smoothly, gaining momentum. The boy hadn't made a bad job of the start, anyway. Perhaps he took in more than I imagined, said Coley to himself.

He fixed his eye on a vast grey expanse, stretching away parallel to the course they were on, and appearing like a long rectangular field of some kind of close undergrowth with curling tops. What the devil could that be? He didn't remember putting down anything like that. Whatever it was, it didn't look anything like the real thing, now that he was down to scale. A breeze stirred small clumps which seemed to ride clear of the rest, and it came to him that, of course, this was the strip of carpet he'd laid down on one side of the room, always insisting that people should walk only on this if possible, to prevent breakages.

If that was the carpet . . . he rushed across to the other window, just in time before the engine started to take a corner to see the top of his son's head, bent over the controls.

It was miles away! So huge! So . . . dare he admit it to himself . . . grotesque! The line of his parting, running white across his scalp, showed to the man in the cab like a streak in a forest, a blaze consequent upon road-making. A house could have been hidden behind the hair falling across his forehead. The shadow of his son on the burning white sky behind was like a stormcloud.

Brian disappeared from his view as the track curled, and Coley shook his head, as if he could clear away these images as a dog rattles away drops of water from its fur. 'It's not like me to imagine things,' said Coley fiercely. All the same, beads of moisture stood out on the back of the hand which clutched a lever.

He sensed a slight acceleration. The telegraph poles were coming by now at more than one a second. He felt the use of his injured arm returning, and with it a return of self-confidence. 'I wonder if, when I return to my normal size, the bruise will be to scale or be only, quite literally, a scratch?'

He was about to resume his jacket, since the wind was now considerable, when the train turned again and he lost his balance. In falling, the jacket fell from his hand, and was whipped away out of the cab.

Unhurt by his fall, but irritated by the loss of the jacket, Coley pulled himself to his feet and swore: 'Hell of a lot of bends on this railway,' as if he were perceiving it for the first time. 'Anyway, that doesn't matter so much, I can put up with a fresh wind for a while if he'd only think what all this bloody light is doing to my eyes. Tone down the ruddy glare, can't you?'

As if in answer, the suns were extinguished.

For an instant the succeeding blackness was complete.

The express forged almost noiselessly through the dark. Coley fumbled for handholds. 'That's a bit inefficient,' he muttered. But the totality of darkness was not for long. Simultaneously, and Coley imagined Brian studying the switches, all the lights in the houses and stations and farms and windmills, and so forth, were flipped on.

'That's really rather nice to look at!' said Coley, appreciatively. 'I always knew I'd done a good job there, but it's only now that I can see just how good. I don't think they can complain there,' he went on. 'I think they'd admit I've looked after that little creature comfort.' He was referring to the little people with whom he had populated the world in which the attic express was running.

He also thought, as the walls of the attic vanished altogether: 'If he hasn't noticed that the old man's no longer sitting in the armchair behind him he's not likely to now. It would be rather good to slip back into the chair before the lights go up again. I'll have to watch my moment as soon as he's had enough and stops the express.'

They sped through a crossing. Coley, looking down on it, and at the figures massed by the gate, observed a solitary figure in a patch of light, waving. Whimsically, he waved back. The expression on the face of the waving man was one of jubilation. His smile reached, literally, from ear to ear. 'A cheery chappie,' remarked Coley. He was beginning to enjoy himself.

At a comfortable pace the express swung into a long straight which led into the area described on the posters and signboards as Coleyville. It was the largest and best equipped of the five stations. Coley thought that Brian must see it as an inevitable stop. Interesting to see whether he could bring it in to a nice easy check. The passengers might be assumed to be taking down their suitcases, and dragging on their coats, and would be resentful at being overbalanced.

Far up ahead Coley could see the platform approaching. He could make out the long line of people waiting to climb aboard. A representative body of folk, thought Coley, I got in a good cross-section of the travelling public for Coleyville. Then, flashing down the hill, on the road which would cross the track just this side of the station in a scissors intersection, Coley saw an open sports car. It was coming down at a frightening speed, and should reach the junction just as the express went through.

'The young monkey!' breathed Coley, 'he must be getting into the swing of it.' For a moment he tensed, until he remembered that on this crossing there was a synchronisation which would automatically brake the car. A high, whining metallic noise filled his ears from the single rail of the roadster, which abruptly cut off as the car was stopped.

'From eighty to rest in a split second,' thought Coley, 'that's not too realistic. Not the boy's fault, but I'll have to see if I can't improve on that.' He also noticed, as the express moved slowly through the crossing, that there were no features on the face of the roadster's driver. Not even eyes! 'No use telling you to look where you're going!' shouted Coley. The square-shouldered driver sat upright and motionless, waiting for the express to be out of his way.

The express stopped at Coleyville.

'Perfect!' exclaimed Coley, 'just perfect!' He wished he could shake Brian's hand. The boy must care, after all, to be able to handle the stuff in this way. His heart swelled. He thought for a moment of stepping off at Coleyville and watching from the outside for a while, and then pick her up again next time she stopped. But he couldn't be sure the boy would bring her round again on the same line. And this was far too exhilarating an adventure to duck out of now. He stayed.

He leant out of the cab and looked down the platform at the people waiting. It was a mild surprise to him that no one moved. There they stood, their baggage in their hands or at their feet, waiting for trains, and doing nothing about it when one came. He saw the guard, staring at him. The guard's face was a violent maroon colour, and the front part of one foot was missing. He had doubtless good reasons for drinking heavily. Immediately behind him was a lovely blonde, about seven feet high, and with one breast considerably larger than the other, but otherwise delicious to look at. At her side was a small boy in suit and school cap. He had the face of a middle-aged man. Farther on down, a toothless mastiff gambolled, at the end of a leash held by a gentleman in city suit and homburg. He was flawless but for the fact that he had omitted to put on collar and tie.

Coley rubbed the side of his nose with his index finger. 'I never expected to discover that you had such curious characters,' he said ruefully. The guard stared at him balefully, the blonde proudly. The express moved out of the station. Coley took his shoe off and hammered the glass out of the right-hand foreport. It was too opaque for proper vision. He smiled as he thought of the faces of the makers if he should write to them criticising. Being Germans, they'd take it seriously, and put the matter right in future.

Beyond Coleyville the track wound through low hills. Coleyville was a dormitory town, but on the outskirts were some prosperous farms whose flocks could be seen all about the hills. A well-appointed country club lay at the foot of the high land which bordered the east wall, which was continued in illusion by a massive photograph of the Pennines which Coley had blown up to extend most of the length of the wall. It was, in Coley's view, one of the most agreeable and meticulously arranged districts in his entire layout.

By the fences of the farms stood children, waving. Yokels waved. Lambs and dogs frisked. A water-mill turned slowly. It ran on a battery, but looked very real. Plump milkmaids meandered to and fro. 'Lovely spot for a holiday,' thought urban Coley, sentimentally. He leant far out of the cab window to have a better view of the whole wide perspective, and almost had his head taken off by a passing goods train.

It came up very softly, passing on the outside of a curve. Coley withdrew his head only because he happened to catch a slight shadow approach.

He leant his face against the cold metal by his window.

'Idiot!' he said to himself in fright and anger.

The goods train went by at a smart clip. There were only about five trucks on it, all empty.

'Steady, old chap!' he apostrophised his son, under his breath, 'don't take on too much all at once.'

For the first time it occurred to him that it might be a good thing to be ready to skip clear in the event of danger. Brian was operating very sensibly at present, but a lapse in concentration . . . a vague chill passed down Coley's spine.

He looked back at the train on which he was travelling. It might be better to pick his way to the rear coaches.

He took three strides and launched himself on to the tender. Landing, he tore his trousers on the rough surface which represented coal nuts. It was very slippery and he almost slid right over it altogether, but he contrived to dig toes and hands into the depressions and check himself.

The express was moving along an embankment. Below him he could see the figures of young women in bathing suits disporting themselves about a glass swimming pool. Uniformed waiters stood obsequiously about, handing drinks to shirt-sleeved gentlemen under beach umbrellas. In the context of night-time the scene appeared macabre and hinting of recondite pleasures, particularly when the white legs of one of the beauties, protruding from under a glistering, russet bush, were taken into account. She could have been a corpse, and none of the high-lifers caring.

Coley wriggled forward cautiously over the hard black lumps. He wished now he'd stayed where he was, since the strong wind was more that he had allowed for.

He scrambled to a sitting position on the hard, pointed surface of the tender. Beyond the country club, looking ahead, were the mountains. He sought about for the secure footholds he'd need before making his leap off the tender into the gaping doorway of the Pullman behind, but decided to postpone the effort until the express had passed through the long tunnel. There was a long gentle declivity on the far side, a gradient of 1:248 he'd posted it, and he'd have a more stable vehicle to jump to. Besides, in the tunnel it would be dark.

He remembered himself one Sunday morning making the mountain secure above the tunnel. The trouble he'd had with that material, nailing it in firmly without damaging any of the features of the landscape built on to it.

Those nails!

Some must protrude into the tunnel itself! He'd never troubled himself about them. There had always been plenty of clearance for the trains themselves. But for him, perched on top of the tender? He looked round desperately to see if he might still have time to make his leap.

But he remembered too late. The tunnel sucked them in like a mouth. He rolled flat on his face and prayed.

It was not completely dark, though very nearly so. A vague glow came through at one section where a tricky bit of building had been finally effected with painted canvas, and in it he was lucky to spot one of the nails and wriggle clear. The other he never saw. The point, aimed perpendicularly downwards, just caught his collar, as it arched upward over his straining neck.

He was jerked up bodily. It was very swift. He had no time to do anything about it. For a second he seemed to be suspended on the very tip of the nail, then the shirt tore and he was delivered back on the train.

He landed with a vicious thump on some part of a waggon some distance below roof-level. Something drove like the tip of a boot into his knee and he doubled over against what might be a rail. He clung to it. He couldn't tell where he was, but he could hear a wheel clicking furiously beneath him. Gasping from the pain of his knee, and a dull throb between the shoulder blades he hung on and waited for the end of the tunnel and light.

It came suddenly.

His first feeling was relief that he had been thrown almost on the very spot he had chosen to jump to before the train entered the tunnel. But this was succeeded by a stab of anguish from his back as he raised himself to his feet in the doorway of the Pullman. He put his hand behind his back and found first that his shirt had split all the way to his trousers. He allowed it to flow down his arms, and held it in one hand while he probed his back with the other.

'Ye Gods,' he murmured shakily, as he examined his hand after feeling his wound, 'I must be bleeding like a stuck pig!'

Slowly he converted his shirt into a great bandage, wrapping it around his chest, under his armpits, and tying it below his chin, like a bra in reverse. While he was doing this, grunting as much from astonishment at his predicament as from pain, the express accelerated, and as it thundered along the decline his horror at this was added to the confusion of his feelings.

'I must stop this,' he said thickly. 'I must signal the boy to cut the power off.' He reeled into the Pullman. On the far side he seemed to remember there was a flat truck with nothing on it but a couple of logs. Perhaps if he got astride one of them he could make himself be seen.

From nowhere appeared the colossal torso of a man. It was white-coated, but the face was mottled, a sort of piebald, with only one deeply sunken eye, and the other the faintest smear at the point of the normal cheekbone.

'Get away! Get away!' screamed Coley, striking out at it wildly. One of the blows landed high on the man's chest. He teetered a moment, and then, without bending, went over on his back. The material from which he was made was very light. He was no more than an amalgam of plastics and painted hat.

Coley looked down at the prostrate dummy and rubbed his bloodied hand over his forehead. 'No sense in getting hysterical,' he warned himself. He stepped over the prostrate figure, twisting to avoid the outstretched arm. He observed with revulsion that the fingers on the hand were webbed, a glittering duck-egg blue. Coley ran his tongue over his lips, tasting blood. 'Take a brace,' he admonished himself, reverting to the slang of his schooldays, 'don't let your imagination run away with you.'

He staggered amongst the conclaves of seated gentlemen, forever impassive and at their ease in armchairs, content with the society in which they found themselves, unimpressed by the increasing momentum of the express, welded to their very chairs. Coley shot a glance over the gleaming carapace of one stern hock-drinker and out through the window. The variety of the landscape was flickering by with alarming speed, becoming a gale of altering colours. The coach was beginning to sway.

Coley broke into a run. The roar below him apprised him that the express was travelling over the suspension bridge. The bridge had been his pride, a labour of months, not bought whole, but built from wire and plywood in his leisure hours. He had no time now for gloating.

'I must get him to see me or I'm done for.'

But beyond the Pullman he found another waggon, a restaurant car. In his haste he had forgotten that one. He dashed down the aisle, grabbing tables to steady himself against the rocking of the train as he went. They must be up to seventy now. Or rather about four miles an hour, he realised with bitterness.

Leaning a moment over one of the tables, he saw that the lamps in the centre were bulky, heavy-looking objects. He heaved tentatively at one of them, and it snapped off at the base. The diners, with their hands in their laps, stared on across the table at each other, untroubled by the onslaught of this wild-eyed Englishman. The Englishman, naked to the waist, his shirt sleeves dangling red and filthy down his chest, his body flaming now with a dozen bruises, stood over them a second clutching the lamp to him, panting heavily, then turned away and reeled on down the aisle. Down his retreating back the blood was flowing now freely. The shirt was inadequate to check it as it escaped from the savage wound he had sustained in the tunnel.

This time when he emerged at the doorway of the carriage he found himself looking at the open truck on which were chained four logs. He flung the lampstand ahead of him and it landed satisfyingly between two of the logs. He gathered his ebbing strength for the jump.

He was just able to make it. He caught his foot in one of the chains in mid-flight and crashed down on his face, but he saved himself from disaster by flinging one arm round a log. He sat up immediately and looked about him.

For a moment his vision was partly blocked as yet another train flashed by in the opposite direction. 'Oh God, what's he playing at?' whispered Coley, 'he can't handle so many trains at once!'

The express was almost at the end of the long straight. It slowed for the curve right, at the bottom. For a brief time after that it would be running directly under the control panel at which Brian was sitting. That would be his chance to make an impression. He hauled himself astride the top log and waited.

The express took the curve at a reduced pace, but squealing slightly nevertheless. Coley could sense most of the load concentrate on the inner wheels. Then he could see his son above him.

He waved frantically.

Brian seemed to rise slightly from his chair. His shadow leapt gigantically ahead of him, stretching forward and up on the slanting ceiling. Behind his head the glare of the Anglepoise lamp was almost unbearable. Coley was unable to make out the features of his son at all: there was only the silhouette. He couldn't tell if he had noticed anything.

With almost despairing violence he flung the lamp. He saw it speed in a low parabola out over the road which ran parallel to the track, bounce on the white space of Brian's shin exposed above his sock, and vanish in the darkness beyond. The enormous figure rose farther, towering now above the speeding express. Coley was sure now that he had been seen. He made desperate motions with his hands, indicating that he would like a total shut-down of power. The boy waved. Coley turned sick. He stared down at his hands, pathetic little signals of distress. The probability was that the boy couldn't even see them.

But he should have been aware that something was wrong. Surely he must see that.

They tore through another station. They were taking the curves now at speed. They flashed across the scores of intersecting rails of the marshalling yard. The noise was like machine-gun fire. He saw another unit come into play; a two-car diesel slipped away south in a coquettish twinkle of chromium.

'He's showing off,' thought Coley grimly, 'he's going to try to bring every bloody train we've got into motion.'

He knew now that the only way he could save himself would be somehow to get off the train. If only he didn't feel so hellishly bushed!

Coley was never tired. Other people seemed to be tired for him. In every project which he had ever undertaken his adherents had flaked away at some stage, forgotten, like the jettisoned elements in a rocket flight. Hector Coley himself drove on to arrive at his object in perfect condition. But now he was tired, and he felt himself nearing exhaustion with his loss of blood and the battering he had taken.

There was just a chance, he thought, of a stop at Coleyville. The boy had evidently taken in the importance of that one. He'd postpone the final effort to get clear until Coleyville was reached.

He leant over the cold metal of which the log was made, and embraced it like a lover. The metal was cold and refreshing against the skin of face and chest. Through his blurring vision he saw again the great grey plain, and the approaching scissors intersection before Coleyville. Once again the smart little roadster ground to a peremptory halt at the crossing. Other cars halted behind it.

But the express did not this time slacken speed. It went through

Coleyville at sixty. For a fleeting instant he saw again the maroon face of the guard, the giant blonde, the malevolence of the middle-aged schoolboy. Those waiting waited still. Those who had been waving waved on. Then Coleyville was gone, and the man on the log recognised that he would have to jump for it. He thought ahead.

Wistfully his mind passed over the swimming pool of the country club. If only that had been water! He winced at the appalling idea of crashing through glass.

But where else could he make it? Spring on to the roof of the tunnel, as they entered? But no, the mountain above was too sheer; it would be like flinging himself against a brick wall. Then he remembered the trees which overhung the long straight beyond. He'd been in the Pullman last time they'd gone under those. But he might be able to grab one and hang from it long enough to let the express pass beneath him.

He fainted away.

When he came to he found that the express was emerging from the tunnel. He wondered how many times he had made the circuit. Several times, probably. Looking across the countryside from this high vantage point he could see on almost every track trains and cars travelling, east, west, south, north.

He felt a cold wind blowing now powerfully across the track. It was horrendous, roaring. It threatened to drag his very hair out by the roots. The shirt sleeves were flapping like mad, trapped seagulls. He twisted his head to face the blast and looked on at the final horror.

His son had quitted the control panel. He was now squatting, setting a fan on the long grey meadow of carpet. In the whirlwind everything light in the landscape was going over, the waving figures of the yokels and children, the flimsier structures of paper cottages. The station at Coleyville was collapsing, while the people on the platform waited patiently.

Brian smiled. Coley saw him smile.

Then, as he thought that he must be obliged to relinquish his hold and be blown away to destruction, the boy picked the fan up again, and placed it where it always had been.

But he did not return to his seat at the control panel. He went out through the door, and shut it behind him. The noise as it slammed was like a shell exploding.

The express went down the long straight through the suspension bridge and towards the curve at the bottom and reached a hundred miles an hour. Coley watched the overhanging branches of the trees sweep towards him. He climbed on to the logs and steadied himself with his feet braced against a knot to make this last leap. He realised that he would have to make it good the first time, and hoist himself well clear of the onrushing roofs of following coaches.

Red, yellow, brown, green, the trees suddenly showed.

He made his effort.

He felt the spines run through his hands. Then the branch broke, and he was jammed in the doorway of the next carriage.

He pulled a spine which had remained in his flesh clear, then lay there. He was broken. He waited for the express to derail.

But it did not derail. It swooped on the curve and screamed round it. Almost exuberantly it hurled itself at the next stretch running below the now abandoned control panel. Behind him he heard but did not see the last light trucks and petrol waggons go somersaulting off the track. For a moment there was a grinding check on the express: the wheels raced, then a link must have snapped and the wheels bit again. They surged forward.

The clatter as they started across the marshalling yard began again.

Coley got up quickly. The will which had devastated board rooms, concentrated now in his tiny figure, was the only part of him which had not been reduced to a scale of one in three hundred. He remembered that before getting on to the express at the outset of this misconceived adventure he had sunk almost to his knees in the foam-rubber ballast on which the track was laid. In the marshalling yard there was acres of it! He stepped back on the log-bearing truck and looked quickly about him.

'Foam-rubber,' he said to himself, 'not ballast.'

He flung himself out, as if into a feather bed.

He lay for a moment luxuriously. He watched the express disappear in the direction of shattered Coleyville. He sighed. What a close thing!

Downstairs, Brian was buckling on his raincoat. His mother watched him anxiously.

'I think your father would prefer it if just this once more you helped him with his trains. It's a bit late to go out.'

'No, he sent me away.'

His mother sighed. She looked forward to an uncomfortable scene with Hector when he should deign to reappear. He probably wouldn't even eat his dinner and then be even more bad-tempered because he was hungry.

'Don't be long, then.'

'I'm only going out to Billy's. We're going to watch for a hedgehog he says comes out at night in his garden.'

'All right then, but be sure to wrap up well.'

Coley hauled himself to his feet. He stood alone, a figure of flesh and blood in a world of fakes.

'I shall never play with them again, not after this,' he said quietly.

It was a decision, but it was accurate also as a prophecy. A sibilant hiss was all he heard of the diesel before it struck him. It was travelling at only three miles an hour, or call it sixty.

It killed him.

Before he died he thought: 'How wretched to die here like this, tiny, probably not even found! They'll wonder whatever became of me.'

He wished he might have been out altogether of the tiny world which had proved to be too big for him. It was his dying wish.

No one doubted that it had been murder when Hector Coley was found stretched out across the toy world which had been his great hobby and pride. But so battered and bloodied and broken a figure could only have resulted from the attack of a maniac of prodigious strength.

'He was still playing with the models when he was surprised,' reported the Inspector. 'The current was on, and about ten of them had come to rest against his body. To be frank, though, he looked as if about ten real ones had hit him.'

RECALL

'We have literally all the time in the world,' said the Governor, 'but, as a matter of convention, here in the Final Cycle, we do try to press on.'

His audience looked for him with pleasure and excitement. They were not sure whether to expect him to materialise. The voice was suave but formal, a trifle donnish. Each man and woman looked about with curiosity for the others: it would be interesting to discover who had come through the Cycle of Rejections.

'Happy release, Governor,' said Philip, in formal greeting. Around him he heard the phrase murmured simultaneously on other lips. He was sure Margot's voice was amongst them, and he thought he heard that Vickers chap who had been so pessimistic about his chances, having failed twice.

'So it was, my friends,' replied the Governor. 'I have decided that we are all sitting around a swimming pool, large enough for immersion, but not to suggest violent exercise.'

He began to be visible to them, sitting astride a stone frog.

Philip sat back in a deck-chair and stretched out his arms luxuriously. A drink appeared in his hand, and he nodded gratefully. He felt a delicious sense of privilege.

Margot dived, and the water appeared only just in time to accommodate her. Philip pushed back his chair, as a few drops fell on his faultlessly creased slacks, and shook his head admiringly. She had endless cheek. She stood up in the pool, in her Balmain evening gown, pushing her hair back from her face, and laughing up at the Governor.

'What a smashing pool,' she said, 'for the spur of the moment.'

'Your confidence in me is a compliment,' said the Governor. 'I beg your pardon for not having slipped you into a bathing suit at the same time, but it seemed, relatively, to be of secondary importance.'

'Oh, that's all right,' replied Margot, 'if nobody minds, I'd just as soon be naked, anyway.' She unzipped the gown and swam out of it, then took the sodden bundle and threw it with an effort towards the edge of the pool. Metamorphosed into a peacock, it skimmed above the water and, gaining strength, flew slowly over the heads of the group towards the nearest tree.

'Thank you!' cried Margot, pulling herself out of the pool to sit on the verge, 'that was beautifully done! How lovely it is to be fat!'

'I asssure you that that is subjective,' said the Governor; 'at the time of your suicide you were excessively thin.'

'I had to be. I was a model. Do you know, I think if I hadn't been so absolutely skeletal I might never have done it.'

'But you have no regrets?'

'Oh no! How can you ask such a question?'

'It was a happy release,' they all intoned.

'So it was, my friends,' said the Governor, 'and I am made happier to see our Margot so very, very happy.'

The lineaments of nine other people sitting and lying about the pool were now definite. They had been nineteen at the dinner in the Cycle of Rejections. Philip was astounded that the whittling away should have been so severe. And yet Vickers had got through. There he sat in his evening dress, his boiled shirt bulging like a spinnaker, as if he had sailed through on that alone. His hairy hands were clasped about his knees, and he rocked slightly, losing his balance at last and leaning back hurriedly to blink self-consciously through his thick spectacles at them all looking at him.

Cotterill, the banker, defenestration. Hildyard, the bailiff, cleaning his guns. Captain Agar, sub-omnibus. Doradita, overdosita. Mrs. Tranter, overexposure. Dr. Wiggs, shaving. Stevens, the boxer, auto-immobilised. Vickers, the journalist, cyanide. Margot, trying to go ashore before land was in sight. And he himself, a pact with Imogen in a car with engine running in a sealed garage.

And Imogen then? Not made it!

He stared round again, expecting her to make a late appearance, which would have been in character. 'You'd be late for your own funeral,' he had once said to her, and very nearly she had been. But evidently this time she would not appear at all. There was not so much as an opaque shadow to represent her. He felt a slight blow glancing off the carapace of his happiness. They had come through so much together that it seemed unnatural to lose her now, but he had no intention of being upset at all, much less unhappy, and he looked at Margot, forgot Imogen, and lost her for ever.

Like a reproach, that blessed dog, which had been asleep in the back seat of the car, trotted forward and placed both forepaws on his knees. Trust him to have joined the pact and qualified for the Final Cycle. His moods only varied from happiness to ecstasy, so there was not the remotest chance of ever leaving him behind.

'What a lovely little dog!' exclaimed Margot. 'He reminds me of my Butch. I couldn't bring him with me when I went up to town to live because I think it's so cruel to keep a dog in town. He's much better off here, with all the room in the world to play in!'

'It was a happy release,' they all muttered, in some embarrassment.

The Governor frowned. 'He'll have nothing to complain of,' he remarked grudgingly.

'Not only the dog,' chirped Margot, 'but all of us. It's so idyllic here that I've a good mind to cheat just to stay on here for a time.'

'That would be inadvisable,' replied the Governor. 'I can reveal to you that those whom I cannot forward will return to the First Cycle, where their whole case is reconsidered before they are even allowed to restart the Progress.'

'Like Snakes and Ladders?' queried Margot innocently.

The Governor smiled. 'You might notice variations.'

'What a tease!' she murmured reflectively.

'But I have no fears on that score,' proceeded the Governor, 'you will find the Final Cycle very simple. It is rather as if you had already taken your B.A. and all that is required of you to earn the M.A. is to keep your name on the books. I would like you all to recapitulate in your own minds the events preceding and following the death trauma, and then, in your own time, to let me know whether you have any hesitations. When you are sure that you wish to move on from Limbo, perhaps you would like to enter the pool?'

'Consider me in already,' said Margot. 'Limbo's been lovely, but I do think its atmosphere of cheesecloth is a bit overdone. It's all right here, but some of the Cycles have been fearfully obscure.'

The banker said nothing, but rose to his feet. He was instantly clad in swimming trunks of a vivid russet colour against which gleamed a saffron pattern of fronds and leaves. He plumped softly into the water and surfaced like a piece of balsa which is so sodden that it scarcely wants to float. He burbled gently as he swum slowly up and down. The dog ran excitedly up and down, hoping at some time to make contact.

Captain Agar said: 'I've never gone back on a decision, sir, not even a bad one. The outcome has shown that I assessed the situation accurately. I'll take the plunge. If you could see your way to issuing me with the appropriate kit I'll be happy to take the two steps forward. Oh, sir, one trivial request if I might make one? A tan, sir?'

Tanned, magnificently muscled, Captain Agar dived, and swam two lengths underwater before surfacing.

'What a lovely brown bottom!' breathed Margot. 'I want one too. Thank you! Could the rest of me be brown too?'

'There have been a great many of you this year,' said the Governor; 'just before recess I tend to take requests rather literally. But the matter can soon be adjusted.'

The tan spread all over Margot.

'Just in time to hide my blushes,' she remarked.

Stevens the boxer got to his feet. He put up his hand.

'Where we're going, guv, shall we need money?'

'Fortunately not,' replied the Governor, 'as you'll have no pockets to put it in.'

'That's all I wanted to know,' said the boxer. He climbed slowly down the steps into the shallow end.

Doradita, the dancer, when she stood up, was instantly in a bathing suit, with a halter neck and flying panels, but she looked down at herself uncertainly and then up at the Governor.

'I'm afraid,' she said, 'that a swimsuit is not any use to me because,' she explained, 'I am frightened of water. I am more frightened of water than I am of anything. I am more frightened of water than I am of being forgotten by my public.'

'You were,' corrected the Governor, 'and incidentally you might like to know that your guilty public have now taken you to their hearts.'

'They have forgiven me?'

'They believe they were the cause. It is being said you were hounded to your death.'

'Then I shall dance again! For those who were born and died without the chance of seeing me!'

'Very likely,' replied the Governor drily, 'and for those who had the chance and didn't take it as well.'

She stood at the edge of the pool and took an attitude, evidently about to favour them with a sample of her talents immediately. Mrs. Tranter, sitting just behind her, hidden from the Governor, gave her a tiny shove and in she went.

'In the case of actresses,' observed Mrs. Tranter, 'enough is as good as a feast. In my case there is little to say. I went out to look for my husband on a frosty night, and I am still looking for him. He is presumably ahead of me, so I shall go on looking. If he is behind me, why then, he will have to look for me. I'll go into the pool now, if those who mean to follow promise not to jump on top of me. My children thought it a huge joke, but I abhor high jinks when swimming. I'm sure the Romans never indulged in horseplay in their gracious little baths.'

'You will shortly have an opportunity of seeing for yourself,' said the Governor. 'Why are you hesitating? Please tell me everything.'

'A bathing cap, do you mind?'

'Of course. I'm sorry that I can't oblige you with a Roman model. There were none.'

'If, where I'm going, none will be available, would you be good enough to make mine last for ever?'

'Would you lend it to a Roman matron?'

'If she lent me her bath, and asked nicely, I suppose I should.'

'In that case, Mrs. Trantor, yours is the Universal for the concept Bathing Cap.'

Mrs. Tranter inclined her rubber-capped head gratefully, and Margot whispered: 'Imagine! And it's three years out of fashion before she starts!'

The four men who remained uncommitted had in fact pushed themselves farther back from the pool, which was overflowing.

'Oh, I hope you won't think I am trying to force your hands,' said the Governor apologetically, 'by making the pool come out to meet you. Immersion is entirely optional. Simply, I've provided this silly frog with a spout in its mouth to pour the water in, and omitted to provide the complementary outlet.'

The dog was rushing up and down, barking excitedly and lapping at the water round its paws at the same time. Then suddenly its tongue was rasping over the grass. It looked up in astonishment and raced after the receding water. Almost it went in.

'Like yourselves, gentlemen,' said the Governor.

'I'm suffering from one embarrassment,' said the Doctor. 'It is the only flaw in my perfect happiness. It concerns Mr. Hildyard, who was once my patient, and what I have to say might be construed as a breach of confidence.'

'Say on, sir,' said Hildyard, 'I think I know what you are leading up to.'

'I had occasion to persuade Mr. Hildyard on a previous occasion not to commit suicide. I must ask him to forgive me for having delayed his progress.'

'In so far, Doctor, as we are now able to accompany one another, I forgive you with all my heart,' replied Hildyard. 'Shall we now join the others?'

'Willingly,' said the Doctor.

They shook hands gravely, and entered the pool.

'Buck up, slowcoach,' said Margot to Philip, 'the water's gorgeous. Warm as pie.' She scooped up a little, and flicked him with it.

'It is in fact just under blood heat,' said the Governor.

Philip looked across the pool at Vickers, who was striding up and down, looking not at all happy, looking like a man who was hearing voices elsewhere. The Governor said to Philip:

'Is it possible that only curiosity restrains you?'

Philip flushed. He nodded. 'Still, that's fair,' he protested, 'considering Mr. Vickers was a journalist. And if he knows something that I don't, I'd like to hear it. . . .'

'Yes,' said the Governor, 'I think Mr. Vickers will have to tell us what is disturbing him.'

'I'm not going to listen!' cried Margot. She reached out and grabbed the dog. 'I'm taking him with me,' she said, 'so do join us!' and with the animal under her arm she launched herself out into the water.

Like all those who had already gone in, she thereafter seemed disconnected, floating up and down, seemingly oblivious of those on the banks.

'I hear voices,' said the journalist thickly.

'I was afraid that might be the case,' said the Governor, 'it has happened before.'

'They are calling me,' said Vickers wildly.

'The voices of your loved ones,' agreed the Governor.

'What do they want from me?'

'Perhaps a great deal. Perhaps only an evening's entertainment.'

Philip stood up nervously. He walked to the edge of the pool. But no bathing suit was put on him. He seemed to be ignored by Governor and candidate. He understood that he had asked for an explanation and must now get it.

'But how are they doing it?' asked Vickers.

'Don't fight it,' said the Governor, 'and you will learn. We must both come with you, though.'

Briefly they all three showed in a room where people sat about a table, their hands all linked in an unbroken chain. Philip saw pale, startled faces gaping up at him. The sensation was horrible. As quickly as it came it was gone.

They were all again sitting by the peacefully tinkling pool.

'A seance,' gasped Philip; 'may I be forgiven for ever having played at it myself!'

'My son! My daughter!' said Vickers.

'They have contacted you through the machinations of their friends. More by accident than design,' said the Governor, 'but now that the contact has been made, you have an alternative.'

'I don't want to make any more choices,' said Vickers. 'In every Cycle I have had to choose and choose and choose again. My decision to quit life was itself an agony, but each Cycle has given me a choice worse than the previous one. Don't force me to make another!'

'You can enter the pool, and for ever break the contact,' said the Governor, 'or strengthen it, by returning to the First Cycle, where they may, of course, keep you.'

'And even if they did not, would I have to go through all those trials again?'

'It is the immutable system,' replied the Governor.

'Why did they pursue me? Is there no other way out?'

'One way, yes.'

Philip felt his happiness ready to disintegrate, like a crystal sphere which is perfect but on the point of sudden dissolution into a thousand fragments. He looked longingly at the water.

'I have to know it,' said Vickers.

'They want a message from you. Tell them to follow you!'

Philip, in his faultless suit, made a supreme effort. He hurled himself out over the water towards Margot and the dog. Momentarily he saw Vickers nodding, and then he was in the water, and striking out vigorously, hurtling down a boiling torrent, Margot and the others bobbing close by, rushed swiftly away from all knowledge of the decision, by the waters of oblivion.

KISS OF DEATH

The first tiny nudge of disappointment was inflicted on her by the day itself. The day had come, but James had not.

Surprisingly, she had slept well. She had obviously not moved all night. She was as firmly pouched in her side of the bed as toad-in-the-hole. The side James preferred was undisturbed. His dressing gown and clean pyjamas, aired and unbuttoned to make it easier for him, were still on the corner where she had hopefully laid them the previous day.

It was light, so it must be late. She was too snug to reach for her glasses so she could read the clock, but she was aware of a sky the colour of gun-metal, and sounds of the house next door, of shouting, and a radio, and hammering, and all the Kellow children getting into their stride.

The answer was a dog, if James would permit it. If she had a dog, of the kind that sleeps on the landing and comes when called, she might not mind so much the long absences which her husband's work enforced. But she knew there would be difficulties. Dogs smelt, shed hairs, came in season, were not allowed in supermarkets, bit people, cost money, died and broke your heart, needed feeding, could not be left, dug up the garden, came when not called, lay on the bed, ate the curtains. . . . The list of objections was endless, and if James did not want the dog he could even invent a few more.

The dog, which in her imagination was a well-groomed intelligent beast, loving her with bright, expectant eyes from the rug by the bed, passed through several phases of ill-nature and squalor and finally receded altogether into the distance. It receded as far as the Kellows' garden, whence in fact she could hear their dog excitedly clamouring for action. She sighed and hitched herself swiftly up against the bedhead, and reached for her glasses with one hand while drawing her dressing gown over the cold surface of the eiderdown with the other. Putting her feet into her slippers, she switched on the radio and heard the announcer telling his audience that snow had spread now over most of the country, while her view through the window confirmed that it had reached London and the south-eastern counties.

With a lot of drifts about, James, of course, would have taken the sensible course and broken his journey in some good road-house. He would come on in the morning. Only thing was, she apostrophised the covers as she pulled them tight again on her side and tucked them in, he might have phoned.

She dressed. 'He did not want to wake me up. How considerate!'

She sat at her kidney dressing-table to do her hair. There were tiny flecks of something on the mirror. She huffed on them and polished until each had gone, the mirror was flawless, and the division between reflection and reality was a matter of experience rather than perception. As she huffed her breath condensed in a faint cloud in the frosty air. James liked every room in the house to be warm, except the bedroom. Then she sat, when the cloud had vanished, still making that moue with her lips, looking at her reflection making the moue back at her. Two small top teeth pushed her upper lip out slightly anyway. She passed her little finger lightly over her lips and found them smooth and warm. She had kept her complexion well: most people who did not know would not have guessed that she had reached forty.

When she had made herself up she cleared the top of the dressing-table. She disliked the swimming-pool green of thick glass, so the walnut surface was exposed. She disliked petit-point. '*Vieux chapeau*', she said to James when discarding to the top of the cupboard her wedding gifts in this genre. She kept nothing on the glossy walnut top but a pin tray and a trinket box, because they did not slide, and because James would have frowned if she had banished them after he had 'lashed out on chased silver'. Then she took the weekly inventory.

In the middle drawer she checked over her creams and powders, the varnishes all together in a chamois-leather folder, her perfumes and mascara, lipsticks, eyeshadows, clipper, tweezers, brushes, tissues, and cotton wool. A paperback volume on a new diet was extraneous, had no business to be there, and out it came.

Ticked off complete in the right-hand top drawer were hair accessories. Curlers, rollers, setting lotions, tail-combs and brushes, hand mirrors, side-combs, kirby grips, nets, sprays, conditioners, hatpins, a switch, and a hairbun.

James would have his breakfast before he started, and with breakfast, inevitably, a newspaper. A newspaper would contain something he doubted and he would retire to the lounge with other papers to cross-check. If the crisis persisted in his mind, he would pen a letter to the editor. Thinking that he would be absorbed, she nevertheless opened the door, so that she should not miss the ring of the phone if he should think to 'put her in the picture'.

The top left-hand drawer was the millinery department. She was well off for handkerchiefs, using and fancy, 'show and blow'. Chiffon scarves filled a casquette, and the remainder of the space was occupied by artificial flowers, a couple of velvet chokers, a bow, and a perfume sachet. The suspender belts, wandering waifs, she transferred to the top right-hand drawer, until next week when she would decide if they should join stockings, or garters and slips. The top right-hand drawer now stuck a bit, being overfilled. 'Oh, damn you, James! Where are you now? Do come home before the weekend has gone.'

She was running a little low on stockings, but there was no immediate cause for concern. Those bulking the front of the container, whole and using, were tied with a central knot, looking like frail, dormant octopi. The stock for evening wear was very diminished, and was smaller still than it appeared for the bottom three strata of crinkling packets were the indiscreet letters from the boy at the hotel in San Remo, such a long time ago. 'Well, James, you wished him on me.'

Finally she glanced over the lower right-hand drawer. A few pairs of lace pants, slips, a box of chocolates with the cellophane unbroken, three packets of mentholated cigarettes, at the back the glistening holder for a Dutch cap, like a large oyster shell, some fancy soap, and a gold-mesh evening bag. When she came downstairs with that on her wrist James knew that she expected him not to count his coppers. 'I'd settle now for a glass of Spanish wine at the local, and make it last, James you beast.'

There was a place for everything, and everything, as usual, was in its place. There was no need to go to haberdasher's, nor chemist's, before the shops closed. There was no housework to be done – it had been done and done, and done again, to the point where Molière's miser would have had a heart attack. She would, of course, go about the house on a tour of inspection, but as she closed the last drawer she knew that it was a question of spinning it out, to make the time pass until James's car pulled in at the drive. She looked out of the window, and the snow showed bland and smooth and lovely. There were wrinkles in it that she would vaguely have liked to pull out, but it would not for a long time need the brush and crumb tray. It gave her immense pleasure to look at it spread away over the line of gardens, like a cool coverlet over the restless limbs of a thousand fevered hobbies.

She went downstairs, adjusting a stair-rod on the way, and looked at the snow again from the lounge window. The Kellow children were already out, rearranging it.

She did not make breakfast, not wanting to be discovered in the middle of it, but she brewed a pot of tea, and stood with her cup in the window watching the children next door. She liked them, but she liked them on their side of the partition between the gardens. Whenever anything was broken they followed the doctrine of collective responsibility, and each owned up to the crime personally, so that it was impossible to discover the real villain. She was always frightened that James would do something a little too severe to one, or even all, of them, forgetting that she had the rest of the week to live 'cheek by jowl' with the parents. Today they had the little Hallsmith girl with them, what was her name, Annerley? A cheery little soul, and very chic in cutaway coat and leggings. Hallsmith was something in something which took him a lot to the Continent. He dressed his daughter out of boutiques on the Rue Rivoli, while his wife was condemned to be a frump off a peg in the High Street. James always called her Mrs. Hallmark to her face, which was so incongruous that everybody within earshot was embarrassed.

She had made enough tea for two, just in case James. . . . Now she drank one more cup than she wanted, not to waste, which would still leave just enough. . . . The children were starting, of course, on a snowman, presumably a snowman, though it was only a hump of snow at the moment. Much the best thing, infinitely preferable to hurling it about and perhaps frightening one of the littler ones: these things began by being jolly and always ended in tears. James one winter had returned a snowball attack with such violence that the wretched youth had stopped, under the impact, as if shot. . . . No use keeping the tea any longer. It would taste as if stewed. . . . She washed out the pot, but left everything ready on the draining-board.

Then she went around the house, checking, checking, checking. The Dimplex heaters set at sixty-five Fahrenheit, the money for the window-cleaner on the window-sill because James hated these sundry interruptions, the hot water in the bathroom coming through quickly enough, the flush animated, the new books from the library in the lounge, the thrillers on her ticket, the general books on his (although he would read only half of one of the thrillers he liked the librarian to think of him as a man of serious tastes), and the linen clean and put away, and the fuses all sound, the larder sufficiently well stocked to last a time even if the snow piled up roof-high, and the glasses in the cocktail cabinet shone (all held up to the light, because if there was one thing he hated, and there were a few score things, it was lipstick on a glass), and the Gilbert and Sullivan records put to the front of the holder, and the barometer tapped and set so he could know before driving away again what was portending, and the accounts made up for his inspection. There was nothing to buy, there was nothing to clean. 'I am ready for parade, James, when you are.'

Thinking this, her eye in the direction of projecting corners and surfaces which might hoard dust, reached the light, and there in the bowl . . . Fiendish intruders! The insects had died, and their corpses together left an ugly, diffuse patch. She almost flew for the stepladder, with shaking hands removed the bowl, emptied it into a little can brought for the purpose, polished the inside, switched on the light and thrilled and horrified herself simultaneously by the brilliance of the revised illumination. She had lived with this gradually dimming glow, not noticed the deterioration. Out of the skies, literally, her confidence had been attacked! The tiny patch cast a monstrous shadow, and she had not seen that she stood in the midst of it. It was the idea that something wholly unexpected, plain enough if she only knew how to look, was waiting to upset her, that did in fact begin to upset her.

She walked into the lounge and sat down by the telephone, and thought furiously. She considered the entire range of her housework, although she had only now completed a physical inspection. She picked up the receiver to wipe out the cradle, and then remained holding it, wondering if she dared call the Bull, near Royston, just outside Cambridge, where James would almost certainly have stayed. Only to ask them if he had yet left. If by any chance he was on the point of leaving, however, he would be furious. Gradually she lowered the receiver, and gently, almost as if James would hear the faint click as it returned, she replaced it in its rest.

'James, if you're held up, or if you're not coming at all, you could, with such a little effort, let me know, and I could make something of my weekend. As it is, I can't get started. Perhaps if I do get started on something brisk and considerable, you will turn up suddenly, just as some people say that the best way of keeping the rain off altogether is to carry an umbrella.'

She took out the lists and questionnaires she had from the motivational research unit for whom she worked, and drew them up with her pad, and her pen, alongside the telephone. But before she had dialled one number it occurred to her that these conversations lasted, and that *if* James tried to get through he would be huffy if she seemed to be incommunicado. He hated these 'projects' of hers, and she had even known him interrupt from the extension upstairs, and say the most awful things to the stranger she was interrogating. And with this thought rushed in the feeling of guilt at interrupting *other* people's weekends with a lot of nosy questions, which was quite irrational, seeing they were always more willing to talk on Saturday than at any other time, and were far more relaxed.

She pushed all the apparatus away. 'If you come now, James, there is still a whole lot of weekend left. Some wives, after all, never see their husbands for more than Sunday, so whatever time you come today I could say that the Saturday bit is a bonus.'

She was over at the window again. The snowman was rising now, not very evenly, but evident at least as a purpose. It was obviously going to be one of those very big ones, which look as if they must have needed scaffolding to complete. And there, once again, facing her, just like the insects in the bowl, was a matter overlooked. She realised it when she noticed the children casting about for more snow, having scooped up most of the building commodity which had fallen in their own garden. They were looking at the snow in her drive. It lay thick there, having drifted slightly against the garage door. James would be unable to put the car away! She leapt up and ran.

She took with her the dustpans and scoops and the shovel from the shed. She called to the surprised Kellow children. 'Come on, let's all have a go, shall we, there's plenty of snow over here. Let's form a little gang and organise it, shall we?'

The children accumulated round their formless tower of snow and stared. They did not want her taking over their snowman, but they wanted the snow.

Seeing them undecided, she drove the shovel in and cleared a deep groove with one quick lunge. By comparison with shaking it off branches and sweeping a few handfuls off the top of a wall this was obviously easier. The eldest, a boy called David Kellow, in jeans and sweater, ran forward saying:

'*I'll* use the spade, Mrs. Best!'

The other children quickly followed. To prevent unhappiness amongst the smaller she found herself obliged to go back into the house to search for more tools. She returned with the pan from her weighing machine and the shovel from the coal-scuttle and a large ladle.

They all worked enthusiastically, if not efficiently. They soon collected more snow than was strictly necessary. She retired for the second time to divest herself of jacket and cardigan. She made them all some hot chocolate. A lot of time passed. The drive was clear. She reminded herself that she must keep an eye on the clock, to remember to get the roast in the oven. Obviously James had not stayed at the Bull. Obviously he had decided conditions were against driving. He would be coming on by train instead. He would not come until after one. All the same, he would be pleased to see the drive cleared.

Freeing the garage doorway from the last lumps of ice caused by all of them treading the snow down, she found the tiniest mite beside her.

'I'm hiding!'

'Oh, I see. Who from?'

'The snowman. I think he's ugly.'

Over by the snowman the other children were exulting.

'I'll bet he's the biggest snowman in London.'

'I'll bet he's the biggest in England.'

'I'll bet he's the biggest in the whole world!'

'Silly! They don't make them except in England.'

'They do too.'

'I suppose you think they make them in Africa, then?'

'Well, I know they make them because Ronnie Peters was in America and he made them.'

'Yes, well Ronnie Peters is a liar. And you are too.'

'I am not a liar.'

She walked across and broke into the argument.

'It's a gorgeous snowman,' she said, and full of the warmth and relaxation of action she suggested: 'But I think we should give him some clothes, don't you?'

They waited.

'Wait here,' she said, and went back indoors.

She turfed out some of James's old things that she had been wanting for a long time to throw away. The sports coat and tie he would not mind about, she thought, but she felt a bit uncertain about the hat, so she set it very gingerly on the snowman's head, with the feeling that if he did get annoyed it might still, after all, be salvaged. With some of his clothes on, it reminded her a lot of James, and she followed a mischievous impulse when she altered the features and gave it a moustache of orange wool to make it a great deal more like James.

The children turned away. They saw that, after all, what they had originally feared had happened. She had taken over the snowman, and stamped her own wishes on it. They disappeared to find some other game, leaving her to hunt about the Kellows' garden for the tools and for the mugs which she had lent them. As she did so, she knew that Mrs. Kellow was watching her through her kitchen window. Embarrassed, she withdrew to her own house without finding the last mug.

Then she decided she had left the cooking too late. She decided that James might have caught an express, though she had never heard of one on that run before. So she rushed about the kitchen, scarcely giving the oven time to warm up before she shot the joint in. It was a leg of lamb, and as soon as it was hot she suddenly remembered that she had meant to take a couple of gigot chops off the haunch end before roasting the remainder. She looked with agony at the clock, and sawed frantically. Then she found she had mint but not fresh mint.

'Don't flap! Don't flap! Don't flap, don't flap don't flap don't flap don't flapdontflapdont . . . *Don't Flap!* What's the matter with you? There's hours, even if he does take the express. Sit down and read the paper. Can't. Wrapped the potato peel up in it. Too wet and soggy and horrid now.'

But there is always a magazine. At last with the joint sizzling peaceably, and the magazine on her knee, with nothing to do until the time came for putting on the potatoes, and then the greens, she had a lull, a period of peace. Once she looked up sharply, as the sun came out, and she thought she saw James. But, of course, it was the snowman. She had herself identified it with James. She bit her lip and concentrated on a recipe. Funny how in magazines the meals looked more predatory than the guests who were supposed to eat them.

And then the time arrived when she began to worry about holding the joint back, in case it were overcooked when James arrived. She turned down the oven, and put out some glasses so that they could have a quick one before going straight in to eat. And then that time passed too, and she put the glasses away. He would just have to do without a drink.

She would hold the meal as long as possible. Already, looking at it, she imagined it was getting a bit dry.

At two o'clock she had her own meal. It *was* dry. She ate it with short, savage, grinding twists of her jaw, occasionally stopping in mid-morsel for several seconds, looking straight ahead into some dark tranquil corner, like an animal which distrusts what has been given to it, or who fears interruption but gets on with it just the same.

The sunshine was brilliant now. The water was flowing down the outlet pipes and down the eaves in a continuous bright trickle. It was going to be a quick thaw.

She went into the lounge with her book, and turned the pages over until she found that she did not know what the author was talking about, and went back twenty to learn again. Re-reading, she fell asleep. And woke to find the snowman gone.

It was the first thing she noticed. She sprang to her feet. She had the weird sensation that James had come and gone away again.

The sun was no longer out. Reaching the window, she realised that it was not that the weather was turning beastly again, but that night was almost come. It always irritated James when she said: 'Night is coming.' He would correct her by saying: 'You mean the day is going. Darkness is merely an absence of light,' just as he admonished her if she spoke of 'the cold getting into her bones'.

'The cold,' James always said, 'is only an absence of heat. It is not itself anything at all, so it's wrong to speak of it as something positively lethal.'

The snowman was gone. Perhaps the children had demolished it. Children seemed to like knocking things over as much as they enjoyed putting them up. She had probably been the same herself when young.

She wished the snowman had been there, though, all the same. She had enjoyed putting him up, even if he was not, speaking scientifically, anything at all. Or had she got hold of the wrong end of the stick, thinking that way?

It was getting really dark, though it was not all that late yet, and if James were to come now, why then, by the clock at least, a fair portion of the day remained to be enjoyed. If he came the first thing his headlights would pick out would be the snowman.

No! The snowman was gone. She remembered the snowman as if he still existed; making him had been the bright spot of the day. That is, if she had made him, if he had ever existed.

It seemed to her that she saw the snowman at the window. Hastily she switched on all the lights. She ran around the house turning on all the lights, in case she imagined again the Snowman, or No man.

No man at home! Would it go on for ever like this? If she only knew that he wasn't coming she could bear it.

At that moment she decided that James would not be home. She stopped waiting. He would not come. 'You can stop away as long as you please, James. Just hope to be lucky, and fit in with my plans.'

She heard the door going. She tore into the hall and flung herself into his arms.

She felt the cold getting right through into her bones.

BREAKAWAY

What a lark! What a shake-up!! What a one-eyed, two-faced, three-card, fourpenny opera!!! And one more! for luck. I am literally *unstuck*. I'm adrift, cut off, disconnected, and all stations to bedlam. I'd like to see their faces when they come puffing up over the glacier looking for a kind word and a noggin, and find I've decamped. I can just hear old Magnus grumble. 'That slippery twister! That Tom! He'd pinch the skin off your coffee while you made him toast. We were mad to leave him in charge of the whiskey. But I never thought he'd make off with the blinking continent.' That's what it amounts to, I've pirated most of the removable part, anyhow. They'll be choked when they stand on Mount Billy and see what's happened. They'll eff, they'll blind, they'll call me all the bastards. But, boys, I couldn't help it. So help me now, God, I wish I were with you to share and share alike. I don't want all this stuff. It's more than even I want. Believe me, the ice-cap broke up without my assistance. I had no part in it.

Friday, 16th.

I'm a little ashamed of the preceding entry. Outbursts like that have no business in a daily log. I was light-headed, must have been, as a result of the shock. It was so far ahead of the forecast. I should have had another six weeks yet, clear, before any possibility of disruption came. I was taken completely off my guard. When the thing happened I cowered in the tent, not wanting to know. But I knew. It broke even through the noise of the storm, that appalling, triumphant roar as the tongue of the glacier broke free. At the very point of impact, as it tumbled on the sea-ice, there must have been already a fault. The iceberg seized its chance. It had waited long enough, but when at last it moved it made itself felt. My world shuddered, and gave in. I could not force myself out of the tent to look at that great dark bulk on the northern side. I felt it, and feel it, as some malevolent creature, oozing south over the centuries, holding back the main impulse, and then suddenly leaping forth on a frantic journey across the ocean. I was alone before, but somewhere across the ice were Magnus, and Whittaker, and Peel and Kenny Symes, and out beyond them the spearhead of the expedition. I was not really alone. Now I am, subject to the purposes of an ancient tyrant. Today I went out and looked at him. He is swinging slowly round, to be the promontory of my continent, the prow of my strange ship, the vanguard of my unplanned flight.

Saturday, 17th.

In a fortnight *Polecat* is due, so the lads have nothing serious to worry about. The greatest danger to me is that they should have relied on that fact, and prolonged their stay. Then they'll put the news about that their Base Camp is behaving frivolously and half a million quid will be spent retrieving its valuable caretaker. There should not be much doubt about my adventure, since the whole coastline will be transformed, nor any difficulty in spotting me, as I sail for sunnier climes on a ship of several million tons displacement. I'm not the biggest ever; I remember Whittaker talking about one at the end of the last century about the size of Corsica. That was at the other end, Antarctic capers, and hove to off the Falklands. But I must be up there amongst the contenders. Something to be thankful for, anyway. Nothing quite so magnificent on the books at Lloyd's. No engine, no anchor, no compass, no ruddy rudder. No functioning radio. Christ, I was a silly bugger not to let Whittaker check the set over before they went. 'I'll manage, I'll manage,' says pig-headed old Tom, and within two days it was playing me up, and conked out altogether on the fourth. But plenty to eat and drink, and no worries about warmth. Stabilisers functioning superbly: no reasons for seasickness. Like a summer cruise. Wish I had a girl along in shorts to play quoits with. We are moving along serenely now, with no disturbance but the hollow booming of old Tyrant up ahead, eagerly beavering his way through the spray towards his southern frolic. Let him put it where he wants, he's in charge. We've left the storm behind; Magnus and the boys should know all about it in a day or two, while the sun just flirts his tail at us then goes down again, enticing us, the old tease. We're big and strong, we can shed an awful lot of weight before we go sick, and in these cold seas we may even pick up as much as we lose. The test will come later, when we go to battle with those soft, soupy, seaweedy, southern seas. SSSSIZZLE! I'm eating well, and I read a lot. Dornford Yates. What a boy, that Jonah!

Sunday, 18th.

Stretched my legs, and my imagination with them. I'd been cooping myself up, most of the time rolled up like a wretched rabbit, self-hypnotised, waiting for the killing stroke. Today I've been out on a tour of inspection, and it was a good thing to do. It cheered me up. We're bigger still than I thought, and a lovely permanent blue colour. Oh we do look cold, right down into the heart of us! When I look all round and see us spreading out so gigantically I feel proud, and when I go on to think of five times that amount, a massive reserve, sturdily buoying us up from below, I am almost exultant. Old Tyrant, his head up high there in front, knew what he was doing when he joined forces. We won't half give off a fog when they try to wear us down. We're not in the melting mood. Hell, we've ice to spare for the cocktails when I invite the flag officers of the Southern Squadron aboard off Rio! Tomorrow I shall move camp. Shift in a little closer under the lee of old Tyrant and get the benefit of his protection from the wind, from one quarter at least. I may as well have my pick of the stores now. They're hardly likely to bother with them when they take me off. Checking through the inventory I see some mad fool has itemised capers, and in fact stocked capons, and until now it has not been noticed. Nobody can say the expedition was under-capitalised! All the same, I shan't eat too many of them: I don't trust them, and I hope to knock out a few more kids yet.

Monday, 19th.

Postponed the move. Conditions were too disgusting. Wind as constant a pressure as gravity. Ripping the snow layers off like the blankets coming off a bed. When I get home I'm going to spend one entire day naked in a deep armchair with my feet braced on either side of the hearth, while the fire warms my crutch. No casual callers. Mr. Tom Harris is dictating his story to a corps of naked newshens. All ticket. Police turned hundreds away.

Tuesday, 20th.

Light almost as bad today as yesterday, but getting about not such a strain. Literally picked my way half a mile up the slope behind the camp, roping myself to successive pick anchors, which I've left for future use. Confirmed a suspicion I tried to put away from myself yesterday: a chunk of my domain has gone. A square mile perhaps, detached but still visible to the east. Well, it was a heavy sea. I should consider myself lucky that I never followed Magnus's advice and pitched camp in that sector, as he originally suggested. He thought that in a hollow like that I would have a natural protective perimeter, but it seemed too vulnerable to drifting. The dogs would have liked it, of course, poor little sods. They're taking the whole thing very well, perhaps a bit puzzled by having no work to do. I don't see much prospect for them, but they'll eat hearty while they can. We'll all shift directly the wind dies away. I'll be glad to have them. I shall never get across this hard ice, now that it's all exposed, without their help. With any luck I shall manage the whole operation in four trips. Old Tyrant hasn't altered in the least. Every line on him is the same as when I first looked. I wonder if he'll resent it when I start poking about in the hem of his robe.

Sunday, 25th.

I've been installed now since Thursday. Of all the stupid reasons for thinking Tuesday's might have been the final entry – I MISLAID THE BLEEDING PENCIL while shifting camp. Now that I've got it I've put it on a string and hung it round my neck. We all got one before setting out – part of an advertising stunt. Mine's a 2B, but for several days it's been a not 2B. I put this down not because I think it smart but because since I missed the pencil the phrase kept going through my mind, nagging me half insane. At the back of it all must have been the terror of erosion, of losing everything that I have, little piece by little piece, my ice, my gear, my mind. I looked every bloody where for it, turned everything upside down, made a spectacle of myself for the dogs' entertainment, I contemplated hunting through their fur for it, it had to be somewhere. Where was it? In the flag, the Union Jack. Christ knows how it got there. Probably fell out of my top pocket when I was wrapping up my dirty laundry in it. Then, when I fell into a grim mood, I began seeing the bundle in the flag like a cadaver ready for burial, as they commit the dead to the deep. To make the fish stand to attention, I suppose. But I undid it all and tried to change the idea of the flag that was tormenting me by using it for a tablecloth. As the centrepiece, vital as dinner, was the pencil. Come back to the land of the living. All the same, I shall chuck the flag away. It makes me uneasy.

It took two days to make the switch. It was more of a sweat than I expected it to be. I seem to have collected a fantastic amount of junk. I kept thinking of the day that we moved out of London for the house at Pagham, and Helen and I fought all day long about what we should throw away. You never use them, Tom, you never use them, she said of two-thirds of my possessions, and then it was my turn to say you've used them enough, you've used them enough until we collapsed on the sofa laughing, even when the removal men were trying to carry the sofa out. So it was here, except that I had no one to fight with, or laugh with. In the end I left very little behind. I even brought most of the books, though I shan't have time to get through very many more. Old Tyrant made me quite welcome, and revealed a nice little scoop like a Norman arch, where I could dig in. I'm getting quite fond of him. Most giants are gentle when you get to know them.

I'm not sure of our position, but I estimate we have come five hundred miles. I must look out my bikini. Shirt-sleeve drill will soon be in order.

Monday, 26th.

Birds, of some sort. They came and had a look, but did not stay. Snooty beggars. Better stuff elsewhere, I suppose. I hope it's near.

Tuesday, 27th.

More birds. Dogs chased them off.

Wednesday, 28th.

Depressed. Can't be bothered with cooking. These fancy meals now strike me as grotesque. No birds today. Sea-birds and Scotsmen turn up all over the world, but it doesn't necessarily mean that the living is getting easier.

Perceptibly smaller all round. I'll have to get out the Sellotape soon and start sticking bits back on.

Thursday, 29th.

Something amiss with old Tyrant. He's making queer groaning noises in the night. Having trouble with his guts. Rather eerie. I feel sorry for him. He's come so far, looked so indomitable keeping his face firmly towards his goal through the worst of the angry north, and now that the air is blander and the sea smoother he's beginning to falter. He would probably be glad to cast off the great mass of ice behind him, which he's dragging along now like an old nobleman at a royal funeral heaving his train along. I can't sleep with the macabre music sounding through his body. I read all the time, William Burroughs, and Henry Miller, and Kafka and Donleavy, and Nelson Algren. Marvellous escapist stuff about drugs and alcoholism and homosexuality and anxiety in cities. Quite unlike real life.

I hate the sea. It never lets up. We're getting a sustained barrage of rollers now, hitting us in the rear. They're coming up over the top. One of the dogs was swept away today. Silly chap would keep rushing out and barking at them until a bigger one than usual came along.

Sunday, 2nd.

I can no longer risk leaving the proximity of old Tyrant. The whole ice behind us is as smooth and worn and dangerous to walk on as oiled marble. It has taken on the general conformation of a clover leaf, and the sea comes smashing up through the gaps to spout skywards at the apex of each fissure. The site of the original camp has vanished entirely, surrendered to the invading sea, and now, like a collaborationist, forms part of the enemy which attacks us. I love the ice, I shall always love the ice. When I am home again I shall live where the winter is hardest.

Tuesday, 4th.

For the love of heaven, where are you all? Does everybody fly today?

Wednesday, 5th.

Sighted a ship around midday. But it stood well away from us and was hull down in no time. What must they think we are? An enemy of some sort, I presume, just because we're bigger than they are and can't manœuvre much. I wished I had not jettisoned the flag. I was thrown into quite a state when I realised they were keeping their distance, and such a distance! Even the dogs noticed I was in a bad mood: they skulked away into the remotest corners still available. But when I'd had a couple of liveners from the bottle I saw the matter differently. I am at least in the sea-lane and there should be plenty more traffic along shortly. It's early in the season for icebergs in these seas and the crew on that liner must have had a powerful shock. Later in the day I cheered up enormously, the more I thought about it, and went into a frenzy of preparation for the rescue. I've constructed a sort of raft and moored it at the base of old Tyrant. It stands on the runners of two sleds. I should be able to get it into the water with the three surviving dogs in a couple of minutes. When everything was in order I took advantage of the last of the sunlight to shave and brisk myself up. I'm not a bad-looking fellow, best on this berg, anyway, once the fungus has come off my chops, no offence intended to the dogs, but they are a little long in the snout. Old Tyrant seemed almost to approve: I shall miss the old chap. If it weren't for the probability that some literal-minded skipper who rescues me would have me clapped under observation and tied to the bunk for raving I'd suggest they take him in tow and deposit him on some nice blizzard-lashed shore. He's had a good innings, but I'd like to think he had a few mellow autumnal years ahead of him, with adventurous souls taking photographs of him for the glossy magazines. One of Nature's Crowns Imperial, and all that. (He's flattened out on the top now, where the sun's been beating down on his bald pate.) For all that I owe him, though, I'd rather be with you, Helen, and I promise you that you've got your Tom at home now, never more to muck about with ice except in the way of tiny blocks in the sundowner.

Thursday, 6th.

The bastards! Oh, the bastards! If I could urge old Tyrant into the steel belly of one of your transatlantic minnows I'd do it. But you're all scuttling out of the way as fast as you can, as we go lurching hopelessly on. I tremble with rage. I can hardly get this down. There was I, preening myself on a successful exploit, bringing the blinking mountain to Mahomet, thinking of a good spot to appear to advantage while the cushioned softies on the liner took their photographs, and all the ship had hove to for was to watch us get blasted. It all happened so quickly: I was scaling the blind side of old Tyrant, was halfway up, when two of their planes came over, and let go their bombs. It comes back to me now. The Ice Patrol keep the sea-lanes safe. Two sticks were enough. The whole issue disintegrated like a meringue. I don't know what became of the dogs, I hope they got theirs cleanly. I can still see fragments of the raft bobbing about amongst small pieces of ice which trail pathetically alongside us, like creatures bereft of their protector, but still hanging on for a kind word. I don't know how to muster up energy much longer to write: the sea is pressing closely all about us, hugging us warmly to death. I suffered some minor injuries during the bombing from flying ice. Blood from them runs down the sticky sides of old Tyrant.

Friday, 7th.

Spent a terrible night, hanging on, hanging on, trying to *melt* myself into a secure groove, with the wind trying to get in under my belly and pluck me off. I believe old Tyrant will roll any time now. The sea must be sapping his base fast with every mile of warm water he staggers through. He's rearing and plunging. Top-heavy, I'm sure. Twice during the night I had to climb back several yards, and try again to take root. Now the sun's up high and pouring it on. He's sweating like a mad, wrestling, dying thing. The water is running off in all directions. The sea all around us is vacant. They're all still scared of us. What of? We're nothing but water! I try to think this warmth is the warmth of your body, Helen. In that I would happily dissolve. You protested when I joined the expedition but you never thought I went as a lemming. It's cold on this berg, this bloody iceberg. I hate the ice, I hate the sea. Fine time to start whining about the cold. We're careering along madly now that we're travelling so light. Either that, or the wind's getting up. A moment ago the sun was all around me. Now it has gone again. I don't know whether I want it to go or stay. We're turning, slowly. The underpart is emerging, smooth and hateful. How long can I go on, trying to ride it in this ridiculous fashion, like a bloody performing seal on a ball? How quiet every change is. I suppose when we do really roll it'll be like coming awake as you turn over in your sleep. Hope I don't stay awake long.

MANY A SLIP

There is nothing against Peterkin Lock.

He has always been a boy to make the best of things.

A good opinion of him could be found in any quarter. In anybody's ledger he would be entered on the credit side – for manners, for looks, for effort.

There is nothing against Peterkin Lock.

He is not even dull. He was equipped with enough brains to give his parents hope, his mentors satisfaction, and his friends a fair return on their goodwill. They would agree of Peterkin: nobody's fool.

There is nothing against Peterkin Lock. After repetition, the proposition still holds up. *Nem con.*, it hardens into fact.

He is good-looking enough to have around, without exciting suspicion. He has stayed out of debt. On the basis of the statutory amount of application he got through his examinations. Where morality was in question he has always given due consideration to the opinions and prejudices of his family. He celebrated the Christian festivals, he generally turned out for teams at short notice when someone dropped out, he paid his round, sang his verse, and thoroughly looked forward. He looked people in the eye when he spoke to them, and people liked him.

His case incites to a belief in malice. Peterkin was abominably teased.

His ancestors were some sort of marauding invaders, corsairs, who outstripped their supply lines and settled early on the idea of a commission in the Regular Army. Who, among those in the pavilion when it rose to his hundred for the Public Schools against the Army at Lord's, would have guessed that a hammer toe would one day debar him from appearing for the other side? He consoled himself with a Blue at Oxford and a niche in a merchant bank.

A hammer toe! To alter the course of a life! Well!

Some publicity was given to the matter of the Leinz inheritance, but the main points of the story are worth recapitulating. Aunt Tabitha Lock married late and unexpectedly. Her husband was a wealthy German named Leinz. The marriage was as happy as it was short: Otto and Tabitha were immersed in one another to the exclusion of politics and people. He died and she had almost everything that was his. But with the war which soon followed Tabitha found that she was now still left to herself for having been married to a German. Her nephew Peterkin gave an early showing of his impeccable manners by not allowing the family hostility to affect his partiality for his aunt. He was sent to stay with her in the country as a form of evacuation and amused her by building an air-raid shelter, which he told her was 'the safest place in the world'. It was this phrase which made the headlines fifteen years later when she died, and named Peterkin her chief legatee, as everybody expected. But the charming, unworldly old lady, in her will, directed him to look 'in the safest place in the world' for his major share of her fortune, and when the site of the ancient shelter was located, and the primitive structure investigated, it was found that she had buried bank-notes for him in a sack, and that they had rotted away. Peterkin commented bravely, when the extent of the loss was apparent: 'My fault, I suppose, for being so sure of my own plans.'

Well said, but does it go far enough?

Peterkin read Modern Greats at Oxford, and out of the hundreds of late-night conversations of his second year he brewed up a serious little topic of his own for publication. It was not in fact assembled and printed until some time after he had gone down, but it was his theme, his thesis, and his contribution. He looked forward, when it came out, to some mild appreciation and a modest buttressing to his status as a responsible member of the establishment. It was his return to the State for his education. But in this, too, his tail was tweaked. Lock on 'Sumptuary Laws' appeared in a silly season and various newspapers which normally devote little space to books of any sort picked it up and made a story of it. Peterkin was being tipped as a likely leader for an M.C.C. touring side, and his book instigated a spate of wild puns under the general heading of 'Lock's Declaration'. In one of these articles the writer said: '. . . his arguments were as far over my head as his fluent sweeps soaring over square leg, so I bowled him one wide of the subject and got on to the topic of the forthcoming tour. . . .' There were commentaries more frivolous still, and in this atmosphere the serious weeklies took fright and ignored the book altogether.

Once again the built-in hitch is obvious, invisible to Peterkin though, until he faced the disappointment.

These separate incidents, widely spaced in time, begin to explain, when seen together, why in the City the first comment expected of him on any new project is: 'It looks all right on paper.' But they can all, in one form or another, be traced through public records, and place no strain on the credulity of archivists or researchers. The malign influence, if this is the correct theory, stayed within the rules. But the final item is the clincher, deriving from the victim himself, where, in their excess of zeal, hostile imps revealed their interest.

The weakness of Modern Greats, which is made up of philosophy, politics, and economics, is that an alpha economist may be a gamma politician and anything down to an omega philosopher. This was Peterkin's case. When the men were gathered in his rooms in College he was accustomed to having an audience if he chose to talk on, perhaps, Brace on 'Seed-Crushing', but confined himself to peripheral comment if someone raised the ghost of Mill on 'Good Form', while he was an altogether silent claret-muller when the spur was Strawson on 'Logic', and 'P' and 'not P' were particularised. After the visit of Loserowitz, when the alpha philosophers were shredding 'The Metaphysical Concept of Nothing' into its component nothings, Peterkin just went on and on and on thinking about Appearance and Reality. He seemed, unfashionably, to be stuck with it. It was a great relief to him when the conversation moved, as it generally did, to the Common Pursuit, otherwise 'Women'. As a matter of courtesy, all were in this field allowed an alpha rating.

Peterkin knew that he was not entitled to a high grading. He felt a fraud. Though in an undergraduate society he could get away with it, he did not see that any man was justified in pontificating on 'women' until he had contrived, at least once, to seduce a woman. This, so far, he had failed signally to do.

Women liked Peterkin as an escort because, transparently, he was 'safe'.

As the terms succeeded one another, ever more rapidly, it began to seem to Peterkin, listening to the lurid experiences of his friends, that in the whole university he alone had never been to bed with a girl. Even those coming up for the first time were able, apparently, to report on one or two successes. Though he detested, in principle, the attitude of scalp-collecting implicit in his friends' anecdotes, he was bound to acknowledge that the promiscuity of modern young women contributed hugely to it. He might have been able to reconcile himself to it more easily if they had not held their promiscuity in check so successfully when he was the candidate for honours.

In a woman's eye there was nothing against Peterkin Lock. His family was good, he spent freely but without ostentation, he gave some thought to the organisation of an occasion, he talked interestingly, and he even listened. He made her feel that the evening was reliably placed in his hands, and he intimated that his high regard for her would not be lessened if she succumbed. But she did not succumb. Either circumstances, or Peterkin himself, always provided a safe-conduct for her out of the minefield elaborately sown. She went home feeling that it had been so easy that she was willing to let him have another try, and, before he was able to prevent it, she was a great friend, and the whole project shown up for a colossal fantasy.

Each time that the pattern was worked out in its entirety Peterkin thanked his lucky stars for saving him from a gross social blunder. He would not have liked the virtue of one of his friends on his conscience.

All the same, the accumulation of more and more evidence of this kind only made it more imperative to Peterkin that he lay somebody. He listened very carefully to his smoother friends, and decided to change the direction of attack.

The outcome was explosive. A woman of a certain age, chic, sophisticated, fell into conversation with him in the cocktail lounge of an hotel, and found they had so much to talk about that the separate themes could be best explored over dinner in her flat. 'So much less stuffy than a provincial restaurant.' Peterkin was delighted to hear Oxford described as provincial and followed like a lamb. Metamorphosed into hopeful wolf, the lamb was clipping his cigar when her husband, a P.T.I. at a nearby R.A.F. station, burst in and started swinging. It was a set-up. The lady curled up on a divan and enjoyed the fight. She had seen several undergraduates hammered over the years. Peterkin, famous for opening his shoulders when facing fast bowling, was better able to handle the husband than he would have been able to handle the wife if there had been no interruption, and he claims to have had the best of it. But it was a Pyrrhic victory. He was left with just enough strength to get out of the house, find his way to his college and walk through the gates without causing comment in the porters' lodge. As he hauled himself into his narrow, coenibitical bunk, it occurred to him that perhaps, after all, the best company in bed would be his own thoughts, and that Morpheus had always made him welcome.

For some time after this incident he adopted the attitude of a man who is sadder and wiser, and impressed his friends tremendously with the cryptic comment that 'the game is only rarely, on very special occasions, worth the candle. By your account of it, you seem to have had beginner's luck.' It would have been considered a gross breach of taste to have challenged a friend to unpack such a statement.

He then walked into the long shadow thrown by Schools, and the problem receded to the back of his consciousness. But it returned with the craftiness of a boomerang when he had set aside the subfusc he wore for the examinations and put on in its place a variegated fancy dress for the triennial Commemoration Ball.

The only characteristic that a Commem Ball has in common with a Carnival is, generally, that it is a marathon performance. But this year the Ball Committee seemed to live up to their fanciful titles. The Mahdi Gras presided over a raffish triumvirate whose imaginative schemes seemed at first likely to sink the reserve fund in one quick swoop. Their plans certainly, when matured, obliged them to price the tickets at a figure which was so prohibitive to state-aided students that most of the college was unable to attend. They were able to proceed however, because the very same thing attracted a large number of outsiders. The Mahdi himself postulated a Carnival, the Captain of Dancing made a personal call on the leader of the orchestra at the Hammersmith Palais itself, the Vizier of Visas issued complementary tickets to half the cast of a touring musical, and the Sheikh of the Shekels declared that for his part he didn't give a damn: in under a month he would be a Customs officer in Malaysia somewhere. *Fiat lubricia, ruat coelum.* . . .

Members of the Eight, still in training for Henley and reluctant to amuse themselves, were nevertheless required to strip to the waist and pole tented punts up and down the Cherwell. Enough fairy-lights were distributed about the quads and gardens of the college to illuminate the fleet. It was all very pretty, and ridiculous too, unless, like Peterkin, you saw it through unfocussed eyes, in the aftermath of Schools fever. He took a girl called Elaine, who would not ever be as beautiful again, not even on her wedding day. So he says.

But Elaine could not be persuaded to eat enough supper to contain the champagne, and was an early casualty. When she complained that the high hat of a Welsh Witch, her role on this occasion, seemed to weigh a ton, Peterkin was concerned, because it was of papier mâché, but suggested she take it off, and hoped for the best. But when she made the same complaint half an hour later, at which time the hat was lying under a potted palm, Peterkin realised he must send her home.

He was walking back towards his rooms, disconsolate, with the salty taste of Elaine's tearful farewell still on his lips, when he saw her. She was standing in the penumbra surrounding the shadow of a group of monkey-puzzles, and she was trying to attract some deer. She had engaged their attention, but they were still standing motionless, watching her for further clues, their soft eyes warm in the floodlights. At Peterkin's approach they cantered, but quietly, away into the darkness. Once or twice a swift flicker of brownish movement in an interval between trees showed that they were still thinking of pursuit, and then they were gone altogether.

She turned with an exclamation of annoyance.

'Now I've lost my deer!'

'I've just lost my dear,' replied Peterkin.

'You look more like a poet or shepherd than a deerkeeper. Keeper of the Queen's Eclogues!'

'Mine was sloshed, I'm afraid. I've put her in the charge of a disapproving cabbie.'

'Oh, I see. It's puns, is it? Do you always go on like that?'

'I should do. Some people say I'm too hearty for a real wit.'

'There you are again! It's not the puns I object to. It's the Shakespeare. I've only just finished a whole season of the bard.'

'Barred he is, from now on.'

'If that's off the cuff, it's pretty good!'

'Say, rather, a chip out of the rough,' he said, adopting an attitude, and flicking an imaginary ball out of his wide Elizabethan ruff.

'Heavens! No wonder the deer ran away. I shall too, if this goes on!'

'I hope you won't. I'm sorry. As one of your hosts it was very rude of me to show off. In that costume you show off very well, by the way.'

In answer she bobbed him a slight curtsy.

She was dressed as a Spanish dancer. The flouncing skirts, dense with sequins and flowers, flowed behind her as she moved. By contrast with their tidal quality, her full figure, closely followed by the tight black bodice and high gloves, showed firm and, in Peterkin's description, 'landmarky'. By her voice he thought her 'youngish', though the veil which concealed her face, hanging from the high head-dress, prevented him from confirming this.

There was this pause, while she too looked him over. Then she said:

'If you're one of my hosts, won't you tell me your name?'

'Peterkin Lock.'

'More kin than kind, I can see.'

He flushed. 'Why? If you think Peterkin so——'

'Oh shush! Touchy man. I only mean that if you were kind you would ask me to dance, especially as you've lost your partner. A host can hardly go to bed before his guests, you know.'

'And you? Have you lost your escort?'

She laughed. The laugh put him at his ease. There was something, claims Peterkin, almost timeless about that laugh, as if she were entirely accustomed to smoothing away social difficulties with it.

'There are no escorts in the theatre, darling!' she exclaimed, 'we're *all* on our own.'

'Oh, you must be——' he began, suddenly understanding.

'Yes,' she interrupted swiftly, 'one of the troupe. I'm . . . no, I'm . . . Isabella.'

'It's a lovely show. If you lift your veil I'll tell you if I thought you were the prettiest.'

'In that case I shan't lift it. I'm only the best singer. But I'm not going to prove it. I'm going to enjoy myself. I'm going to dance with you, may I?'

And so they danced. To the music of the big band in the Big Quad, and to the music of the little band in the Little Quad, and later to a mixture of both, on a canvas spread on the lawn of the Fellows' Garden. It is reasonable to suppose that they talked a great deal, more fancy than fact, though Peterkin remembers little of what was actually said. Who ever does remember?

And later they had had enough of dancing and went on the river. Later they had had enough of the trees, and the water and the cold of the river. He remembers that she said: 'When I'm back in London they'll all notice that I'm terribly moonburnt! The moon sees right through this costume, right through, right through. . . .' And later she had had enough of the Ball and said that she thought he lived in a frightfully artificial world, for her part she'd be frightened she'd just fade away altogether in such a rarefied atmosphere. She, an actress, said that! Peterkin, frightened that this was her preliminary to a sudden withdrawal from the whole occasion – he had noticed that she acted instantly on any caprice that came to her – suggested that they 'adjourn to his rooms for a warming toddy'. Today he will still use a phrase like that, even with his heart thumping as he perceives that she will raise no objection.

It was beginning to be dawn. The Chinese lanterns, still lit, looked two-dimensional. About the lawns there were couples, seated on the grass and on chairs, the girls sometimes half-asleep, sprawled over the white shirt-fronts of their men, who looked now more like boys.

The lights were still on in his rooms. The decanter and the glasses had been laid out by his scout and were all clean and untouched.

He closed the door behind them. Then he opened it again

immediately, and first closed the heavy outer door.

'Are you expecting a rioting mob to force its way in?' asked Isabella.

He said painfully: 'We call that Sporting our Oak. When we close the outer door that means we're working and don't want to be disturbed.'

'Oh, I see,' she said, 'but I understood you to say that you had taken your final examinations. Doesn't that mean that you have no more work to do?'

'It only means that I'm officially an educated man.'

'Oh!' As she said it she opened her lips as if she were officially expelling an illusion. 'I *am* impressed.'

He walked back into the centre of the room to join her.

'I don't think I want a drink,' she said.

He put his arm round her waist. The phrase he had rehearsed in his mind was: 'To come to bed with me now would to be set a crown upon a most aristocratic evening,' but the words which actually issued from his lips were:

'Please lift your veil now, Isabella, so I can see what's beneath it all.'

She twisted out of his enclosing arm, and walked without answering round the room, looking at his pictures, and at the photographs in frames, and at his books. Eventually she reached the doorway to his bedroom and tentatively opened it and looked cautiously in. She opened it wide and entered. He followed.

She looked about this room in the same way.

She said: 'You really mean seven veils, don't you?' and then: 'As long as you don't think I'm feeling guilty because I didn't sing for my supper,' and again, still musingly: 'And it's time you came out of that ruff yourself, if you have no more brave Elizabethan words to say,' and finally, as if coming to a decision: 'Well now I'm sporting my oak, to them at least,' and she turned to the wall the photograph on his bedside table showing the University Eleven coming out to field at Lord's.

Peterkin does not recollect undressing, but he imagines that he divested himself without ceremony, because he does recall only lying under the covers watching Isabella while she removed the 'seven veils'.

His stomach tightened suddenly as she kicked off her high-heeled shoes. She was at a stroke a couple of inches shorter, back on her own heels, unwrapping the beautiful heavy outer skirt. He was motionless, looking at her in the soft white bell of underslips. The outer skirt she laid carefully over a chair. The underslips she stepped out of, one by one, and left to lie where they fell. Slighter and slighter she seemed as the white mass of them piled up about her. At one point he had moved up tight against the wall, feeling it cold and dank against his naked back, with some nervous consciousness that it was a narrow bed, and that the two of them would barely fit, lying alongside one another. But the problem diminished with each garment.

In the increasing light of the growing day the outline of her limbs seemed at last to be clear beneath the several slips which still remained to her.

She was, after all, a very delicate, frail creature. There was not very much of her at all.

Any time now she would join him, and he would be at peace.

She faced him directly. 'Won't be long now. Thank you, Peterkin, for a lovely evening!' Her voice was tiny, a murmur like a leaf on the window-sill.

She loosened the tape of the last slip, and raised her gloved hands to the veil.

'Stop! Stop!' cried Peterkin.

But she raised the veil, and in the first streak of sunlight Peterkin was up on one elbow, staring down at a heap of clothing, on the top of which, in the draught entering by the half-open door, the veil of her head-dress fluttered demurely.

SEARCHLIGHT

—Batista, you know me. I insist.

—Useless, to know you.

—But we have been together.

—Too long.

—No! In the field we were together.

—In the field was different.

—No! I tell you no.

—José, you are a son of a bitch, and it happens to a son of a bitch, as to a real man, that his sins catch up with him.

—I am not arguing, but I am not afraid.

—You are a son of the North. It may be that you are not afraid.

—Have I not said so?

—And you are a son of a bitch. It may be that you are lying.

—Because we were in the field together, that is why I do not punish you for talking to me like that.

—You could not punish me without a gun, and your gun has been taken away from you, José, my little son of a twisted crutch. You are not trusted with guns, and that is why you are on the searchlight.

—You too, Batista, are on the searchlight.

—Because we were in the field together, I am detailed to be on the searchlight and keep you company.

—But I am not afraid of what they may do to me.

—Then why keep talking about it?

—Because I want answers different from the ones you've given me.

—You are like all those whose mothers have crept away into the *matto* to give birth, you want the world to be other than the way it is.

—No, not much, Batista.

—Very much, José.

—I ask only respect.

—Respect! Woolly-headed, wild thing you are . . .

—Where are you going?

—I am going to spit, to add my little bit to the disrespectful sea below us. Respect, the bastard says, as if each day did not bring in some new cause for contempt. You, José, are so respectful that if you were to find your father you would tie a weight to his stones and make him run until he left them behind. I have heard you say so.

—You know me, though. You know whether I meant that.

—I know, and I have looked after you, as if you were as precious to me as my own boots. But, like them, you are done now, and I must apply for a new issue.

—All the same, I am not done, and I am not afraid.

—All the same, you have done up your buttons, since the Lieutenant spoke to you.

—Then I undo my buttons!

—What a most valiant, unbuttoned, messy bastard!

—Let the Lieutenant come!

—The Lieutenant will come when he is ready.

—I too shall be ready.

—And you will screw him, I suppose, being unbuttoned and ready, as a mark of respect.

—One button I had undone. One!

—One is enough to change everything. One bullet, one screw, and now one button.

—I shall leave the fatal button undone.

—Because you know the Lieutenant will not come until after you are ready to do it up again.

—How do I know that?

—You know because I have told you.

—No, no, no, you have not told me, Batista my friend. I do not know that the Lieutenant is engaged elsewhere.

—Cloth-eared peasant, slovenly vagrant, I have told you, I have told you that he is down below there, with his cap off by now, while he touches up Cat's Nails.

—There below, in the shadows?

—There, or there, or there, where I am pointing. There is

nothing to see, but perhaps if we listened we might hear those nails of hers, those long pointed nails clicking in his scalp like knitting needles.

—Let us listen, Batista, oh yes, what a joke!

—What do you hear?

—I hear the crabs clicking as they run across the sands.

—Those are her nails, José. What else?

—I hear the waves, washing in the hollows of the rocks below these walls.

—Those are her kisses, washing in the hollows of his eyes, and ears and neck. What else, unwanted child?

—I hear the tearing wind and the fine sand rustling over the rocks.

—You hear his tearing hands, impatient with her rustling, satin underwear.

—What a joke, Batista! Do you think they are really there?

—I swear it.

—What do you know about it?

—Twice a week she slips out of her employer's house, there, the big flat-roofed one between the American Hotel and the convent, and she stands in the archway formed by those palm trees, and she waits for the Lieutenant's signal. . . .

—What signal could she see at that distance?

—The searchlight, of course, fool. The Lieutenant commands the searchlight, does he not?

—What a dog! He uses Army equipment for such a purpose?

—When the light settles for a few seconds on the statue of the first Governor, there on the island in the bay, she knows it is safe for her.

—What impudence!

—But how simple.

—Simple impudence! The Lieutenant waits under the walls of this ancient fortress like a dog by a dustbin. He knows that if he waits long enough some bitch will come by he can mount.

—No, no, José, have I not explained to you that our Lieutenant does not wait? He is a pedigree dog. He gives the signal, when he has dined, and looked over his master's house to see that all is quiet, and has found one ignorant servant with a button undone when on duty, then only he gives the signal that he is ready to serve her. A dog with class. He gives the signal, and she comes.

—The searchlight.

—The searchlight. Just that, and no more. But how superb! Think of her there in the garden, looking out across the bay. The evening traffic rolls by, others on their way to assignations in the centre of the city, and for a moment their headlights flick across the garden and are gone again. The ships are at anchor, and all the lights of the greatest do not seem more than the candles on a cake when she looks over at the fortress and sees our great searchlight stroking the clouds. How powerful our Lieutenant must seem to her then, how kind of him to deign to lower his great light for a few seconds, for her alone in this city of millions. It must be a marvel to her. Don't you find it, José, you rock lizard, a lush picture to moisten your dry mind?

—She may be moist, the whore, there where he'll make her moister yet. But I stay dry, Batista. The searchlight belongs to the nation. It is here to play on the skies, and pluck out the enemy aircraft, not to play about on her thighs.

—Poor old José! No enemy aircraft has flown over our shores for more than forty years. Then it was only the soft old Zeppelin.

—I think you are teasing me, because you know I am upset by the matter of the button. There are no steps opposite the big house there. It is too high there to jump down on the beach.

—I agree. And that is how I first spotted her. She runs down the road for a distance, her feet bare on the tar, which is still soft and warm from the heat of the day; she crosses over opposite the point of the last lifeguard tower, and comes down those steps to the beach, and from then on she is only a plump shadow tight against the wall. You might see her once as she leaps the sewer outfall, but thereafter she is invisible, except to our dog, who descends with his tail wagging. So pretty to think of!

—I would want more confirmation.

—We were in the field together, you who have to make do with José for Christian name and surname both, and when did you know me move before I am sure?

—And you found actual, visible proof?

—I found what will do for proof until I see the soles of her feet shining white as her coffee-coloured legs press about his neck. I found a picture . . .

—You have kept it, the picture? Let me see!

—I have not kept it. I would have needed ten men with shovels and a truck to keep the Lieutenant's artwork. I would have needed to scoop out a ton of the beach in one place to keep it. And really, to give you my poor opinion, that of a man without much education, that of a man who generally believes the world more beautiful than the copies that are made of it, the beach was more beautiful before the Lieutenant drew on it.

—I wish I had seen the drawings. The dog drew in the sand? What a joke! I love you Batista for making so many dull nights gay for me.

—You would have made nothing of the drawing. It was of a face, simple and potato-shaped, without ears, as children draw them. The nose was long, with a moustache and heavy eyebrows and a small beard.

—The image of the Lieutenant. How I hate him when you describe him so accurately.

—I was describing the picture. But in fact I think it *was* meant to be a self-portrait. There was a wide mouth, which half swallowed the nose.

—Proof! You call this rubbish proof?

—Because your spine is out of true, because your knees bruise one another, because you have the yellow eyes and poisoned teeth of a bastard, do you think all men are so ugly? How many mouths are there like that, stupid?

—But yours is the bastard's mind, Batista, if mine is the bastard's shape. How do you know she liked the picture the Lieutenant drew for her?

—With a sweep of the foot she could have destroyed it, as did later the discreet sea.

—I would not have waited for the sea. I would have destroyed it as soon as I saw it. I would like to destroy him too. I wish we could turn the big gun on them both, now!

—The smallest range of the big gun is half a kilometre, José my dear one. Cat's Nails and her Lieutenant are only just down there, possibly not more than a hundred metres from us.

—Prove it! Prove it!

—How can I prove it more? José, you are mad. Do you want me to lead you to them in the dark? Find them on this huge beach? Two tiny people out there, holding their breath as you trudge clumsily about all round them. One person more like, by now, out of your range, hideous, jealous, unbuttoned bastard!

—But the searchlight, Batista, that would find them! We could turn the searchlight on them!

—Oh now! What evil ancestors gave you such an inspiration?

—But, Batista, it could be done. What do you say? Shall we try?

—And catch them. We would light them up for all to see.

—Yes, yes, how he would then regret that he ever commanded the searchlight.

—But, José, the searchlight belongs to the nation. The nation has waited so many years for you and me to catch one plane defiling our pure sky . . .

—Let the nation wait for ten more minutes.

—Why not, old friend? Listen a minute. Do you hear planes?

—I hear nothing. I hear only the Lieutenant's voice.

—Speaking sweetly to her?

—Speaking filthily to me.

—Then first dim the light while I turn it about.

—I shall dim it gradually, lest he should notice the difference.

—Yes, if you want, but I believe we need not worry overmuch. Why should he be noticing the searchlight at such a time?

—Until it springs upon him! It will be like a whip over his exposed back!

—It will be like a gun! It will be, after all, as if we hit him with a gun.

—What a joke, Batista! How glad I am to share it with you.

—Share it as a comrade in arms, though. I insist. You are about to avenge an insult to the uniform. So do up that button.

—I will. You ask me as a comrade, and gladly I respond. You see the difference in me when I am approached civilly. How's that now?

—Very neat, for a hook-nosed crow. How handsome you are, when properly turned out. It suits you, to have that button done up.

—Is everything else ready? Shall I give it the full power?

—One moment, before we fire. I shall train the ray on the nearest lifeguards' tower. That way we cut the beach in two. They will not be higher up than that, for fear of being observed by people strolling on the promenade. And they will not be much lower because the wet sand might interfere with their pleasure. He would not want to come back with rheumatism in his extra leg.

—My hand is shaking on the dial. Stop making me laugh, Batista.

—Dim out altogether, as I lower the aim.

—It is extinguished. The battle begins.

—I have the tower in my sights. Are you ready?

—Yes, Batista. Will you concentrate the focus?

—No, that will be for you. But not yet. Stand by.

—What a pleasure! Imagine his dismay.

—I said stand by.

—The unit is ready for action.

—Then, my José, spit once and give it the full power!

—At maximum. What do you see?

—Wait. The beach is uneven. Follow the line to the tower without letting your eyes jump. It looks white hot. Anything in it would sizzle. The red flag for a dangerous sea flies over the tower. How's that for a good sighting, old fellow?

—But, Batista, they are not in it. We have missed them!

—But not the tower. Keep cool, we shall have them.

—The Lieutenant will know what we intended. He will come for us and chase us round and round this fort like a firework on the fourth of June.

—I don't think he fancies us. Cat's Nails is lovelier than the two of us put together. I could go three times in her without uncoupling. And the Lieutenant is younger than me.

—We're dead.

—Not yet. Don't panic. Be ready to alter the focus as I rake the beach.

—It will be a court martial. Last month there was one flogged, and he had been a corporal.

—The risk makes it more exciting. Having something to lose is the thrill of gambling.

—I would rather be answering only the button charge.

—All or nothing now. Steadily and surely to move the ray down the beach is the best way. The only way.

—First let us quickly expose all the higher slopes. To make sure that he is not even now on his way here.

—No, no. That would give him a chance to break for safety without crossing the light. He will not attempt to run through it, and if she does we shall instantly pick up the flash of her bright wings, the butterfly.

—How quiet it is. I can hear my heart thudding.

—Never mind your heart. Listen for theirs.

—It is still enough for that, even.

—The whole city is waiting. Up there on the promenade people must have stopped, wondering what it is all about. Now steadily and surely . . .

—Quick, quick. Look, what's that? Shall I focus sharp?

—Nothing but a boat. Without oars. Being on the beach, it has no need of oars.

—And that? Surely that must be them.

—A couple of folded umbrellas. Here come the tables.

—They're there. Beyond. I see them, Batista.

—For a four-eyed man you see very little. This is a buoy.

—I know what they've done. They've crept under that sail.

—Would you do that, José? If so you must be a very flat, narrow-gutted soldier. Think how tight the fishermen peg out their sails when they mend them. Done deliberately to test for strain, and to stop the wind getting under. They are more solid than the wind, old friend.

—We shall not find them. You have been wrong from the start.

—We shall find them.

—I see nothing now, and already the ray runs parallel with the sea. Why have you stopped?

—Do you not see their clothes? Look at his boots, standing up beside them. I bet they'd like to walk off without him.

—Batista, it's true. It must be. You are a genius.

—And here she is, running for them! Watch her breasts bounce. What a splendid creature! What a marvellous instrument this searchlight is. How it lightens her, whitens her. Pure as a flame she looks with the searchlight on her. What a miraculous machine, this bitch of a searchlight. I never loved it so much till now.

—She's got them. She's away with them!

—Scooped them up while still on the wing. Spectacular! If I had four hands I would applaud.

—Follow her quick. She'll get away.

—Yes, but nor far. She won't leave the country. We know where she works.

—After this I would not go within a street of those nails of hers. She'll grow them even longer, and file them even sharper, hoping to meet us.

—Who knows if your instinct is right? It may all turn out very different. She will know at least that we are not common, ordinary men. If we had been would we not have bathed her in light all the length of her fearful journey home? But we have spared her, and she will be grateful.

—The Lieutenant will not spare us.

—We have not yet got to the Lieutenant. It is his turn next.

—He is separated from his uniform.

—He is separated from the whole world.

—I think I see him, on the edge of the ray.

—Yes. And on the edge of the sea. The small waves are about his ankles.

—Pitch the ray straight on him now.

—No, José, not for a little while yet. How impatient you are.

—The wind is getting up again. Listen to it crying in the rocks.

—Yes, it is. Thank you, old friend. Would you reach me my coat? I don't like to take my eyes away. He is wondering what to do next.

—He must be getting cold.

—We are no nearer to him, now that I have moved the ray to the water's edge. He must be up to his knees.

—He dived. He went in under a wave.

—When I swim I like to begin that way. One plunge, and you are accustomed to the sea.

—He is swimming. He is already quite a distance from the beach. He must be a very strong swimmer.

—Maybe. But then, of course, the current will take him outwards.

—How long do you think he means to stay out there?

—Till he realises that there is nothing for it but to come in and collect his clothes. If you were to run down, José, they would not be there when he came in for them.

—No, Batista. I think differently. I think, watching his bobbing head, that he is trying to swim round the fortress and come up on the officers' private beach, and so sneak in to their quarters without being shamed.

—Well thought, José. That idea had not come to me. Of course it is what he must do. Well done, you are using your ogre's head for thinking. We are still a great team, José mine.

—I am afraid, though, that if he succeeds with his plan we have played our last game together.

—A game is not lost until it is won. Be ready when I call on you.

—I cannot see him at all.

—He is there. We cannot see him, but he is there. Now I shall have him directly. I see him, José. Concentrate your focus.

—Ah!

—Have you ever tried to outstare our searchlight, old friend?

—I have too much respect for my eyes.

—You have too much respect for everything, José. But in the matter of the searchlight you are entirely right. The Lieutenant sees nothing. What do you see?

—I see only his head, twisting as he goes in one direction then another.

—You see only a porpoise, José, playing with the human light. What do you hear?

—I hear the Lieutenant calling for help.

—No, you hear only the gulls crying as they stream inland before the wind. What do you see now?

—The porpoise has gone. Vanished.

—You bastard. You've confused the poor creature with your terrible light. He may never come back.

—And the gulls are silent.

—Well, I for one am glad. It will soon be time for our relief, and those birds often keep me awake.

—I shall not sleep.

—Please yourself. If you do not, you will be very tired tomorrow.

—Up here, of course, with the searchlight.

—To go through all the same routines, night after night, Batista.

—Yes, that is our calling. But it has its consolations.

—Tell me one. Only one, will do.

—We can train the searchlight on the statue of the first Governor.

—Use the searchlight still, as a signal?

—No sense in wasting a good idea, ugly old friend, so ugly that you must always sit behind the light.

—But the new Lieutenant may order us not to.

—Well, no one can predict what the new Lieutenant will do. But if he turns out, begging your pardon, to be a bastard, we shall have to think of something else.

ALSO AVAILABLE FROM VALANCOURT BOOKS

Michael Arlen	Hell! said the Duchess
R. C. Ashby (Ruby Ferguson)	He Arrived at Dusk
Frank Baker	The Birds
Charles Beaumont	The Hunger and Other Stories
Charles Birkin	The Smell of Evil
John Blackburn	A Scent of New-Mown Hay
	Broken Boy
	Blue Octavo
	A Ring of Roses
	Children of the Night
	The Flame and the Wind
	Nothing but the Night
	Bury Him Darkly
	Our Lady of Pain
	Devil Daddy
Thomas Blackburn	The Feast of the Wolf
John Braine	The Vodi
Jack Cady	The Well
R. Chetwynd-Hayes	The Monster Club
	Looking for Something to Suck
Basil Copper	The Great White Space
	Necropolis
	The House of the Wolf
Frank De Felitta	The Entity
A. E. Ellis	The Rack
Barry England	Figures in a Landscape
Ronald Fraser	Flower Phantoms
Gillian Freeman	The Liberty Man
	The Leather Boys
	The Leader
Rodney Garland	The Heart in Exile
Stephen Gilbert	The Burnaby Experiments
	Ratman's Notebooks
F. L. Green	Odd Man Out
Stephen Gregory	The Cormorant
Ernest G. Henham	Tenebrae
	The Feast of Bacchus
Thomas Hinde	The Day the Call Came
Claude Houghton	Neighbours
	I Am Jonathan Scrivener

James Kennaway	The Mind Benders
Cyril Kersh	The Aggravations of Minnie Ashe
Gerald Kersh	Fowlers End
	Nightshade and Damnations
Francis King	Never Again
	The Dividing Stream
	The Dark Glasses
C.H.B. Kitchin	Birthday Party
	Ten Pollitt Place
	The Book of Life
Hilda Lewis	The Witch and the Priest
John Lodwick	Brother Death
Michael McDowell	The Amulet
	The Elementals
Oliver Onions	The Hand of Kornelius Voyt
Dennis Parry	The Survivor
	Sea of Glass
J.B. Priestley	Benighted
	The Doomsday Men
	The Other Place
	The Magicians
	Saturn Over the Water
	The Shapes of Sleep
	Salt Is Leaving
Forrest Reid	The Garden God
	Following Darkness
	The Spring Song
	Brian Westby
	Denis Bracknel
Andrew Sinclair	The Facts in the Case of E.A. Poe
	The Raker
David Storey	Radcliffe
	Saville
Russell Thorndike	The Slype
	The Master of the Macabre
Hugh Walpole	The Killer and the Slain
Keith Waterhouse	Billy Liar
Colin Wilson	Ritual in the Dark
	Man Without a Shadow
	The World of Violence
	The Glass Cage
	The Philosopher's Stone
	The God of the Labyrinth

WHAT CRITICS ARE SAYING ABOUT VALANCOURT BOOKS

'Valancourt are doing a magnificent job in making these books not only available but—in many cases—known at all . . . these reprints are well chosen and well designed (often using the original dust jackets), and have excellent introductions.'

Times Literary Supplement (London)

'Valancourt Books champions neglected but important works of fantastic, occult, decadent and gay literature. The press's Web site not only lists scores of titles but also explains why these often obscure books are still worth reading. . . . So if you're a real reader, one who looks beyond the bestseller list and the touted books of the moment, Valancourt's publications may be just what you're searching for.'

Michael Dirda, *Washington Post*

'Valancourt Books are fast becoming my favourite publisher. They have made it their business, with considerable taste and integrity, to put back into print a considerable amount of work which has been in serious need of republication. If you ever felt there were gaps in your reading experience or are simply frustrated that you can't find enough good, substantial fiction in the shops or even online, then this is the publisher for you.'

Michael Moorcock

Lightning Source UK Ltd.
Milton Keynes UK
UKOW02f2146120814

236810UK00002B/17/P

9 781941 147269